PRAISE FOR
CUBICLES

"The enterprising story of three women, Margaret, Faulkner and Joyce, who initially seem to have nothing in common, but are drawn together in a cryptic sort of way . . . Packed with Spencer's delightful storytelling."

—*Black Issues Book Review*

"With a tone like *Dilbert* spiked with vitriol . . . *Cubicles* is perfect for the exhausted worker bee who realizes that Mr. Paycheck is the best thing about the job. And that if Ms. MasterCard didn't own your bank account, you'd tell that she-wolf of a manager your opinion of her people skills."

—*USA Today*

"The complicated office politics in *Cubicles* will make you laugh out loud."

—*Book Street USA*

"Exceedingly well-executed . . . Spencer transcends the African-American 'girlfriends with men problems' genre and touches upon more substantial and universal themes. On one level, *Cubicles* may be enjoyed as an engrossing story of the challenges facing African-American women in the corporate workplace. But its implications are broader than that. It is about women and men of all races struggling to survive within, or to break out of, the compartments or cubicles of their economic, social and personal lives. With *Cubicles*, Spencer has exceeded the bright promise of *When All Hell Breaks Loose*."

—Fort Worth *Star-Telegram*

"*Cubicles* is an entertaining read for working women sorting through a little drama on the job."

—*Upscale*

Cubicles

A Novel

Camika Spencer

ONE WORLD

BALLANTINE BOOKS • NEW YORK

2008 One World Books Mass Market Edition

Copyright © 2002 by Camika Spencer

Published in the United States by One World Books, an imprint of The Random House Publishing Group, a division of Random House, Inc., New York.

ONE WORLD is a registered trademark and the One World colophon is a trademark of Random House, Inc.

Originally published in hardcover in the United States by Villard Books, an imprint of The Random House Publishing Group, a division of Random House, Inc., in 2002.

ISBN 978-0-345-50643-6

Printed in the United States of America

www.oneworldbooks.net

OPM 9 8 7 6 5 4 3 2 1

IN MEMORY OF

Bertha Johnson Gray
Cletus McGilbray
Edna Gray
Mr. and Mrs. Cephus Williams
Chuck Rogers
Wanda Gail Ballard
Donna Hue Walker-Patterson

DEDICATED TO

Jacqueline Jones-Harvey,
the woman who encouraged my creativity,
pushed me to achieve academically,
and has been my mother's support
when no one else believed.
"T.A.G.! I'm it."

ACKNOWLEDGMENTS

To my professional support, Melody Guy, Beth Pearson, Liz Fogarty, Matt Bialer, Manie Barron, and all friends (new, not so new, and to come), family, bookstore owners, readers, and students who have been with me through this journey. We are all in this universe together. I don't take you for granted. Thank you for what you give unselfishly. And to Terry Williams for helping me really be truth, love, and peace. You will always be appreciated, truthfully, lovingly, and peacefully.

INTERNAL JOB POSTING

Job Type: Corporate Services Adjustment

Company: Meridian Southwest / Downtown Office

Job Title: Manager, Customer Operations

Salary: 55K

Contact: Joyce Armstrong
Fax: 972-555-6611
Mail Slot: 12B/8th Floor

Duties: Manage and implement all programs designed to enhance employee productivity, communications, and operations quality. This includes training, scheduling, creating, and implementing such operations. 20% travel. Must have advanced communications and negotiation skills, teamwork ability, must be time-oriented, and able to accurately document implementation and progress.

Requirements: Bachelor's degree in Communications or Business preferred. Science and Administration majors applicable. Two-year minimum experience in high-end customer relations or equivalency. DRISCOLL, Excel, Outlook, and ACIS experience needed.

Faulkner

"Meridian Southwest Telephone, how can I help you today?"

"Is this Faulkner Lorraine?"

"Yes, it is."

"Well, Faulkner Lorraine, we spoke earlier and I need my phone service turned back on right now! I can't wait a minute longer."

"Can I have your first and last name, please?"

"Don't play games with me! This is Jonnie Coleman. Y'all know me by now!"

"Mrs. Coleman, may I please have your account number?"

"Two-one-four, five-five-five, twenty-seven-forty-three."

"Can you verify your address?"

"It's the same address that it was when I called you people an hour ago. Twenty-six-seventeen Banneker Lane."

"Mrs. Coleman, according to your account, you have an unpaid balance of three hundred—"

"Kiss my ass. I don't owe you people nothin'! I paid my bill!"

"Mrs. Coleman, it shows here that we have not received a payment from you in three months. The computer records indicate you have been given two extensions and the—"

"You is a goddamned lie! Them computers don't

know nothing but zeros and ones. I sent a payment two weeks ago! I remember because I used one of them stamps with Mary Bethune on it. I mailed it in, so you musta lost it."

"Mrs. Coleman, we need proof of payment before we can reactivate your service. Can you provide a check stub or confirmation number?"

"You think I have time to be hunting down those check stubs and running back to this pay phone? I don't have no car! Why don't you come and pick me up since you want to help me so much! All I want is for my god-damned phone to be turned on!"

"Mrs. Coleman, your service will not be reactivated until the balance on the account is paid."

"The phone company gon' make me come down there and hurt somebody. That's what this is boiling down to, an ass kicking."

"Mrs. Coleman, if you continue to use offensive language, I will have to terminate this call."

"You black bitch. I don't care what the hell you do—" *Click!*

That was the fourth time today I'd given Mrs. Coleman the uncut version of Mr. Dial Tone. It was never a desire of mine to hang up on her, but each time she called, that's how it usually ended, as if she wouldn't have it any other way. Earlier today, she called me a "skank ho" before I pressed the wrap-up button on the phone and disconnected her call. I didn't even know what part of a ho the skank was, but coming from Mrs. Coleman, I knew she wasn't telling me how much she liked me. I usually kept my cool because even though Mrs. Coleman's bark seemed worse than her bite, I never doubted that any of our irate customers were one bullet shy of coming up here and creating some tragedy for the evening news. Especially now, with the way the world is. People are losing their jobs left and right, not to mention recession, war, and the not-so-global crises like house fires and child abduction. Too many people are at the end of their ropes, and I'm not trying to give anyone a reason to let go of what little piece of rope they're holding on to.

I took my ear set off and rubbed my ear to get the blood circulating again. After wondering for a second why I dealt with this madness from day to day, I rolled my chair away from my desk, extended my fingers, and balled them as tight as I could into fists and back out again, allowing the tension to escape. I looked at the wooden nameplate on my desk and frowned. Underneath my name were the words "Team Lead." Sometimes I wished it read "Support Representative," like it used to. Being promoted isn't always something to brag about, and today I couldn't even see the worth in having the position. The back-and-forth episodes with Mrs. Coleman weren't anything I couldn't handle, but they quickly got old. I mean, I'd been with the Conflict Resolution Department of the phone company for four years, and dealing with customers like Mrs. Coleman was the absolute worst part of the job, not to mention having to deal with that drama while being cramped in a three-sided workspace the size of a compact car all day. I don't know whose bright idea it was to increase workspace by creating cubicles, but he obviously still had an office. Don't misunderstand me—the people here were great, the benefits wonderful, and I enjoyed what I did, for the most part. I'd been Team Lead for two years, with the company five years, and I was looking to move up into management soon, but sometimes, it just didn't seem worth it. There were days when the idea of putting my belongings into a box and walking straight out of here was so overwhelming, I had to get up and take a walk just to tell myself that I was here for a reason and that my bills wouldn't stop coming just because I'd quit a decent job. It was the frustration of dealing with customers who try to curse and back-talk their way out of an overdue bill that pained me, because I knew that my team and I were hired to take all the shit that comes with a person who is mad because his phone has been disconnected, not connected soon enough, or who's been overcharged on his bill. We handled the absolute worst accounts the phone company had, both business and residential. If people wouldn't pay, didn't pay, couldn't pay, hated to pay, or paid late, they dealt with us. Sometimes it was like telecommunications Vietnam around here, but the six of us got the job done. Gail Perez, Brenda Jones, James Hardy, Carmen Estrada, Margaret Eddye, and I were the people who made up the Meridian Southwest Conflict Resolution Team. What the customers didn't seem to understand was that we were held personally responsible for everything that went into our computer systems, and all the yelling and cursing in the world weren't going to sway things from our point of view if they weren't presented in the form of a cashier's check, money order, or cash. Sure, if it was our mistake then it was all good. What customer was going to call back if his bill was a few dollars short or if he wasn't charged a reconnect fee? But when it was his fault then all hell broke loose and we were the ones in the trenches defending a billion-dollar enterprise against the common man.

I could only guess what mean, bitter Mrs. Coleman did with her money to keep from settling her account. Maybe she had a gambling problem and was spending her social security checks on casino boats down in Louisiana. I let my mind wander, like I do about so many of our customers, and began to imagine where she lived and what she did all day besides call the phone company. West Dallas, maybe? There were some suspect spots on the west side, but maybe she lived on the south side. Hell, she could even have been in those run-down apartments I saw along Gaston Street, headed into one of the wealthier areas in East Dallas. I imagined her as a small-framed old woman with leathery, dark skin surrounding squinty eyes, yellowed and dull from years of cigarette smoke and late-night socializing at the club. She'd be the type of woman who wore her hair pulled back in a gelled-down, why-even-try-it pigtail. One thing I didn't have to wonder about was the way she spoke. When she talked, her grammar was broken and devoid of any sign that she'd ever paid any attention in school as a child. I figured she was one of those women who spent her time not wondering where she'd gone wrong, but rather blaming everyone but herself for any of her disappointments. Or she could easily be a woman who was simply trying to make ends meet and kept coming up short. I decided that it didn't matter where she lived, because Mrs. Coleman could very well be a wealthy woman who simply was not paying her bill. Maybe she called and yelled because that was the only way she knew how to express herself. Maybe she was lonely, and found a connection in the relationship she had with us, regardless if it seemed like a backward form of adoration. She knew us each by name. She knew our voices, even if one of us was feeling under the weather. Sometimes, if she called enough, she could tell who was absent. The funny thing was that it was no secret we tolerated her more than we should. Maybe we enjoyed it in some strange, Whitney Houston–Bobby Brown sort of way. Whatever the case, every time she came in on my line, it was the same thing: I asked for her information, she cursed, I threatened to hang up, she cursed more, I disconnected the call while she cursed. And with each episode, I'd have to take five minutes to regroup; ten, in some cases.

I let my hands rest on the keyboard of the computer.

My fingers and neck ached, so I wiggled them again and did a few neck rolls before getting back to the grind of documenting Mrs. Coleman's call. Her file had become such an active part of our database that I'd created a shortcut on my desktop to get to it quicker.

I ate at my station sometimes and it was obvious. Several of the letters on my keyboard were dirty. A mustard stain was on the space bar and several crumbs of toast were sprinkled over and in between the keys. The keyboard desperately needed cleaning. A bottle with barely a swallow of sweet, fruity drink teetered near the edge of my desk. I touched it lightly and watched it fall noisily into the trash can. Two points. Several stacks of folders caught my eye and made me frown. They were pay adjustments that needed to be input into the system so the billing department could modify accounts. A medium-sized, yellow Post-it rested on top of each stack, and in bold, black Sharpie marker were the words DUE THURSDAY. Considering Thursday was yesterday and I'd already avoided them all day today, I knew the billing department would be blowing up my phone line and e-mail on Monday. I had been in training meetings all morning, not to mention this afternoon I'd spent four phone calls battling Mrs. Coleman. I hadn't had time to delegate the work, until now. The line closings would have to be turned in by Monday in order for MSCOT to get their April bonuses, and for the accounting division to get their quarterly reports in on time, so they held first priority. I closed my client-assistant tool on the computer and opened Excel. I clicked on the file I needed to work in and placed the hard copies near my keyboard. The document opened and a blinking cursor waited for me to input the information. The close of the quarter was always hectic, and management was notorious for giving me things to do at the last minute. Although I was beginning to think it wasn't management but simply my boss, Joyce Armstrong. It seemed as if she'd been assigning me more and more work to do, with no consideration given to my current workload or state of being. Of course, I took it as a good sign, a sign that a promotion was coming soon . . . real soon. Otherwise, why would she be doing it?

A medium-pitched voice spoke over the cube wall where I sat. "Sounds like Mrs. Coleman called you everything but gracious." It was Gail Perez. She sat in the cube next to mine, which gave her sufficient leverage when it came to being in my business. We would have been cubemates had it not been for the wall between us. She stood, leaned against the partition, and laughed as she commented about the call. I couldn't tell if she was taking a break or if she was about to leave for the day. I looked at my watch; we still had twenty minutes before quitting time. She stretched, making a noise that echoed between a dying cat and a growling lion.

I stayed focused on my work at the keyboard, not giving Gail the satisfaction of taking a break to talk with her. I had work to do. "Yup, and I was told to kiss the same ass she had last week and called the same black so-and-so I was two weeks ago. Nothing new with that woman." I grabbed the stack of pay adjustments and handed them to Gail. "Here, take care of these for me."

Gail took the stack as she hung lazily over the divider. "It's Friday and you're still dishing out work. Don't you ever take a break?" Gail didn't wait for me to answer. She wasn't interested in starting additional work so close to the end of the day, like I needed her to be. She wanted to chat and continued talking about Mrs. Coleman. "She came in on my line before I went to lunch today, and I was every rat-faced MF in her book," she said, laughing. "I wonder if she calls because she doesn't have anything else to do. Hell, it ain't no secret she has no plans on paying that bill. Maybe we should take her address from the database, find her house, and go get our money. That would be a trip."

I laughed, still focused on what I was typing. "That would also put us in the unemployment line, and I don't think three hundred seventy-two dollars and twenty-six cents will pay either of our rent."

Gail shrugged. "I don't know about you, but it'd be worth it for me. I don't come here every day to be talked to like that. I'm from the 'hood and I can get with Mrs. Coleman."

I agreed with Gail. Mrs. Coleman had gotten out of hand, but I wasn't ready to go Adolf Hitler on the woman. I exhaled. "Eventually she'll stop calling. People like that don't last long."

"Well, she's lasted three months, girlfriend, and I'm willing to bet that as long as old Jonnie don't have nothing better to do, she'll be bumpin' her gums on our phone lines." Gail returned to her desk, shifted some papers around, opened a file drawer, crackled some more paper, and began crunching on something.

I asked, more bored than curious, "Those Doritos?"

"You know it." She smacked. "Gots to have 'em."

Gail ate at least two grab bags of Doritos a day, guaranteed. It was her favorite snack. "I just wish they'd find a way to make the powdered cheese stick to the chip," she said between chews. "When I get to the bottom of the bag my fingers are orange and crumbs be all over my clothes. You would think after all these years they would figure out a way to keep the cheesy taste without the cheesy mess, like a new-wave, for-the-millennium Doritos or something. Platinum Chips."

My eyebrows rose. "Platinum?"

"Girl, yeah. A Platinum Chip would be just what I need, and I believe it'd be simple to make. Instead of adding the cheese later, all they would have to do is put the cheese in the meal that is used to make the chip. Then, after the chips are ready, they're blown so all the excess crumbs are gone and, wah-lah, a nonmessy yet extremely cheesy Platinum Dorito."

This time I stopped typing and stared at the partition as if I could see Gail. "Blown? What do you mean by blown?"

Gail's voice huffed, "You don't get it. See, when the chips are coming off the conveyer belt, they would have these huge fans blowing the excess cheese from the chip."

"Oh, I see." I continued typing. "Interesting concept."

"See, I got vision over here. I got vision. You know, I thought of the smokeless and greaseless cooking grill before that boxer, George Foreman. I was outside one day grilling some fajita chicken and it started raining. That's when it hit me that I needed a utility that would cook like a grill without me having to be outside. I also needed something small, not like a conventional stove. I told my husband about it, but he's more of a carpenter than electrician, so he couldn't figure it out, but I knew that if I could take a class on thermonuclear heating, I could get the grill invented." Gail bit into a chip. "But I don't have that kind of time. I got work, a husband, and kids. George beat me to it and now, every time I turn the television channel to the Home Shopping Network, I want to roll over and die because that's my money he's making. *My* money."

I stayed quiet, not wanting to spark up a conversation with Gail about her many inventions and all the people who pulled her ideas from under her. Just last week, I'd found out compact disc players, shower gel, and wireless phones were all her original ideas. Her latest idea was a pitch she was working on to send to Mattel toys called Trucker Barbie, complete with an eighteen-wheeler truck that smelled like grease when you opened the trailer doors. I wasn't sure if mothers were ready for their little girls to start dreaming of the day when they could graduate high school and enter trucking school, so I wished Gail good luck on her proposal, but emphasized how important it was for her to keep her job here until she had her check from Mattel in hand.

Gail was my coworker and friend, but she was situated faithfully between ghetto and ghetto fabulous. Her actions rarely spoke louder than her words and she was what I considered a true woman from the 'hood. From the gold tooth and feather-tail, finger-wave hairdo (which didn't always flow down to the center of her spine) all the way to her five-color-per-nail manicure, which she changed every other weekend. She talked loud, conversed too long on personal calls, spent long minutes away from her desk, had been caught sleeping a few times, left early on Thursdays to catch happy hour, and felt business attire included matching open-toed sandals, no matter what time of the year it was. If the shoes were black or navy blue, then they need not apply to be a part of her wardrobe.

That was Gail Perez, five years younger than me, and at twenty-three years old she was married interracially and had two kids and a job that paid her less than twenty-five thousand a year. Gail had worked in customer service for a year before she was promoted to MSCOT and enrolled in the training program. Our manager, Joyce, didn't like her and never had because Gail was a faithful gossip. The woman couldn't keep her lips closed to save her own life. Before she was moved to MSCOT, she was caught up in a few he-say, she-say incidents, and Joyce was adamantly against her joining the team. But Gail looked good on paper, she was swift when it came to learning, and for the most part, when she worked, things were good as done. It was getting her to work that was the issue. Honestly, I thought an upward move was what Gail needed to get her away from the bad habits of the drippy-lipped customer service reps. I'd learned in college that environmental changes are conducive to behavioral changes. So much for college; I should have listened to Margaret Eddye, the wisdom of our group, when she said, "You can take a monkey out of the jungle to keep it from swinging on trees, but that don't mean it won't be swinging on your chandelier. It's still a monkey." She was right, but I was still hopeful. Gail showed me every now and then that she was a necessary component of MSCOT. I was the only person that had kept her from being moved back to customer service, because she spread other people's business and her work ethics were like those of a child with attention deficit disorder. Once, her name came up in the middle of a rumor involving Joyce and Mr. Price, who was the VP that supervised the entire customer relations division for Dallas and six other offices throughout the Southwest. The day Joyce called Gail into the office and had me sit in to witness the conversation wasn't a good day. Gail immediately denied involvement until Joyce played back a phone conversation that busted Gail in the middle of her "I didn't say anything" speech. I was embarrassed for Gail. Joyce insisted on demoting her but I convinced her that MSCOT needed Gail. I highlighted Gail's ability to handle irate customers and the fact that she hadn't missed a day of work. Joyce relaxed, but warned me that next time, Gail wouldn't be escorted out the door by herself, hinting that I would be sent packing with her. That's when I had to make a conscious decision to distance myself from Gail. I still considered her to be someone with a great deal of potential, but I couldn't let that great deal of potential get me fired. I hoped Gail knew better than to get involved in hearsay regarding Joyce, because Joyce wasn't one to be played with, and I'd be pissed to lose my job because Gail couldn't keep her mouth closed.

Margaret

Most of the day had been calm. I only had two customers who tried to give me grief about their phone service. And although I'd had to attend ACIS training, it turned out to be easier than I expected. These new computer program upgrades were getting a bit advanced, but the new client server interface we were being trained on was pretty easy to manipulate. The program did everything. All I had to do was a bunch of pointing and clicking. I didn't know how much longer I was going to be able to keep up with the technology or the pace of this job, though. My husband, Lester, was ready for me to retire, but the time wasn't right. Our daughter, Lisa, had moved back home with her two little girls, Nicole and Shylanda. I was buying more groceries, Lester was using more gas in his truck to take them to school, the bills were higher, and I just couldn't see me retiring from the phone company when our budget was being strained. It wouldn't be so bad if Lisa was doing a little something to help out, but she wasn't working, and getting her to do simple things around the house like washing dishes, picking up after the girls, or keeping their bathroom clean was like pulling alligator teeth. She was spoiled and part of that was my fault because she was an only child. But I'd always tried to teach her responsibility. She didn't have many friends growing up, but I'd always talked to her about the importance of sharing and consideration. I didn't know what had gotten into her since her man put her out and she had to move back home, but I found myself having to follow behind her to make sure she did what she was supposed to do when it came to those babies. Now she had two additional mouths to feed, and she was a fool to think Lester and I were going to sit around and be parents all over again.

Thinking about Lisa reminded me to make a call. I took the phone book from underneath my desk and flipped to the *S* section. I looked under "Schools" and found what I was searching for. I dialed the number as I prayed to myself. It was a prayer that reminded me that Lisa needed patience and understanding during this time. A woman's voice answered after the first ring.

"Milestone Business School. This is Malinda, how may I direct your call?"

"I need to know how can I find out if a student is enrolled."

"That's admissions, ma'am. I'll transfer your call."

With one click, the receptionist was gone and I was listening to Frank Sinatra do a popular version of "Fly Me to the Moon." The song reminded me of the night Lester and I drove to New Orleans on vacation back in '78. He pulled over onto the side of the road, outside Baton Rouge, and made me dance with him. I remembered being scared to death because the police in Louisiana were like pit bulls, but nothing happened as Lester led me from the car and turned the radio up loud enough to be heard from outside. He held me close and we kissed like we were kids all over again. Those were the good days.

"Hello? Hello?"

"Oh, yes. My name is Margaret Eddye and I was calling to find out if my daughter is enrolled there as a student."

"What's her name?"

"Lisa Eddye."

"Middle name?"

"Jeanette."

"I don't see a Lisa Jeanette Eddye on the student roster. Maybe we can find it under her social security number. Do you have that?"

"Yeah, hold on." I dug through my purse and pulled out my address book, where I stored all the family's personal information. I gave the woman Lisa's social security number and waited. Something inside me was already telling me that Lisa hadn't done what she promised to do. It wasn't long before my gut feeling was confirmed.

"No, ma'am, I'm sorry, we don't have her in our database."

"Is it too late to enroll?" I asked.

"Yes, the semester started two weeks ago. We are taking admission applications for the fall."

"Okay, thank you," I said and hung up. Things were getting stressful at home, and soon enough, I wouldn't be able to keep protecting Lisa from her father. She was wearing out her welcome and my sympathy. She'd been nothing but a headache since she'd moved back, lying about this and that, leaving without telling nobody, and being just plain lazy, but I was the one who kept Lester at bay whenever her lack of responsibility became an issue. I didn't want the girls to witness their mother being treated like a child, nor did I want them to see Grandpa yell. We didn't know what to believe with her anymore, but I knew way more about her transgressions than her truths. If Lester knew half the things she'd done, she'd have been out on her rump long ago, but I protected Lisa. I protected Lisa when she didn't know she was being protected because she was a mother and didn't need to be on the street struggling with those girls. She didn't know I would be calling the school, but I would make a note to ask her about it tonight.

As I gathered my things to go home, I closed my eyes and prayed a small prayer for safe travel and for Lisa to have an acceptable answer regarding her not being in school. Maybe she'd changed her mind and enrolled in community college. I'd know soon enough.

Joyce

Fred Price called me into his office just as I was walking out for the day. I had a nail appointment and wasn't up for one of his calculated beleaguerings. I hurried toward the stairwell, careful not to rub against the dusty rail. Taking the stairs from the eighth floor to the twelfth floor was good exercise and I liked the challenge. I could still do the small distance without so much as breaking a sweat or panting.

He was on the phone when I stepped into his plush office, which was several hundred square feet larger than mine, with plush Berber carpet instead of flat. He waved me in and motioned for me to close the door and have a seat. I smiled, followed his wave to the seat, and sat down, waiting eagerly for him to close his call. There were several degrees on his wall. His bachelor's and master's certificates in business hung neatly near his Naval Academy framed certificate. A photo of his wife hung to the left of the bachelor's degree. She was a younger woman with a short, feathery hairdo and deep green eyes. She was pretty, but I could tell from the look in her eyes that she wasn't a happy woman. They were morose and lifeless. Fred probably treated her like he sometimes treated me, with no appreciation for what I contributed to his being an executive. I felt sorry for her for the simple fact that she had to deal with him every single day. He took a lot for granted.

Five minutes later, he hung up. "Joyce, I hope I'm not keeping you from anything pressing." He smiled. His teeth could use a good bleach job, but I didn't let his un-attractive smile distract me from why I'd been called to his office.

"As a matter of fact, Fred," I replied, "I was about to leave for the day, but anything for you." I smiled and crossed my legs, a good strategic move for a woman who was five-feet-seven with legs that could easily compete with Tina Turner's.

"I won't keep you long, then." Fred sat back in his seat and looked at me. He glanced at my legs before returning eye contact. "I need a full financial and performance report on MSCOT. I have to present it to the executives a week from Monday."

Fred was two snaps from getting a puzzled look from me. He had all the information he needed to do the report, and the last time I checked, I wasn't buying European-made suits so that I could do his job for him. This man had a secretary. I smoothed my skirt, relaxed my breathing, and put on my serious, business face. "Fred, I'm currently taking care of ACIS training, as well as DRISCOLL operations. I have a team to run."

He smiled again, but this time it was more forced than sincere. "And you're doing a great job, Joyce. You're a go-getter and your attitude over the years has been more than exceptional. I know this seems like more responsibility, but we're all in over our heads around here. There have been cutbacks—"

"We haven't laid off anyone in our department. As a matter of fact, this so-called recession that the country is experiencing hasn't affected our operations. Southwest Meridian is even holding its own against deregulation. We're doing just as much business as Bell South and Verizon. Surely you don't think I don't know what's going on with the company I've worked for most of my life."

"No, Joyce, but I'm getting more pressure from the executives and I could really use your help on this." His face went from false-friendly to damned near ominous. "Joyce, I need you to do this report for me." His blue eyes eased up as they scanned me. I knew this look. Had dealt with it before.

My stern look met his. "And what do I get, Fred? How long have I been asking you to promote me? I should have been an executive six months ago."

He rested in the high-back leather chair and appeared to be surrendering. I noticed the Italian design on his tie. "Joyce, I'm working on it. I just need you to be patient with me. I assured you—"

I stood up, remaining calm. "I'm sick of your assurances. You've been stringing me along just like Mr. Loomis did."

"That has not been my intention." Fred rose and slammed his hands flat on his desk. His face became flushed. "Sit down!"

I remained as I was, wanting to storm out of the office but feeling caught between obligation and annoyance. Whatever the case, I wasn't scared and I wasn't backing down.

Fred's face had gained some color. "I said, sit down."

I straightened my jacket and sat down, crossing my legs at the ankles without taking my eyes off my boss.

He sat down in his brown leather chair and crossed his arms on his desk. "Don't you ever take that tone with me, Joyce. My sole intention is to ensure that you get the promotion you're after, but there is a process to everything. I know you deserve to be promoted and I will make sure that you are. What I'm asking of you is a favor. It has absolutely nothing to do with you and me and what we have unsaid between us. Do I make myself clear?"

I pursed my lips, still keeping my professional composure. Fred didn't wait for me to answer. He could see it in my face: I couldn't play hardball with him without losing my job, damaging my reputation, and airing my own dirty laundry at the same time.

"I need the report a week from Monday." He placed a disk at the end of his desk. I reached over and picked it up. "Thank you, Joyce."

As I stood, Fred cleared his throat loud enough to catch my attention. "How is Faulkner Lorraine working out? I've been hearing wonderful things about her."

"Faulkner is a bright woman," I shot back. "She's going to make a great manager when I'm promoted. I like her. She's diligent, and she keeps MSCOT in line. Why do you ask?"

"I'm thinking I need to keep my eyes on her. As a supervisor, it's my job to know who works under me. We can't afford any slackers."

"Faulkner will surprise you. She's working when no one else is."

"Sounds a lot like you, Joyce." He smiled. "That's what we need. More people like you, who are committed to keeping this company on top. I'll be making a few visits to the floor to keep tabs on the team." Fred looked at some papers as I stood wondering if he was through talking about nothing. I stared at him long enough to realize how much I didn't like him. He was arrogant and condescending. He was the kind of man who would eat the last piece of food on earth without so much as offering a crumb to a starving child. If he could not personally gain something from a deal, then there was no deal. He'd built his fake life on it. For the brief moment that I looked at him, I regretted knowing him the way that I did. He raised his head and stared at me as if I'd just walked into the office. "Oh, you can leave now."

I stepped from the office in a funk, but highly composed. His secretary, Frances, watched me as I breezed past her desk. "Have a good weekend, Ms. Armstrong," she said. Her skin was as dark as my mood right now, and her soulful voice and blond extensions made me cringe. It turned me off to see women with extensions in their hair that didn't blend with their natural hair color. It defeated the purpose. I didn't understand the logic. Sometimes, I caught myself wondering how she'd gotten a job as an executive secretary looking like something from a rap video. I didn't acknowledge her. Ignoring some of the people around here usually worked better for me. It kept me from telling them how I really felt about them.

I took the stairs back down to help me cool off. Fred had never shown any interest in Faulkner, now all of a sudden, he wanted to know how she was doing. The thought crossed my mind that Fred might be considering Faulkner for a promotion. I liked Faulkner's spirit and I did what I could to make sure she could handle the type of politics that came along with moving up in a large, growing company, but I also did it to benefit myself as well. I gave her extra work to do, and I gave her my extra work. I made her stay late, so that my numbers were turned in on time. She worked hard at making my image shine. I was molding her, but I wasn't going to allow that to supersede what I was trying to do for myself. She was sedulous but she still had a lot to learn. She hadn't been here as long as I had, and if Fred thought he was going to promote her before I got my executive position, he had another think coming. I liked her, but I'd make her quit before that happened. I headed back to my office, knowing exactly how I was going to get out of doing this report. Delegation was one of the greatest perks to being in management.

Faulkner

By the time I finished the incident report regarding Mrs. Coleman and the line closings, I had ten minutes left before quitting time. I decided to clean my space before I left. I put the paperwork in a folder and placed it on the file cabinet in my main cubicle. I had two cubicles: the one I sat in and the one across from me, where I usually conducted interviews and kept all my paperwork in order. The cubes were nice but I wanted my own office; to be able to close myself away from everyone and get some uninterrupted work done was my personal corporate wet dream. However, it was a rare commodity on the call center floor to have two cubes—those who had two were usually people in middle management, like myself—but I hardly considered it special. We were all still worker bees. It seemed like everybody was trying to cut back and downsize to save money, but employees were doing double the work at less than double the pay. I wasn't worried, though. The phone company valued me and I always tried to show my appreciation through my work and my work ethic.

I grabbed a cloth and a can of cleaner from the bottom drawer of my desk, no longer able to stand the dust and stains. I sprayed the foamy substance on the cloth and went to work. I cleaned my keyboard, desk, mouse, phone, and computer. Dirt, food, and lint stuck to the wipe like dingy magnets. The sight of the gunk made my face bend. I could see Gail from where I stood. She was brushing more crumbs from her skirt as she talked on the phone. Bits of chips and processed cheese flew from her skirt to the floor.

I could tell from the way she was laughing and carrying on that it was a personal call. She was inputting the pay adjustments at the same time. If she'd stayed off the phone she would be finished by now. I watched her until she noticed me. When she saw me, she hung up.

"You finish the line closings?" she asked.

"I have to double-check them before I turn them in."

"Weren't they due today?"

"Yesterday, but I can't turn them in without checking them first. I never give Ella line closings with mistakes in them. I can't rush just because they're a day late."

"I haven't seen Mrs. Parnell today. She must've been in meetings." Gail stretched her legs and let out a long breath. Her wide thighs made it look as if she had a blue-jean television tray on her lap. She was a short, thick woman with wide-set eyes, a wide frame, and a warm smile. Her pecan-colored skin was smooth and it surprised me that, with all the junk food she ate, she never had a pimple. Gail licked dried cheese from her thumbs. She smacked on it while she talked to me, which irritated me slightly. "Girlfriend, I can't imagine having to take any work home. I barely did that in high school, and I struggled in the training program. I would take those manuals home and they would sit on the

couch till the next day. I don't think I ever read 'em."
She smiled and her gold tooth, designed with the letter
G in it, twinkled. "Not to mention raising two children
who always seem to be into something. Just yesterday
my son put one of his small action figures in the VCR. If
I ever get to your level, it will be a miracle."

I paused in my cleaning. "Gail, you're doing great
work. There's no reason why you shouldn't move up in
this company. You're ahead of a whole lot of people
around here." I touched up spots that I'd missed. "And
my hard work will hopefully make me a better manager
later."

"I know Joyce ain't making this easy on you." Gail
leaned over. As soon as her eyes drew low and she
looked around to see if anyone was watching, a red light
went on in my head: my coworker had just shifted into
gear to gossip. She looked back at me and spoke while
barely moving her lips. "Sharlitha Givens told me that
Daeshun Norris heard about Joyce not wanting you to
have the management position. Daeshun said that she
heard Joyce telling Ella that there was no way in hell you
would get promoted before she became an executive,
and we both know that Joyce has been trying to be an
executive for a while now."

I raised my head and looked at Gail. "That's a rumor,
Gail. Sharlitha and Daeshun work on the fourth floor
with all those other loose-lipped Lucys in customer relations. How would they know about what happens on
the eighth floor?" Sarcasm flooded my tone. Everyone
knew that Sharlitha Givens and Daeshun Norris were
Gail's buddies, and the three of them were the ringlead-
ers of the grapevine around here. They were like walking newspapers. *National Enquirer*s. Half of the things
they said, you couldn't believe. Gail waved her hand and
let it fall over the edge of the cube. "Daeshun's boss ap-

plied for the same job as you and she's been keeping them updated about the position, that's how I know."

"You mean Rebecca Morrisey?" I laughed. "The same Rebecca that got drunk last year at the Christmas party and puked on Joyce's BMW? Gail, it's natural that she would start some gossip like that. I think you should be careful where you get your information. Rebecca is hardly reliable."

Gail sucked her teeth. "Faulkner, I know they talk on four. Hell, the whole company knows that's where you go if you need to find out who is doing what and who's doing who. It's my old stomping ground, but Shar and Daeshun always get the true four-one-one and I think you should watch Joyce. She ain't the nicest person already. She smiles in your face, but any minute now, she's going to stab you in your back with betrayal. I've seen things play out like this on the soap operas over and over. Gossip or no gossip."

"Why would she not want me to have the job?"

"I don't know," Gail huffed as if I had asked her a rhetorical question. "Joyce is selfish and likes to shine at our expense. That could be a reason. Look, these are the facts: ever since word got out that you applied for that management position, Joyce hasn't given you work on time, she's always asking you to stay late to do a job she should have done, she's accidentally lost everything you've turned in, and she insults you on the sly."

"She insults everybody on the sly, Gail." I rolled my eyes and waited for her to say something I didn't know. "We've all been victims of her big-word abuse. It's a shame we have to look up words to find out we're all crumbs to her." I laughed.

"That's true, but don't you think it's a little odd that the job hasn't been filled by now and you're the only person in this company fully capable and ready to be in a management position? It would be blasphemous for her to hire someone from outside of the company. That job is yours and you know it, girlfriend, so why don't you have it by now?"

I put the cleaner away and organized a few things on my desk. I couldn't answer Gail's question right away, but I refused to accept her reasoning. I pulled the day's date off my desk calendar and stared down at the wisdom antidote for tomorrow: *We must accept that everything will happen when it's supposed to happen. This is how we learn patience.* I took in the wisdom and looked at my cube neighbor. "Gail, Joyce is not out to do me wrong. Get that out of your head, and for the love of God, please stop spreading rumors."

"Whatever." Gail shifted her weight and moved on to another subject. "Have you used your vacation time yet?"

"No, but I was thinking of driving down to San Antonio. My dad's sister and her family live on the air force base down there. I haven't been in a while."

"That's where Miguel and I spent our honeymoon." Gail's eyes softened. "Our room was overlooking the Riverwalk, with the moonlight shining off the water and the cool spring air coming in from the patio doors. It was just like on television. Los Lobos performed there that weekend. Girlfriend, after the concert, Miguel was on me like red on Mexican rice." She chuckled and stared dreamily into nowhere in particular. "He didn't waste no time that night. Our son, Sederrick, came along nine months after the honeymoon and his sister was a year and two months later." Gail touched the photo of her kids, Sederrick and Miranda, that sat on her desk next to a miniature sombrero. They were five and four and were beautiful children. Gail flung her hand carelessly my way. "I'll have to tell you about my honeymoon one day, girlfriend. It was a stone trip. Especially what Miguel did with some grapes." Gail giggled like a schoolgirl. "I never looked at grapes the same after that. Can't eat them without snapping my fingers twice and saying to myself, '*Excellente!*'"

"TMI, Gail." I smiled, letting her know she was revealing too much information. "Is your family doing anything this weekend?" I asked as I gathered up my things and prepared to jet out.

"His company picnic is at Six Flags tomorrow, so we're loading up the kids and making a day of it. Then, tomorrow night, his mother is making dinner and I'm gonna have to take my diet pills before we go over there. Girlfriend, Mama Perez be cooking some food. I hurt myself every time we go over there."

"I still remember the shrimp enchiladas you brought to work, Thanksgiving. They were off the hook."

"Yes, Lord." Gail sighed. "She makes the kind of food that a person would sell their children for. I'm going to bring in some of her homemade chorizo and let you taste it. Miguel hates it when I ask his mother to cook for us. He says I need to learn how to cook the way she does." Gail looked at me and pointed at herself. "Girlfriend, how am I supposed to learn to cook when half the time I'm eating? I ain't gon' be able to do it. Who does he think I am? Once I got past the love, I realized that was one of the main reasons I married Miguel. You can't beat Mexican cooking, you just can't."

We laughed.

Gail walked away from her desk headed toward the elevator. I knew she was going down to the fourth floor to get the gossip of the day from Sharlitha and Daeshun even though she hadn't finished the pay adjustments. I would let her get away with it this time because, like her, I was ready to go home.

I e-mailed my best friend, Teresa, and proposed meeting for happy hour. While I waited for her response, I thought about what Gail had said about Joyce's attitude toward me. I tried not to believe it, but some of the points she made had some validity. Joyce *had* been giving me more work and causing me to stay late more often than not, and it did bother me, but not to a point where I was thinking that these were acts against me. Joyce and I weren't close. We never spent time getting to know each other. I didn't know Joyce the way I knew Margaret, who had become like a second mother to me, or Gail, who was like a younger half-sister. Joyce wasn't even like Brenda, Carmen, or James, who also were like family. Maybe I would need to know Joyce to feel the way Gail felt, but Gail didn't even know her. *Nobody* knew Joyce. What I assumed was that Joyce wasn't close to anyone because she purposely distanced herself from the group. It was a great move in the corporate world to remain neutral; at least, that's what I assumed.

The sound of a bell came from the computer, notifying me that I had e-mail waiting. It was from Teresa.

> *Faulk,*
> *A drink is just what I need. These mo-fos at the paper 'bout to make me lose my mind. We can meet at our fav spot in Deep Ellum. I will be leaving in about ten minutes. See you there. I have to tell you about my new assignment too. Ciao.*
>
> *Teresa*

Loaded down with a laptop, satchel, purse, and lunch container, I headed out to meet Teresa. Gail hadn't returned to her desk and a few of the other team members were already gone for the day. The office had quieted considerably. People were leaving, only to sit another hour in five o'clock traffic. I usually stayed late to miss the road rage, stalled vehicles, and bumper-to-bumper confusion, but it was Friday, and I needed a drink like dry grass needed water. Besides, I knew the back streets well enough to bypass traffic.

My footsteps resounded on the gray, marble tile as I walked down the hall to the elevator. I could smell the weekend. I smiled and began humming a party tune as I passed the water fountain and private offices. The elevator opened less than thirty feet from where I was. It was empty and I accepted it as a sign of benevolence. The heavens had opened up and provided me an empty elevator to end my workday. No waiting. No sharing. No end-of-the-day meaningless chatter with people. As I walked by Joyce's office door, I looked at the gold nameplate:

JOYCE ARMSTRONG
Customer Operations Manager

One day, I hoped to see my own name on one of the doors lined along the hallway. As I stood admiring how well my name would look on the nameplate, Joyce's door creaked open. Her perfume preceded her. The multifloral, slightly sharp scent irritated my nose.

"Faulkner, did you complete the quarterly reports for accounting? Ella Parnell called me today wondering when she would receive them." Joyce's voice was low and devoid of conversational tone. She leaned against the door panel waiting for me to respond. Her designer three-piece burgundy dress suit hugged her tall, shapely frame. I could tell it was expensive by its contoured cut and design. Her shoes matched the suit's fabric perfectly and were probably custom designed. Joyce was head and toes above the designer shoe stores in the malls or Galleria. She was a sturdy fiftysomething but could easily have been mistaken as being in her early forties. I envied her for still looking like she could kick ass in a *Soul Train* line. It was obvious that she took care of herself. Her rigid face was loaded with makeup, but aside from the crow's-feet and noticeable veins on the backs of her hands, Joyce was any man's fantasy woman and any wife's threat. She was single, educated, good-looking, well paid, independent, and she owned nice things. Outside of work, I didn't know much about her, but if I had to judge her work attitude against her being single, then I knew why she didn't have a man. At work, she was cold, fickle, and domineering. She liked to be in control and loved showing it.

Now here we were, staring each other in the face, a direct repeat of last Friday, the Friday before, and the Friday before that. I could walk into these moments with my eyes closed. Once again, she was asking me about some work I was going to take home. Work she should be doing. Work she would say had to be turned in before I went home.

I shifted my weight to show her I was in a hurry and that the paperwork I was holding wasn't a Ziploc bag full of feathers. "No. I was going to take them home and check them over the weekend."

Joyce shifted her weight from the panel as she shook her head. "No, no, dear, that won't do. We must get those stacks in by six, checked and in order. I would do them, but my manicurist gets livid when I'm late for my nail appointments." Joyce took a quick glance at her nails, which looked fine from where I was standing, ten steps away from a now closed elevator. Joyce's nails shined like ripe, red apples and they looked like that every day. Who knew when it was time for her to get a fill or a new set? I peeped at my own nails. Two were chipped, one bitten off, and the rest were just there, unpolished, and desperately in need of lotion.

Joyce pulled her jacket close so it contoured her body even more sharply. "I need the closings turned in before you go." It was a charge without options. It needed to be done her way. Gail's comments rang in my head.

I held my breath, could feel my heart pounding against my chest. Heat rose in my head and descended to my toes. I gritted my teeth so hard, any one of them could have chipped and popped down my throat from the pressure. I forced a half-cocked smile. "Sure, Joyce, I'll get on it right away. Anything else?"

Joyce smiled. "Actually, the executives will be meeting a week from Monday, and they need a full financial and performance report on the MSCOT. I need you to have it in to me before then, so I can review it and make any necessary adjustments. I'll e-mail you the details this coming Monday.

This time I did give Joyce a crazy look, but she ignored me. She used her control to avoid conflict.

"I'll look for the e-mail."

She gave a cozy smile. "Very good, dear. I'll telephone Ella and let her know to expect the stack today. Also, check your voicemail later. I may have forgotten some items." She smiled again, and this time the smile held exactly what I spoke of earlier: control. Joyce had it and I was a victim of it. She turned and retreated into her office, flinging her auburn-colored, flipped weave ponytail behind her and closing the door. A few of us knew it wasn't her real hair, but Joyce went to one of the best hairstylists in Dallas. Therefore, she had half the people in the building fooled. Joyce's extension to her natural hair looked so real, I used to believe it was hers until the day she made the mistake of letting her new growth catch up with her and the difference in the textures was evident. If I were as pretentious as Joyce, I'd probably have a nice weave job too. Women were wearing weaves now like it was nothing. In this building alone, I'd seen more sisters wearing weaves, extensions, and wigs as if the hair they were born with wasn't good for anything else but covering up or adding to. I'd gone natural a few years ago and considered myself lucky that, for whatever reason, having extra hair on my head was not an option, but I still respected the talent it took to make synthetic hair blend with someone's real hair.

I hurried back to my desk and tried to call Teresa to let her know I would be running late. When I called, her voicemail picked up. I tried her cell phone and got no answer there either. I'd missed her and now she would be at the club waiting for me, which meant she wouldn't wait long. Dealing with Joyce had caused me to stand Teresa up last week, and from then on, she told me I had a ten-minute grace period. I clicked on my computer and sat back down at my desk. There was no rest for the weary around here. I knew not to have a pity party for myself because this was my own fault. I should have told Joyce how I felt; maybe it would have changed things. I laid the line closings in front of me and began going over what I'd already done. By the time I finished, my eyes ached and I had a few minutes to get the papers to accounting and no time to get to Teresa.

I ran into Margaret Eddye as I hustled toward the elevator. She was carrying a bag with her lunch containers, along with her purse and sweater.

"Faulkner, you're going to break your neck hurrying so fast. Slow down; whatever it is you're trying to get to will still be there."

I put my arm around her shoulder and kissed her cheek. "Trying to turn in line closings. End of the quarter is upon me."

Margaret folded her sweater across her arm. "Ella wasn't here today and she has to look at those papers before she turns them over to her group, so what's your rush?"

I halted. "Joyce is my rush. Joyce is always my rush.

She told me Ella asked about the line closings. What do you mean Ella wasn't here today?"

"Now, Joyce knew good and well Ella was out today." Margaret laughed and patted me on the back. "You should have told her you were taking the closings home, like I told you to tell her."

"I did, Margaret, but she was adamant they be done before I go home. I'll be here with a sleeping bag and a coffeemaker, if Joyce has it her way."

"One day you're going to have to force Joyce to recognize you're capable of doing your job without her pushing her power on you. I think she sees good things in you, but she always has to have things go a certain way."

"Yeah, *her* way," I said.

Margaret smiled. "Be patient, God has blessings in store for you, he does for all his chosen."

The elevator opened and closed without either of us getting on.

"Margaret, you know her better than I do. She's not the easiest person to convince."

Margaret knew I was telling the truth. She'd known Joyce longer than anyone at the company. She trained Joyce, taught Joyce everything she knew. Once, Margaret told me, she and Joyce used to be close, but now they rarely spoke to each other. They were polite to each other, but anything outside of that went unsaid between the two of them. I wanted to ask what happened, but Margaret didn't seem too eager to tell me.

Margaret stopped at the water fountain and took out a medicine bottle.

"What's that?" I asked, giving her just enough time to take one of the pills out before taking the bottle and reading the label. "Verapamil. What is this?"

"For my blood pressure." Margaret took the bottle from me and placed it back in her purse. "The doctor just put me on it."

"Margaret, why don't you retire? Working in your condition isn't good. You need to be at home resting and enjoying being a grandmother."

Margaret smiled. "I'll retire in due time. I'm still young, don't forget; fifty-seven isn't old." Margaret wiggled her body enough to remind me she had a sense of humor. "I still got a few good years left in me. My condition is just that, a condition."

"I know." I smiled. "I just want you to enjoy those years at home resting and experiencing life outside this office building. I'd much rather help you plant that garden you've been dreaming about having instead of seeing you take calls all day."

The elevator opened again. This time, we stepped on. I pressed "L" for Margaret and "5" for myself. I hugged Margaret again before stepping off. "Think about retiring, Margaret. There's no use in both of us dealing with Joyce, right?"

Margaret shooed me away. "I'll see you on Monday. Have a safe weekend, Faulkner." The elevator closed, leaving me staring at its steel double doors. She was like a mother to everyone in MSCOT. She knew how to cure the common cold, told us the best way to remove ink stains from cotton, and she was never one to hesitate to take out her Bible to quote Scripture, or to give advice. Margaret Eddye did everything but follow her own advice and it showed. She was a diabetic and suffered from high blood pressure. She'd even survived a stroke, which led me to believe she could possibly have heart problems as well. She didn't eat right and I'd committed myself to getting her a salad every day to go with whatever she'd brought for lunch. She was married and her husband was one of the nicest men on earth. He brought her to work sometimes, but Margaret mostly caught the bus. She'd never learned to drive and declined my offers to be her personal ride to and from work every day. Her theory was that she didn't need me to as long as she had her husband and the Dallas Area Rapid Transit. That was Margaret in a nutshell: she puts everything and everyone before herself.

I walked the line closings to Ella Parnell's door, which was closed and locked, as I now expected. I placed the papers in the holder on the wall near her door and went back to my desk to officially end my day. As I walked past Joyce's office I stopped again and stared at the nameplate. Sometimes I couldn't stand to look at it and other times I idolized it. Right now, I wasn't idolizing it. I was thinking of ripping it off the door and chucking it down the hallway. She had lied to me about Ella rushing her on those line closings, and because of that, I'd stood up my best friend. I couldn't imagine what else she'd lied to me about just to get me to work late or send me on a wild goose chase. As I headed to the elevator, I finally gave in to the thoughts that I'd been able to fight off until now. Gail was right on the money: Joyce had it in for me. She didn't like me and she was doing what she could to let me know it. She wanted me gone. But why? What had I done to her besides help make her look good? I never meant her any harm in coming to this stressful place and doing what I was paid to do. A part of me still wanted to be in Joyce's corner, but the other part wanted to find out what her beef was with me, if she even had one. A part of me wanted to know why she and Margaret weren't close anymore. I got on the elevator and headed to my car. For now, I would take Margaret's advice and be patient, but I wanted to start digging for answers.

Joyce

Hello, Ms. Armstrong, it's good to see you today. The usual?"

I breezed past Laura, the short, thin girl who'd spoken to me when I entered Master Tam's salon. It was a small place located near Love Field in University Park. I came here because it was quiet, no soliciting was allowed, and the likelihood that my car would still be outside when I was done was highly probable. The massage chair at her station was empty, so I sat in it without looking around to see if there was a wait. I dropped my leather bag and crossed my legs. "Hello, dear," I said, letting out a breath. "I haven't got all evening, I've plans tonight. A manicure and massage will do."

The frail-looking girl took a bottle of nail polish from the glass counter that housed well over 250 different shades. The bottle she carried was labeled "Venom Red," and it was my usual. "Coming right away." She pressed a button on the chair I sat in. The chair began to vibrate and warm up. Tension started to seep from my body. I could feel my bones warm and my toes loosen. The girl removed my shoes and used her slim fingers on my feet. A few of the bones in my toes popped.

"You sure no pedicure?" she asked. "I can do quickly. Your feet feel tired." Her rounded tone made her sound like an Asian Shirley Temple.

Without opening my eyes I replied, "No time tonight.

You take too long on my feet anyway. Just a manicure and foot massage, thank you."

She kept her hands on my feet some additional minutes before moving up to my calves. I'd been dreaming about being in the massage chair all day while dealing with that motley crew at the phone company. Today was one of those days that made me wonder why in the hell I bent down to run MSCOT. It was like running a day care. The team wasn't professional. Gail Perez came to work looking like a circus. She wore a thousand colors a day. Margaret always smelled like a hospital. Then there was Brenda Jones, the woman who didn't belong there because she was too busy trying to be Martha Stewart with her idea-a-day projects that she brought to work. Not to mention Carmen Estrada, the one Hispanic on the team, who never made it to work on time. James Hardy was young, and with youth there was always some issue regarding responsibility to the company that would arise, and I knew I'd be dealing with that soon. The only thing that made me confident in his dependability was the fact that he was an intern, so there was a considerable amount of obligation on his part. Faulkner held the team down, but I was still responsible for everything MSCOT did and I hated that feeling. These were six people who didn't represent what I was about. They frustrated me. I represented being sharp and looking the part. I demanded to be taken seriously at what I did. I would rather have people who thought like me; that way, I wouldn't be second-guessing about who was in my corner.

I wiped work out of my mind and blew off my end-of-the-day blues by letting Laura's hands professionally work their way into my subconscious. I leaned my head back and thought about where I wanted to be tonight, but it wasn't long before Laura's voice inconveniently broke my concentration.

"Hard day, Ms. Armstrong?" Her Cantonese accent was heavy.

"Yes, dear. One of the hardest."

"You should get in the sauna today," she said, smiling. "Make you feel better."

This time I opened my eyes and snapped at her. "Didn't you hear me say I had plans or was I talking to myself?" I paid her to work, not chitchat in that difficult-to-understand, broken English.

Laura fell silent with a smile plastered on her face. Her naive eyes stared at me briefly before returning to what she was doing. She was young. Barely twenty-two, if I had to guess it. She had a model look—smooth skin, high cheekbones, tall, thin frame, and a bright smile complete with a dimple in her left cheek. Her hair, once glossy, black, and flowing, was now cut close to her face, dyed a fiery auburn color, and shaved in the back. Americanized to the bone, but she could still be someone's fashion doll. The black leather pants she wore were out of season so late in the spring, but the cold air in the salon kept me from commenting. Her pink DKNY top looked painted on. It pressed against her small breasts like plastic wrap, and the faux jewels that spelled out Donna Karan's designer marker glimmered occasionally under the salon lights. She wasn't wearing a bra. She didn't have to. Her tits couldn't compete with ant bites. I almost envied her as I remembered the days when I was that young. I'd have on my fitted pedal pushers with no panties and a sleeveless shirt to match. My college friends and I would drive several hours just to catch a party in Tyler, Shreveport, or Nacogdoches, any town near Wylie that had a party jumping.

I looked at Laura again with the fresh memories on my mind. She was cute, but I was much finer when I was her age. Shit, I still was, but it had been a long time since I had gone out. Of course, I used to party at the Cliff

Club in Singing Hills and at Annie Mae's in South Dallas before the young, thirty-something crowd started coming and hanging around. They messed up everything, coming onto the old-school stomping grounds as if they knew what was going on. Those of us from the original days of night stalking used to get our groove on listening to BoDean's local blues band. They played everything, all the favorite blues tunes. I dated the bandleader, Bo, and always got the queen treatment. I wouldn't have had it any other way and Bo knew it. I made sure he knew that there were rewards for treating me first-class all the way. I would slow dance with him and he'd almost lose his mind over me. That was when slow dancing drenched you more with sweat than fast dancing did. People danced so close, they could feel each other's emotions. Groping. Sticky. Those were the good times. Then young people came, the music changed, the closeness changed, and the mentality changed. Those of us who were regulars knew it was time to go when the newly hired DJ played Gerald Levert like Eddie Levert didn't exist. Since then, my life had been different. Clubs no longer catered to the seasoned and sexy. Now it was about the young, fast girls with no shame in letting their butt cheeks hang out. Girls who'd suck a dick for a movie pass instead of a backstage pass and hotel key. Men my age didn't want a strong woman anymore. They didn't want a woman on her own, *with* her own, or at least they acted like they didn't. They want a needy woman. A woman who was good at sacrificing her common sense to make them feel validated, that's what they seemed to really want, but I couldn't pretend to be no man's ego booster. My life was complicated enough without some old pervert my own age trying to run me and treat me like I didn't matter. A brief thought of Raymond, my dead ex-husband, sent chills up my spine. I inhaled a deep breath and focused on relaxing.

Laura grabbed an emery board and started shaping my nails. I looked at her to let her know I was monitoring her. I liked my nails medium length with no curve. It took a long time for Laura to get comfortable with the style I liked and sometimes she'd try to give me three-inch-long tips, and I'd have to start talking bad to her to make her understand. I'd seen the girls come through here with nails as long as an Alaskan winter. I didn't know how they ever expected to get a decent job with that ghetto-fabulous nonsense, not to mention wipe their ass. Maybe it didn't matter to them.

When Laura finished filing, she placed my hands in a glass dish and let them soak. Afterward, she took care of my cuticles, got rid of my hangnails, applied my favorite Venom Red polish, and applied the quick dry. Perfect! I paid Laura seventy-five dollars plus tip and left. My nails were fierce! All I needed now was an old drink and some young company and I knew where I could get both. My house.

Margaret

Zachery, the bus driver, had to wake me up when he reached the stop where I got off. I was ten times tired. Sleep had crept up on me not long after I'd got on and my energy was low. My ankles were swollen and the only thing I could think of was getting home and soaking them in some Epsom salt. When I turned the corner onto my street, I could see my grandbabies playing in the yard. That meant their mother was home. I had my fingers crossed that she was cooking dinner. Lisa could only cook breakfast—scrambled eggs, toast, and bacon—but I'd take it as long as I didn't have to make it. I could tell Lester wasn't home because his truck wasn't in the driveway. He must still be out working on that roofing job. As soon as Shylanda and little Nicole saw me, they jumped up and ran my way.

"Big Mama! Big Mama!" Nicole took no prisoners as she rammed her small, six-year-old body into mine and hugged me around my plump waist as best she could. Shylanda grabbed my purse and food containers as always, carrying them into the house. They waved good-bye to their friends and came in with me. They brought me joy. They were smart little girls. Shylanda was in the seventh grade this year and had always been one of the smartest children in her class. Her favorite subjects were math and science and she had the awards and ribbons to prove it. Her downfall was her stubbornness. She was as ornery as a mule and I had to take a switch to her every now and then for not doing as she was told. Nicole was the total opposite of her older sister. She was the artist of the family. She liked to draw, paint, was always singing or humming some little song. When she recently showed an interest in classical music, Lester and I used some of her college savings to put her in violin lessons, which she immediately took to.

It seemed like every light in the house was on when I walked in. It was still daylight outside and there was no reason for all the lights to be on.

"Where's your mama?" I asked Shylanda. The child didn't so much as look at me. Her lips became tight as she busied herself taking my containers out of the plastic bag and placed them in the sink.

"Sleep!" Nicole rang out. "She's in the den on the couch."

"Lisa!" I yelled out as I placed my keys on the entry table near the front door and loosened my blouse. There was no response. I walked to the converted garage we now called a den and there she was, sprawled on the couch with the lamp on and the television running at top volume. On the screen was a half-dressed woman shaking her booty, while a guy in clothes too big for his body sat talking in rhyme. I tapped Lisa on the shoulder. "Lisa, get up!"

Lisa rolled over and blocked the lamp's glow from her eyes. "What is it?"

"Get up and fix these babies some food." I picked up Lisa's shoes and one of the girls' book bags that was lying in the middle of the floor.

Lisa looked dazed. "What time is it?" She yawned. She sat up wearing only an oversized football jersey and some footies.

"It's time for you to get up." I took the things to the back and placed them in the spare bedroom, where Lisa and the girls slept. When I returned to the den to turn the television off, Shylanda grabbed her book bag and headed to the kitchen table to do her homework. Lisa yawned again as she rose from the couch and walked lazily to the kitchen. Nicole had disappeared to the back, probably to involve herself in some doll play. As I heard Lisa rummage through the pots and pans, I went to my room and closed the door. I sat on the edge of the bed and kicked off my heels. My feet and ankles felt like water balloons. I slid off my skirt and blouse and immediately came out of the support hose. I looked at my ankles and rubbed them. It seemed like they ached all the way to the bone. I grabbed my Bible and headed for the bathroom, where I removed the hairpins from my hair and massaged my scalp. This was my favorite part of the day—I was off work, I'd made it home in one piece, my family was alive, my house wasn't burned to ashes, and

I was able to gather my senses in the bathroom, the only place in my house that I could get some quiet time with myself and Jesus. After I came from the bathroom, I slid on a housedress. The yellow and green stripes didn't compliment me much, but it was comfortable. Both of the girls were at the table, Shylanda still working on homework and Nicole coloring. One of her doll shoes was on the floor. I picked it up and placed it on the table. I looked around the kitchen and saw that Lisa had placed a pot on the stove with three wieners in it. The water was coming to a boil.

"Lisa!"

"She gone," Nicole blurted out.

"She's gone," I said, correcting my grandbaby's English.

Nicole smiled. "She's gone."

I put my hands on my hips and looked at Nicole. "Gone where?"

"To the store to get some bread."

"Nikki, you talk too much," Shylanda said without looking up.

"So! You do too!" Nikki hollered back.

"Calm down this moment and stop arguing with each other. That's not nice, I told you." I walked to the fridge and opened the door. A loaf of bread stared me in the face. I shook my head. "How long has your mother been gone?"

This time Nicole looked at me reluctantly. I could tell she was trying to take her sister's advice, but I gave her my "tell me what I want to know or else" face. "About two hours."

My seriousness changed to amusement. "Nicole, two hours is a long time. I don't think she's been gone that long. Shylanda, how long has your mama been gone?"

Shylanda never looked up from her work. "A little while."

"What's a little while?"

Shylanda shrugged. She didn't like being questioned about her mother. She safeguarded Lisa at all costs. "She put the wieners on and told us to stay in the kitchen until you came out of your room, then she left to get some bread."

Nicole looked over at me. "Big Mama, can I have some Kool-Aid?"

"No, we're drinking water tonight. No Kool-Aid." I opened the cabinet and looked for some canned vegetables to make with the hotdogs.

Nicole sucked her lips, but didn't seem too bothered by not getting her favorite drink. After finding a can of creamed corn, I poured a glass of ice water and gave it to Nicole. She gulped it down in no time.

"Child, you must be thirsty."

"Yup. I'm thirsty all the time." Nicole giggled. "We played outside at school and then I played again at home."

The front door opened and closed. I looked out of the kitchen to see if it was Lisa, but it was Lester. His dirty overalls and dingy white T-shirt had been sparkling this morning. I could see he'd been under someone's car or on somebody's roof. He wasn't ten steps from me before I could smell the dirt on him.

"Hey, ladies." Lester ruffled Shylanda's sandy-colored, curly hair. She frowned and attempted to fix it.

"Hi, Grandpa!" Nicole jumped up from her chair and gave Lester a hug, not concerned with getting herself dirty. He patted her back and retreated to our bedroom.

By the time the girls finished eating, took their baths, and went to bed, it was eight-thirty. Their bedtime was eight. I sat down to find something on television. The early news would be on in thirty minutes and I needed to see the weather. Lester came into the den and sat next to me.

"How was your day?" he asked. His hand rubbed over my thigh.

"Same as yesterday," I replied. "Long but good."

He crossed his legs and put his arm around me. "Sammy damn near broke my truck today trying to haul some sheet metal over to the dump. He tied the rope wrong and part of the metal cracked my window."

"Really?"

"Yeah. I told that nigga he need to learn how to load stuff before he has to buy me a new truck. Shit, it's going to cost me two hundred dollars to replace the window."

I cut my eyes at Lester, letting him know I didn't agree with his choice of words, but he didn't change his choice. I flipped through the television stations without giving them much thought. Lester continued cursing and talking about his partner Sammy, but I wasn't listening too much. I was thinking about Lisa and where she could be.

"Baby?"

Lester rubbed my thigh again, bringing me out of my thoughts. "You gon' cook tonight?"

I responded without looking at him. "There's some chicken from last night in the fridge, Lester, and a hot dog with some leftover corn that the girls didn't eat. Go ahead and microwave it."

"Microwave it? Margaret, I want a cooked meal sometimes. Every time I get home everybody has had a cooked meal but me. Don't I matter around here?"

"Lester, don't start that tonight. I've been on a nine-to-five just like you and I have not eaten since I got home. Microwaving your food isn't going to kill you."

"No, it won't kill me, but it also won't kill you to fix me a meal like you used to. I can remember getting a fresh, hot meal every day. We never had issues about whether or not you were going to cook."

"And I can remember when you cooked for us too. What's wrong with you going in there and cooking?"

"Absolutely nothing, but food tastes better when *you* cook it. You said it yourself, baby." Lester smiled. "I have a knack for burning shit up. C'mon, Margaret, make me something to eat."

"I said there was some food in there. Now you either eat that or don't eat at all."

Lester was unmoved. He leaned over and kissed my cheek. "Then let's go out to eat. My treat."

"I can't go out, Lester, my ankles are swollen. Besides, who's going to watch the girls?"

"Where's Lisa? She's their mama, she can watch 'em."

"Lisa is out."

"Out where? Where could an unemployed mother of two be at a quarter of nine on a Friday night?"

"The girls said she went to get some bread."

"That girl, I swear. I'm going to get in her shit when her black ass darts in that door."

"Lester, please, watch your language."

"A man wants to spend some quiet time with his wife and he can't in his own damned house. Margaret, that ain't right." Lester's voice raised just as we both heard keys in the lock. The front door opened and closed. Lester and I both looked up as Lisa came into the den with a sack in her hand.

"Speak of the devil," Lester said before Lisa was in the den good enough to hear.

Lisa stepped in, half dressed in a miniskirt and gray top that tied around her midsection. She had a brown paper sack under her arm. "Hey, Daddy."

"Where have you been?" Lester asked.

"I went to get some hot-dog buns for the girls."

I cleared my throat. "The girls are in the bed. I put them to bed over an hour ago. They ate hot dogs on white bread."

Lisa snapped. "Well, Margaret, the girls are used to eating their hot dogs on hot-dog buns."

"You better watch how you talk to people, girl." Lester stood up to get his point across. "You don't live in that fancy house anymore with that nigga who barely took care of you. We can't afford little luxuries like hot dogs with matching buns, and the next time I come home and find my wife baby-sitting kids that ain't hers, you might as well start looking for a place to stay other than here, you understand?"

Lisa interjected, "Margaret didn't mind watching the girls while I was gone."

I stayed quiet, even though every bone in my body wanted to grab Lisa and slap her into God's kingdom. She'd left the house without telling me and assumed it was okay to leave those girls unattended. Anything could have happened while I was in the back. I did mind watching those girls sometimes. I did mind coming home every day to a house with children who had to be told repeatedly to pick up their toys and do their homework. I did mind cooking and cleaning behind them, but if I didn't, who was going to do it? Their mother wasn't worth a pot to piss in and it didn't make sense for me to treat them wrong just because their mother was a sorry excuse.

Lester put his finger in his daughter's face. "Lisa, you don't leave your children for two hours to get a loaf of bread. That's abandonment in my book, and I have a right mind to call CPS on you. Try something like that again and that's exactly what I'm going to do."

"I'm a good mother," Lisa argued. "No, I may not have a job or a high school education, but I choose to treat my daughters to some matching hot-dog buns to go with their hot dogs because I think they're special and they deserve nice things. Y'all need to see that."

This time, Lester raised his voice. "Girl, bread is bread around here! This is Oakcliff! There ain't no professional athletes running around this part of town! It's nothing but working men, disabled veterans, and drug dealers. Now, I know you didn't walk up to the Affiliated to get that bread you're holding. I'm your father and I know you. What you need to do is ask yourself if this new nigga that is riding you around without including your kids in the activities is worth losing your daughters over. Lisa Jeanette, you will not live under my roof, disrespecting my wife, and leaving those girls without your adult supervision, do you understand me?"

Lisa stared at us both like we'd stolen something from her. She was thirty years old and a former sales associate at Macy's. She'd met a pro football player, shacked up with him, had his two kids, and watched him return to his hometown to marry his college sweetheart, leaving Lisa with a five-hundred-dollar monthly check and nowhere to go. The sad part was that the guy had six other children as well, so the money Shylanda and Nikki got was barely enough to dress them for the winter.

"Do you hear me, Lisa?"

"Yeah, I hear you." Lisa stormed out of the den and into the kitchen.

Lester leaned down and kissed my forehead. "I'm going to bed."

"You don't want anything to eat?" I asked, not really looking for him to answer.

"No, but I want to take you out tomorrow night. El Fenix sound good? I know you like Mexican food."

"My favorite."

Lester left the room, and no sooner was he gone than Lisa crept back in and sat down next to me. Her legs were too long for the skirt she wore and I thought the tattoo on her left ankle took away from her natural beauty. God only knows why people mark up their bodies that way. I thought it was tacky.

Lisa was Lester's only daughter from a previous marriage. She was half white and half black and stunning. I always thought she should be on television, but Lisa didn't seem to want much out of life if she had to work to get it. She liked hanging out late and letting people do for her. She was dependent and for the most part used her common sense like she was comatose. Her mother lived in California and kept Lisa until the child turned eighteen. Lisa moved to Texas after her mother decided to stop being a mother and followed her lover-therapist to Switzerland, where she was now a palm reader by trade. We'd had Lisa ever since. She was only twenty-four when she moved out of our house and in with the football fella.

"What are you watching?" she asked without looking at me.

"Nothing. I'm waiting for the news to come on."

Silence rifted between us. I'd known this act too many times. First would come the apology.

"Margaret, I'm sorry for leaving the girls, but they love you so much and I really didn't think you would mind watching them while I was gone."

Next, she would explain why she was gone so long and attempt to make me comfortable with a conversational tone.

"The Affiliated was out of bread and I had to catch a ride to the Minyard's on Ledbetter and it was crowded. I couldn't believe it was that crowded on a Friday night; you'd think everybody would be out partying."

Finally, she'd remind me how different I was from her own mother and, then, she'd knock the stake one inch farther into my heart by bringing those babies into it.

"I've never had a mom like you. I was brought up around people who only liked my mother's looks, and she used her looks to keep food on our table and to keep me in the nicest clothes. She didn't cook for me or give me hugs. I didn't get violin lessons and I never had people come to my plays or my science fairs. My girls love you more than anyone in the world and I'm thankful for that. God is blessing me and I'm going to join the church this Sunday so that I can make . . ."

Oh, yeah, I forgot she had to bring God and the church into it as well.

". . . a good life for me and the girls. I'll do better when I start secretary school. I'll be making a little money and I can get a car and things will be right again. Margaret, just please don't let my daddy take my girls from me."

I looked at Lisa like I always do, without too much pity, but just enough to keep me from going upside her head. "Lisa, when are you supposed to start business school?"

"In two weeks."

"I thought you were supposed to start this coming Monday. That's what you told me last week, that you were enrolled and classes would begin Monday."

"I called downtown today and they told me that classes had been pushed back, but I'm registered and ready to start."

As Lisa sat lying to me, I never let my eyes leave hers. "Do you have a plan as to how long it's going to be for you to get back on your feet?"

"Well, I figured I would work and save my money. After I get a car, then I'll find a small apartment somewhere and we'll be out of your hair."

"How much you thinking on paying for rent?"

She shrugged. "Around seven hundred dollars a month."

"Seven hundred for rent isn't going to allow you and those girls to live under safe living conditions, Lisa. You're going to need more than that to live comfortably with two children. You have utilities, food, gas, not to mention things like insurance, a car note, and getting the girls' hair done."

Lisa crossed her legs and I noticed an ankle bracelet that wasn't there when she left and it wasn't there yesterday. I could tell it was a nice piece of jewelry. "Oh, I know," she said quickly. "I will find me a good-paying job."

"When, Lisa? You don't want to go to college and nobody is going to pay a young, uneducated woman a lot of money if she ain't degreed unless she's hookin' and you better not be thinking about that. You could get a job at the phone company where I work. After a ninety-day probation you could get a good career started, and they'll pay for you to attend school."

"I was thinking about going to modeling school instead. You said I'd make a good model," Lisa said, ignoring my current advice for something I'd said ten years ago.

"You were eighteen when I said that. Now things are different. You don't have time to go out and rediscover yourself. You have children and you need a job now. You need your own place soon."

"I'm doing the best I can. Marcus left me in a mess when I moved out."

"You put yourself in a mess when you met him, Lisa, and he *put* you out. I don't want to hear it. I'm tired of you blaming Marcus for your situation. You're always trying to put things on him when all he did was took advantage of having his milk without buying the cow. You always running in behind men that don't want to get to know you. If you'd slow down, you'd see what I'm talking about."

"Can we ever just sit and talk about me without you preaching?"

"No." I exhaled a long breath and rose from the couch, deciding to forgo the news tonight. "I'm going to bed."

"Margaret, I promise to have my stuff together soon. I'm trying, you have to see that."

"Okay, Lisa."

I walked down the dark hallway into the bedroom, where Lester was in the bed snoring. His freshly showered body was naked and sprawled across his side of the bed and half of mine. I went to the bathroom to turn off the light. Lester always left the light on so I could see when I came into the room at night. Before flipping the switch I caught a glimpse of myself in the mirror. I wasn't the string bean I used to be, no, sir. My arms were flabby, I'd developed wrinkles on my face and hands, my rear end was wide, and my eyes no longer held the fascination in them that they used to. I remember being curious and being happy about everything. My skin was smooth but had a puffiness to it that I hadn't been able to get rid of since I'd had that stroke some years ago. My hair, once dark and shiny, was now spotted with gray and dull. I kept it in a neat bun once it had grown past my shoulders. Lester liked it long, so I never considered cutting it. I took my medicine from the medicine cabinet, turned off the light, and sat on the edge of the bed thinking about tomorrow. The linens needed to be washed and the girls' hair would have to be washed too. I'd already decided somewhere deep inside that if Lisa didn't do it, I would. I just couldn't have my grandbabies walking around here looking like they didn't belong to somebody. Nikki had violin tutoring in the morning and Lester's suit would have to be picked up from the cleaner's. I said my prayers and pulled myself into bed. Lester moved in his sleep, flinging his hairy arm around me, giving me a quick feeling of claustrophobia. As I drifted off to sleep the tightness around my ankles throbbed, reminding me that I never soaked them.

Faulkner

There was nothing like a fresh, new, sunny Saturday to combat a long Friday. I lay in bed as long as I could, allowing the April sun to warm my bedroom and fill it with brightness. I got out of bed long enough to let my window up and take in a breath of freshness from outside before I hopped back under the covers. At nine on the dot, the phone rang. I knew it was my mother. She'd probably been up since six, but she never called me until nine each Saturday. It had been that way since I moved out nine years ago. My mother, Gwena Lorraine, was a fifty-two-year-old fourth-grade teacher who was supportive but demanding. She loved to listen, but loved giving advice even more. And if her advice wasn't followed, she persisted until it was. We were close to being like night and day. She spent most of her life telling little people what to do and how to do it, which sometimes caused her to treat adults like fourth graders. I, on the other hand, felt it necessary to speak only when it *was* necessary. I didn't enjoy telling people what to do, let alone little people.

"Hello?"

"Girl, you still in the bed? When are you going to start getting up with the rooster?"

"Hey, Mom. Yes, I'm still in the bed. I'm always in the bed when you call, because you always call before I get up."

"I see somebody was already prepared to get up on the wrong side of the bed. Hard day at work yesterday?"

"Sorry. I did have a bad day. I'm not trying to take it out on you."

"And I wouldn't let you take it out on me. Besides, your attitude is nothing new. Remember, I'm your mother. I realized you had a crankiness about you when you stayed in my stomach a week and a half over your due date. You stayed in there and gave me grief, kickin' and carryin' on like a tyrant. And when you finally came out, boy, were you an ugly little something, face frowning, fists balled up, and determined not to be breast-fed."

"Mom, please don't start."

"So tell me what happened at work."

"I had some paperwork that needed to be turned in, but I never got around to it until the end of the day, and it needed to be double-checked. I'd decided to bring the work home, but as I walked out the door, Joyce caught me and basically told me to get it completed and turned in before I went home, which caused me to stand Teresa up at happy hour."

"Teresa will live. I'm sure she had enough drinks to keep her from being angry at you. It sounds to me like Ms. Armstrong is testing her limits with you."

"She is, but it's no big deal, I can handle it."

"I believe you. Still no word on the management job you applied for?"

"No."

"I keep telling you, Faulkner Michele, to go back and get your master's degree. That way you can be a manager and stop auditioning to be one. Corporate America, and Joyce, will respect you then."

I closed my eyes and rubbed my hands across my forehead. My mother just didn't understand. "I know,

Mom, I know." I rolled over, pulled the covers up across my breasts. As much as I wanted to tell my mother I had no plans of going back to school, I couldn't. "I'll look into it."

"Don't try and pacify me, Faulkner. You said that last time, and you still haven't done so much as call a school and try to see what classes you would need to take."

"Mom, I will look into it."

In the background, my father yelled my mother's name. He called her Gwen for short. He always called her name twice before my mother would answer. I wasn't the only one with a stubborn streak. The first time she didn't answer, but the second time she yelled back without taking the phone away from her mouth. I pulled the phone away until she finished. Thank God for my daddy, because whatever he needed, it was forcing her to end our call.

"Let me call you back. I think your father needs help with the toilet in the front bathroom. He called himself fixing it, but I'm going to call a plumber."

I had fixed my lips to say 'bye to my mom when she just hung up. I hated when she did that. I yawned and hung up too, glad to be free of my mother's tormenting accusations that I was never going to get anywhere in life unless I went back to school. She saw education as the light of the world, but from my point of view, education was behind me. I'd paid all the dues I was willing to pay being bored to death by someone who did things like collect dead bugs for a living and demand that they be referred to as "professor." I couldn't see myself in a classroom mentally masturbating over theories. I wasn't totally against going back to school, because I enjoyed learning and I liked being around other people with similar interests, but I was working now and getting paid good money. This was a matter of occupation, not education. Once I got the promotion, my mom would ease up. But I had to get the promotion first.

I frowned when I dragged myself from bed and took inventory of my apartment, which was in desperate need of some personal attention. Clothes I needed to take to the cleaner's were crumpled in a ball next to the bookshelf, and three pairs of shoes that needed to be in the closet sat under my reading chair. Not to mention my workout gear was trailing from the front door all the way to the bedroom. Keeping late hours at work had me living like a pack rat. The dank smell and darkness I experienced now when I came home had already killed two of my plants, and it had forced me to take my dog, Louis, to my parents' house. He had stayed with me as more of an alarm dog than as company, but my neglect rattled his nerves. He had a bad habit of shitting everywhere when he didn't eat on time, which was at six o'clock every evening. I'd missed feeding him a few days too many, and he paid me back with a vengeance. I came home and found little doo-doo drops everywhere: under my bed, on my couch, in a pair of my favorite shoes, in the bathroom, and even on my CD case. Louis wasn't used to the neglect and I wasn't used to seeing him neglected, but I still punished him with some rolled newspaper before I took him back to my parents' house. Now he barks at me whenever I visit. As soon as he hears my voice he howls and runs under the table for cover.

I cleaned. First, I washed the dishes, swept, mopped, and polished the wood floors then Hoovered the bedroom and took my cleaning to the car. My oil needed to be changed as well, so I made a note to stop by a lube center and have it done. I put my laptop in the car and headed out.

Spring in Dallas is usually warm. As I drove from my uptown loft, headed toward Oakcliff, I could see people out in shorts and tank tops. Thank goodness dropping off the cleaning and getting my oil changed were the only errands I had to run. I was eager to get out and enjoy the weather with everyone else. By the time I got to the lube center, fatigue had crept up on me. Driving and heat had that affect on me. When I stepped inside, the cool air hit me and I could have melted. Some spring we're having, I thought, when the weatherman had already reported weather bordering ninety degrees.

There was a charming elderly couple sitting in the waiting room. From the quick glance I took, as I smiled and nodded hello to them, I could tell they were married (wedding rings), in love (holding hands), and inseparable (sitting close). They were too cute. I didn't know if I was the only one who thought this, but after two people have been together for a while, they begin to look alike. This couple looked like an older version of Cliff and Claire Huxtable. The woman had smooth, nutmeg-colored skin. She was beautiful. Her salt-and-pepper hair was wispy and flowed from her head like cotton candy. When she smiled, her teeth were so perfect I wondered if the pearly whites were hers. If they were, then sister-girl had it going on. Her husband was a few shades lighter, but his skin glowed too. His hair was in a short, salt-and-pepper Afro, with much more salt than his wife's. They both had on matching turquoise jogging suits and matching sneakers. When they smiled, it was the same smile, both flaunting natural-looking teeth, with an immaculate appeal. No gold, no rottens, no gaps, no grime. Twinkling eyes. The woman watched me all the way to my seat. Her manicured nails tapped on the purse that lay in her lap to whatever music was playing in her head.

I opened my laptop and began getting the work schedule together for May. The couple resumed their conversation. I extended my listening for entertainment's sake. It took me no time to figure that they were talking about their granddaughter's wedding, which apparently had been the previous weekend. From being nosy, I heard the event was pretty elaborate, with fourteen bridesmaids, a six-layer vanilla cake with Italian cream icing, and a private reception on a yacht. The elderly woman caught me peeking over my screen. She didn't have a problem letting me in.

"Our granddaughter, Donna, had the most beautiful wedding last weekend."

I typed a few words and returned a comment. "Really? The weather was gorgeous last weekend." I smiled, welcoming her energy.

The woman scooted over toward me. "Oh, you wouldn't believe how stunning the entire event was. Everything was white. A total-white wedding out on Lake Ray Hubbard."

"Sounds like it was beautiful. How old is she?"

"Twenty-four. About your age," the woman said.

I was pleased that the woman thought I was twenty-four. I felt the need to correct her, but let it slide; besides, her husband was already talking.

"She married a navy man," he said proudly. "I served forty years myself." He leaned back with his chest out.

"Preston, that's all you think about is that old navy," the woman snapped playfully. "I hope Marvin doesn't stay in there as long as you did. Donna wants to have kids and get her career off the ground. She don't need to be uprooting every time she gets situated."

Not caring about the tiff they were having, I interrupted. "Your granddaughter is working on a career, huh?"

The woman turned back to me. She seemed glad that I'd asked the question so she could talk about her granddaughter instead of revealing what years of being a naval wife will do to a person. "Yes, she's an accountant."

"Nice career choice." I felt good as I pecked away at the keys. There was still hope for me to have a career and a successful relationship at the same time.

"Are you married?"

I held up the back side of my left hand and wiggled my ring finger. "Nope. I'm working on my career first."

The old man pointed his finger at me. "Oh, you're too pretty not to be married. You mean to tell me not one man has come along and put his claim on you?"

I gave a polite laugh. "No, sir. I have a hard enough time being married to my job." I laughed at my own joke. The couple stared at me, both with blank looks on their faces. I cleared my throat and attempted to give them an honest, less amusing answer. "I think I'll think about settling down in about three years."

The woman leaned over and patted me on the leg. "You know, I was reading in *Reader's Digest* this story about a young woman. I suspect she was young and pretty just like you. She was ambitious and had a good job and she worked until she was in her midforties. Then one day she got fired on the spot without any cause. Even though the article was about her lawsuit against the company, the woman mentioned that she realized she'd spent too much time working and not enough time being in a solid relationship and creating a family of her own. She said when the company let her go, she felt empty." She paused briefly. "Imagine that."

I wondered where she was going with this and why *Reader's Digest* was still in circulation. I figured it would have gotten lost in the shuffle of the more colorful magazines. "You young girls got some slim pickings, but don't get caught up too much in that business world because it can't love you or support you like family. Relationships are important and companionship is a necessity."

I said, "I know what you're saying, but don't you think

now that women have more opportunities to work and make changes in large companies that they should go for it?"

"Oh, honey, I know they should. Women had to fight to get the recognition, but families are suffering because the women are getting younger and younger in the professional world and choosing not to work on stability in a family. Some don't want a family at all. It's selfish how they make all that money and spend enormous amounts of time working outrageous hours and whatnot. Then they turn right around and expect a relationship to be perfect after just a few weeks of dating. That's what I had to sit Donna down and explain to her, that you still have to make time for relationships just like you make time for your job, neither of which blossoms overnight. A strong faith and knowing how to balance is the key."

"It's easier said than done," I said. My screen saver activated and computerized fish began to swim across it. "Men should stay at home, maybe that's the answer."

The old man laughed out loud, causing me to frown. His wife totally ignored him.

"Oh, you young ladies just don't have the patience and that's all you need. When I was in my teens, everything was laid out exactly how it was supposed to happen and we just had to go day by day and wait. You got up, went to school, came home, helped with chores, did your schoolwork, ate dinner, and went to bed. That's what I focused on every day, and if I had one ounce of free time for any boy to come visit, I had to wait for him to get permission from his father, finish his chores, and walk two or three miles to my front porch." She laughed. "By then, it was time to prepare for the next day and go to bed. But everything we did took time. That's just something you all seem to think you don't have enough of."

"We don't," I protested. "It seems like when I get

home, I have just enough time to eat, go over the work I bring home, and take a bath."

"That's in your head. The best thing about being young is that time is on your side, but it's only on your side for a little while. Don't spend it all doing needless things and rushing through. You got fast food, remote controls, next-day service, and a ton of other devices that make you feel rushed, but you can't fall for that. When all is said and done, it will be about what you gave and what you built from a human standpoint, not how many hours you put in or how many times you came back late from lunch."

I couldn't do anything but stare into the woman's deep brown eyes. She had a look on her face as if it were the gospel she'd just told me: *The Gospel According to the Old Woman in the Lube Center Waiting Area*. I felt a little ambivalent, but I smiled at her as if she had shown me the light, convincing myself that this was not some on-the-path lecture that I should go home and change my life for. Don't take it personally, I told myself. The woman probably is just making conversation like all people do. That's it. That's all. The end. What she didn't understand was that the quicker, the better. If you were fast and good, you made more money, and the more money you made, the more comfortable you would be in a world where social security was questionable and retiring at sixty was becoming extinct.

"You remind me so much of Donna," she continued. "You both share the same attitude. She thought the world revolved around that job she had. Poor Marvin didn't stand a chance until she got sick and found out she had a rare blood disorder. She had to take a leave to get better. She had time to think about what was most important and Marvin was there every step of the way."

"She's lucky," I answered. I pecked a few more keys on the laptop to try and divert the woman's attention away from me. I didn't want to talk about this anymore, but I didn't want to be rude. Now I truly regretted dipping into their conversation in the first place. I'd had enough of Ma Kettle's *It's a Wonderful Life* sermon. She didn't know how hard it was to meet someone now. Men were no longer being the aggressors in the dating scene. They were tired of being turned down and turned out, so now, when I went to a club, the men sat and stared just like the women did. Everybody wanted to be approached but nobody wanted to do the approaching. I believed what the woman had said, but it wasn't applicable in the time we lived in. It was important to me that I be stable in my job before having a family. Climbing the corporate ladder was the way for me to secure my future, but this woman didn't agree with that. She didn't know that to be twenty-eight with no children, good credit, and living in one's own place, totally supported by oneself, was a symbol of successful urban survival, and that everything else, including a relationship, came after you got settled. As much as I appreciated this woman's words, I knew they were not for me. Unlike her granddaughter, I didn't have a man wanting to marry me. Having to choose love or career wasn't my issue and I didn't anticipate it ever being an issue. I knew what was most important and nothing could make me think different.

When they called for me to get my car, I packed up my computer, said good-bye to the couple, and rushed home to finish the schedule. The message light on my answering machine was blinking. I looked at the box and saw that I had one message. I pressed the button.

Beep! "Faulk, you know I'm mad at you. I sat at that club for an hour just like I did last week. You'd better be glad we're best friends, girl, otherwise I'd be at your house slashing your tires. Besides, I met a guy and I think this might be the one." The voice broke out in laughter. "This is Reesa. Call me."

The machine rescued the calls. I was now in need of a nap, and no longer wanted to be out in the warm weather. I lit two incense sticks and placed them in the potted plants near my stereo. The mild, sweet scent floated through the room, making me feel less pressed about getting the schedule done, but I was in the mood to do it. I put in my favorite CD, *The Essential Nina Simone,* and sat at the small work area I'd set up at home. My computer desk was positioned in front of a window overlooking a small shopping area and part of the nearby expressway. I opened my laptop and began typing. I never looked up or left my chair until all the information had been put in the computer, triple-checked, and saved. Before I knew it, Saturday was gone and Sunday had crept up. I hadn't had a wink of sleep and my bones ached from my sitting in a chair most of the day. The clock on my desk glowed a steady 3:42 A.M. This time I didn't bother to pull off my clothes. I put Nina on repeat and let her croon softly from the living room. Her deep, melodic voice soothed me. Her singing validated that being crazy was normal and being normal was crazy. I briefly entertained thoughts of going back to school before visions of my next workday overshadowed them. If I just hung in there, Joyce would have to face the fact that I was the best woman for the management job. Sunday ended up being one big blur and before I knew it, the alarm clock was buzzing and it was Monday.

Margaret

I stumbled out of bed this morning and a dizzy spell hit me as soon as I put my feet on the floor. I tried to ignore it, but the room wouldn't stop moving long enough for me to get myself in order, and before I knew what had happened, my legs buckled and I'd fallen against the dresser, bumping my knee on the way down. Lester was out of the bed and over me in the next few seconds. From there, things blurred. When I came to, I was back in the bed. I didn't feel as weighed down like I'd felt earlier, but I was weak and my left knee ached. I pulled the covers back and saw that it had swollen. I tried to touch it, but it was too tender. Half a glass of orange juice and my insulin pills were on the nightstand by my side of the bed. The top part of my gown was damp. I pulled it up to my nose and smelled orange juice. I pieced things together and was thankful that my husband had been there when he was. Lester wasn't in the room, but I could hear his voice coming from the room where Lisa and the girls slept. Minutes later, he came storming in.

"I'm going to beat Lisa's ass when she gets home," Lester mumbled to himself as he grabbed his keys and wallet from the dresser. He hadn't even noticed that I was awake.

"What's the matter?" I'd managed to sit up and sit at the edge of the bed. I looked over at the clock and realized it was 7:52. We all should have been out of the house.

"Oh, baby, I didn't see you. How are you feeling?"

"Okay, I guess. My throat is dry, but I'm good."

"You fell this morning, Margaret, and your knee swelled quicker than I could get you back in the bed. Have you been taking your insulin pills?"

"I'd been feeling good the past few days, Lester."

"Woman, take your medicine no matter what. What if you'd been here alone? It's bad enough you get up and go to work against what I want you to do. I don't want you to go to work today. Call and tell them you won't be in. I'll come home for lunch to check on you."

I wasn't in the mood to hear Lester rant about me or my job. "Where are the girls?" I asked.

Lester paused and looked at me. He didn't like the fact that I was ignoring him, but I was in no mood to hear him comment on my condition. He snatched his cap from the bedpost. "They're in the den waiting for me to get them to school. Evidently, their mama slipped off last night and doesn't seem to think it important enough to be here to get them ready for school." Lester didn't wait for me to respond. He left the room and soon I heard the truck start and pull out of the driveway. Lester didn't operate well under his own frustration and I could only imagine how my grandbabies looked when they left.

I called my doctor to let her know what had happened. She ordered me to come in before noon. Then I called Faulkner to let her know I wasn't coming in. She was immediately alarmed, but I reassured her that I was fine and would be in first thing Tuesday. I'd taken two aspirins and sat at the edge of the bed, letting the silence of the house engulf me. It was the first day in two months that I'd had the house to myself.

Since the girls had come along, the house was seldom

quiet, and in a small way I resented them being here. God, forgive me for even thinking it, but it was true. Since Lisa moved home, everything upset Lester, so to keep him from hollering, I took up the slack by making most of the decisions that needed to be made. What was going to be cooked for dinner, when it was time for the girls to bathe, when Lester had to mow the lawn, and the list went on. It had become that way by default, and it was a role I didn't like having to play. My dislikes ran the gamut from Lisa being a deadbeat mother, all the way to Lester's dirty clothes sitting in the middle of the bathroom floor.

Hearing cars whiz down the street and the voices of children walking to school outside my window, along with the sounds of birds, reminded me of my single days when I'd had my own apartment. I looked around the room, not finding it remotely close to being as much of me as my own space had been. The room where Lester and I slept was sadly in need of a paint job and new furniture. Our old mahogany dresser and bed were ones we'd bought at a furniture store called Levitz back in '79. Four of the six handles were missing on the drawers and it was scratched up pretty bad from being moved so much. I had an antique bedroom suite in storage, but Lester wanted to paint the room before moving the bedroom suite in. He'd been saying he would paint for three years, then Lisa moved in, and ever since, nothing else had been said about it. I figured once Lisa was out of the house, he'd do as he promised.

I slid back into the bed and closed my eyes. The pressure in my knee throbbed as I pulled the covers back over it. I thought about my life for a moment. I wondered what would have become of me if I'd left the phone company years ago when I probably should have. Why did I stay? Why did I choose to go there year after year, watching the woman who used to be my best friend become someone I couldn't stand to be around? That question always bothered me. It rang in my head and I was always praying to be at peace with my decision to remain there and not deal with what-ifs.

The sound of keys at the front door brought me out of my thoughts. A female voice giggled, followed by the low tones of a male voice. It was Lisa and she had a visitor. I rose from my pillow and looked out my window, which faced the street, giving me a sufficient view of the driveway, where a big, fancy utility vehicle was parked. It was white with shiny trimmings on the wheels and black-tinted windows. The giggling and deep tones came down the hallway and were closed behind the door of the room across the hall. I prayed a moment before forcing myself from bed. I asked the Lord to get Satan behind me while I went to go see what was going on in my house.

Faulkner

Being at work early had its advantages. For one thing, the office was quiet and peaceful. This gave me time to do some deep thinking about how the day was going to go, no matter what happened. Today I was choosing to be more assertive and not to have a bad day. Besides giving me a head start on my attitude, being at work early also meant no one could ever accuse me of being late. After I meditated over a cup of hot tea, I looked at my to-do list. Customer surveys needed to be turned in,

I had to send a verification form to Joyce saying that the billing information was correct, the new schedule needed to be posted, I needed a list of everyone who had completed ACIS training, and I would start on the project she needed me to do for the MSCOT review that was coming up. She'd be swinging around here in about an hour. She always perused the floor on Mondays, going from cube to cube, seeing what she could see and making her presence known.

The ringing of my phone broke the silence and startled me. I checked the Caller ID above the number. Private line sprang across the display. Knowing it was a personal call, I picked up.

"Faulkner speaking."

"You can't call nobody back?!" Teresa's voice blurted. "First you stand me up and then you don't return my calls. A sistah can't get no love these days from her best friend?"

"Hey, girl," I said. "I'm sorry, Joyce held me over again on Friday. By the time I finished, it was too late to call you back and I slept all day yesterday. What happened to your ten-minute rule?"

"Whatever, Faulkner, save the drama for your mama. I sat up at that bar for an hour waiting on you anyway. I thought you had been in a car accident or something. The least you could have done was called." Teresa broke out in laughter. "Dang, I sound like I'm talking to my man."

"I tried your cell phone, but you didn't answer."

"I left it at home, Friday. My bad."

"Yeah, your bad." I laughed. "Really, I'm sorry. It won't happen again."

Teresa huffed, "You're sorry, that's the truth. Breaking your back waiting on the promotion you haven't got and probably won't get. It's really no excuse for the way you let your boss dog you, but I'll let it slide 'cause it's your life. I've been listening to you flip your emotions on and off about Joyce since day one. One day she's Jekyll then she's Hyde. I'd be a fool to think you would have given her a piece of your hardworking mind; besides, I wouldn't be your friend if I ragged on you about your inability to stand up to your boss."

Teresa had a way of using the truth to cut and console that I sometimes wished she'd keep to herself. She was forward, but never hard-hearted. She called things like she saw them and never held back when it was time to speak up. Two years at a small paper and three years at Dallas's top news station as a reporter had made her that way. Of course, she was crazy in college, but once she started working in journalism, she became a cutthroat and it extended into her personal life. She spent most of her time like me, behind a computer screen meeting deadlines, and trying to be recognized for her dedication. Some days we'd pack up our portable computers, head to the nearest coffeehouse, and work together in silence, with only the clicking of keys between us.

We spent the next few minutes talking about her new assignment. She'd been assigned to do a national story on New York's mayor. That meant she'd be traveling. She was excited to finally break free from local stories. Teresa was a kamikaze reporter, in my opinion. She covered the stories many of her colleagues dared not try. The newspaper honored her two years in a row for her ability to get a good, newsworthy story. Once, she stayed in a vacant house directly in the way of a tornado, just to write a piece on the emotions people go through during natural disasters. The story was amazing. She'd suffered two fractured ribs and a broken leg during the storm.

"Congratulations," I said. I was happy for Teresa.

"You know I have you to thank."

"Me? Why?"

"Friday I met a guy and he told me that because we'd met, my life would change. If you would have showed up, I would not have given this man the time of day."

"Then why'd you call me barking earlier? I did you a favor."

"Well, you know I had to make you feel bad. I was hoping it would give you the strength to flip your boss off and walk out on her; wishful thinking on my part."

"You hussy." I laughed. "What guy did you meet? I should have known better than to let you go alone."

"His name is Phil Putnam. He programs software."

"Really. How'd you meet?"

"He bought me a drink. I was sitting at the bar and I guess I'd looked at my watch one time too many because he approached and asked if I was waiting on someone. Well, of course I replied, 'Hell, yeah, my best friend is supposed to be here and she hasn't shown up.' I was kind of fired up and didn't pay him much attention at first. But after he bought me the drink and we talked, I became more interested in him. The rest is soap opera stuff."

"Like what?"

"Like we danced half the night, ended up holding hands, and he walked me to my car, where we kissed."

"Girl, hush! You know better than to be kissing some strange man the first night you meet."

"Faulkner, I couldn't help it. He had lips like that rapper L.L. Cool J, and he kept licking them."

"Then you should have offered him some Chapstick or something."

"Whatever. It was just a kiss, stop tripping, you've done worse."

I laughed. Teresa knew me too well. "Did you exchange numbers?"

"Shit, yeah. I wasn't going to let him get away from

me. He's single with no kids and he's been on the same job for more than five years, not to mention he was sweet. You can't beat that with a royal flush. We're going out tomorrow night to see that new Brad Pitt movie."

"Then I should be glad I didn't show up. I've been feeling guilty for nothing."

"Whatever, you missed out. He had a friend with him and he was fine too, just not my type."

"So he didn't have two cell phones and three pagers hanging from his sagging jeans?"

"You're being sarcastic, Faulk, and it ain't working." Teresa laughed. "I think you and Phil's friend would have hit it off because he talked a lot about jazz music and that reminded me of you. You know you're always playing Sarah what's-her-name or Dinah Shore."

"Washington. It's Dinah Washington."

"Same difference."

"No, it's not. What was his name?"

"Who?"

"Phil's friend."

"Greg. I can't remember his last name. I think he said Anderson. But I know you'll like him so I gave him—"

I heard footsteps in my area. Without looking up I moved my hand over to the release button on my phone. "Reesa, I gotta go."

She was still talking when I disconnected the line. I didn't have my headset off five seconds before I felt someone standing near me. I turned around and Brenda Jones was peeking in. I was relieved it wasn't Joyce. I'd made a rule for her never to catch me doing personal business on company time.

"Good morning," Brenda sang. Her green eyes sparkled. She reminded me of a taller, small-nosed mix between Bette Midler and the lady who starred on *The X-Files*. "How was your weekend?"

"Good, and yours?"

"It was wonderful. Craig and I took a quick drive to Hot Springs."

"Arkansas?" I rested in my chair as Brenda nodded, letting me know I was right. I smiled, giving her my full attention. "You and that husband of yours are always on the road going somewhere."

She giggled under her breath as she rolled a chair from the empty cube. When she sat down, her skirt showed her pink knees and firm white legs. She didn't tan because she had a fear of catching cancer, but there were times when even I wished she'd do something to add color to her faded-looking skin. A hint would do. "Oh, Faulkner, this time it was absolutely wonderful." She flipped her straight, naturally red hair behind her ears and filled me in.

"We went to this day spa called Buckstaff, where I got the most incredible massage. The masseuse had huge hands that made my whole body relax. If you ever go, you have to visit the Buckstaff spa. On Saturday night, we had a romantic dinner at this restaurant called Bohemia. They served some really great European dishes. Then we went dancing at a place called the Bronze Gorilla."

"The Bronze what?"

Brenda laughed. "I was wondering about the name too, but they played the best music from the seventies and eighties. Barry Manilow, Gloria Gaynor, Hall and Oates, Patti LaBelle."

"Hmm, sounds like fun."

"Faulkner, it was the best time!"

"I've never been to Hot Springs," I said. It reminded me that I hadn't been on vacation in more than a year. "Where did you two stay?"

"At a bed-and-breakfast about seven miles outside the city. It was on a lake and the moonlight cascaded right into the bedroom. I can't remember the name, but I have a brochure at home. I'll bring it so you can take a look at it."

"Thanks," I said, grinning.

Brenda reached into a bag that she had with her and pulled out something wrapped in butcher's paper. "I made this for you when I was there."

"What is it, a piece of pork loin?"

We shared laughter as I removed the paper from the gift. My mouth fell open when I saw what the gift was. Brenda had made a ceramic utensil holder. It was painted in a patchwork-mosaic style of my favorite colors, brown, green, and orange. I couldn't keep my eyes off it. "Brenda, this is lovely."

"I painted it myself. I got the color idea from Home and Garden Television."

"Everything you've ever made for me is simply stunning. You know I'm not the arts-and-crafts type. When I was in the second grade, we planted pinto beans and my bean never sprouted."

We both laughed. Brenda glowed. I could see it in her rosy cheeks. She was always in a good, productive mood after one of her weekend getaways with her husband. As she continued to talk about her weekend, she stopped suddenly and rose to her feet. Without looking at me, Brenda rolled the chair back to my spare cube. "I'll talk to you later, Faulkner," she said dryly. Brenda shuffled down the aisle with her gaze straight in front of her. Gail came in, lugging her usual Igloo cooler, a sweater, the latest black hair magazine, and two bags of Doritos.

"Hey, Faulkner," she huffed, sounding out of breath.

Gail looked at Brenda and sucked her teeth. "Good morning, Brenda."

Brenda gave a dry response and a half-smile. All the enthusiasm and joy that had filled her voice just seconds ago had disappeared. "Hi, Gail."

Gail watched Brenda long enough to frown and roll her eyes at Brenda's back. She situated her belongings. "Monday mornings are never easy for me."

I sat in my chair, aware of the hostile transfer. "Gail, what was that all about?" I stood and leaned on the wall that separated us. "What's going on between you and Brenda?"

Gail never looked up as she talked. "Nothing. Brenda is just way too sensitive. You know how they are."

"How *who* are?"

"Faulkner, don't act like you don't know what I'm talking about." Gail stared at me like I'd tried to get over on her. "*They. Them. White folk.*" Gail kept going about her business as if talking about white people were something we did every day. I'd never talked to Gail about how she felt about people of different races. She was married to a Mexican, so I assumed she had no racial biases. Hearing her comment negatively about white people had thrown me for a loop.

I disregarded her comments, curious to find out where her prejudice was coming from. "Do you mind telling me what happened?"

Gail paused a moment. "It was really nothing, okay? Last week I was walking down the hall with two of my friends and one of them made a comment about white people. Brenda just happened to be walking behind us and we didn't know it. Anyway, she was dipping in our business and heard some things she shouldn't have."

"You, Daeshun, and Sharlitha?"

"Sharlitha and Tiffany."

"Tiffany Martin?"

"Yeah. Tiffany had some earrings she was selling out of her car and we were coming back from the parking garage. I got the cutest pair of blue hoops. I should have brought the bag in so you could see them."

I reminded myself that Gail and Tiffany weren't even

speaking to each other two weeks ago because Tiffany wouldn't give Gail a ride home. "What was said?" I asked, in an attempt to keep Gail on the subject of what had happened.

Gail huffed like I was giving her a hard time. She stared at me a few seconds with her lips pursed.

"Are you going to tell me or do I have to go and get it from Brenda?"

"Sharlitha said that the white people around here are always trying to regulate, like they runnin' thangs. Then I said something about one of my white coworkers and how she's always running in behind my Team Lead, brown-nosing, and how she's always trying to check people about getting personal faxes. Brenda excused herself into our conversation, I told her to mind her business, we got into it, and that was it."

"Brenda is your only white coworker, Gail, and I'm your Team Lead. Why would you say something like that?"

"Well, it ain't like I was lying. I walk in here this morning and see her grinning all up in your face and she's always going to lunch with you or asking to help you with some work. Hell, she even monitors the fax machine. I know she's just trying to set herself up for Team Lead once you're promoted. But that's going to be my job."

"Gail, I never promised you that you would be Team Lead. I said I would help you in any way that I could to make sure you get moved up. You're a great asset to MSCOT."

"Same difference. I know you have pull, Faulkner."

I rubbed my forehead. It wasn't hurting, but the stress of the conversation made me close my eyes and rub it. "Gail," I said, "you owe her an apology."

"For what?" Gail's neck formed a slight half-moon. "I'm not apologizing to her. It's bad enough she runs around here thinking she's Miss Homemaker, Betty Crocker, with her stringy hair and pale skin. I don't slave on this job every day to be apologizing to nobody, especially no white people." Gail looked at me. The look said a lot of things and her willingness to apologize was not one of them.

"Gail, you owe her an apology," I repeated in the same calm but stern voice. "I know this isn't a secret to you, Gail, but you could lose your job. Your comment about white people was racist and insulting if nothing else. You can't just go around here saying what you want."

"Faulkner, I tell it how it is. I keep it real. I'm not going to bow down for nobody. White people around here are always saying and doing what they want. Just last week, Mr. Price strolled down here and said something racist to Carmen and me. They the reason people like us can't move up."

"What did Mr. Price say?"

"He came down here and was asking us how everything was going. I told him things were fine and then he went to Carmen's cube and observed her for a while. Then he turned his chubby ass back to me and said, "You people were made for customer service and I'm proud of the work that you do.""

"What did you do when he said that?"

"I really didn't know how to take it at first because I know I'm good at what I do and I know Carmen works her ass off. But Brenda was sitting right there and he never so much as looked her way, but when he said what he did, she looked at him and then turned back to her computer like he wasn't there. That's when I knew what he said wasn't right. It didn't feel right to begin with. These white people make me want to holler. They keep us from being successful."

"Joyce is black and she's successful."

Gail released a condescending laugh. "And look at what it's done to her. Has her ass so high in the air, she can't even recognize that without us, she'd be right here answering these phones. She left us high and dry. Mr. Price got her brainwashed."

"Gail, Brenda isn't a Mr. Price. She's not Hitler and she didn't deserve to hear those remarks come from your mouth."

"She's just as guilty, Faulkner. You can't trust them, none of them. At some point they all become racist. I don't trust one white person up here, Brenda Jones included."

"Gail, I think you're jumping the gun a little. No one around here is calling you out of your name."

"They don't have to, it's all in how they treat you and how they look at you."

"Brenda has never treated you as if she didn't like you. I'm sure there are things that I haven't witnessed between the two of you, but, Gail, we know black people who call themselves derogatory names all the time. How do you expect to move up if you're going off on people when you don't have proof that they dislike you?"

"The same way all the other bigwigs do," Gail protested. "The only way to the top is by playing hardball. Joyce is a prime example of what I'm talking about. The other person gets to choose how they will get stepped on, you know what I mean? I know I'm not all that, but once I get some more training under my belt, then I'm going to move up and continue to move up until I'm fully vested, driving a nice car, and dishing out the work instead of taking it."

Gail and I were about to stare a hole into each other. I'd developed an attitude and was ready to write her up for insubordination, but decided to give her one more chance at choosing to stay employed. "It must be nice to think it's just that easy to be ruthless," I said. "Gail

Perez, minus the politics, the bottom line is that you need to apologize to Brenda. You will either do what I'm telling you to do, or you will lose your job. Take your pick."

Gail looked at me with her wide eyes. She'd left me with no choice. I wasn't about to condone her attitude toward Brenda. If she wanted to be that way, whether I agreed with it or not, she wasn't going to do it under me. I sympathized with Gail. I knew there was some validity to her complaint, but Brenda wasn't the right target and Gail needed to learn how to aim her guns, otherwise she'd always remain stagnant at work.

"And remember," I added, "the hardball you throw will be the same one that eventually you will have to catch, if it doesn't hit you first."

"Hmph." Gail fiddled with one of the magazines on her desk. I could tell she didn't want to apologize, but she knew she wouldn't last long under me if she didn't. She looked at me and walked away. "I don't know why you're trippin', because a blind man can see that I just be fuckin' with Brenda. If I really didn't like her, she'd know it."

The phone rang as Gail entered Brenda's cube and began talking. I felt better seeing Gail choose a higher ground rather than getting fired. I put on my headset and pushed the answer button.

"This is Faulkner."

"Faulkner, this is Margaret. I won't be in today, I'm not feeling too well."

I looked at my watch. It was eight-forty. "What's the matter?"

"My blood is up a little so I'm going to go to my doctor and get it checked."

"Do you need me to come get you? I can come if you need me to."

"No, no, don't worry yourself. I have a way."

"Margaret, you haven't been watching what you eat. I warned you Friday when I saw you were eating left-over fried chicken and mashed potatoes."

"That was just once. Besides, I'm fine. It's just that my daughter didn't have the girls ready and Lester woke up yelling and ranting and my blood went up. I'm sure that's all it is."

I didn't believe Margaret, but I decided to let it rest for now. "Okay, but you call me if you need anything and I'll be there. I'll have a salad waiting for you tomorrow."

"Alrighty, that sounds good." Margaret had a smile in her voice.

I disconnected the call and began the day. I was worried about Margaret and determined to get her to retire, but she wouldn't listen to me. I knew if I could get Joyce to lighten up and put aside whatever animosity they had, she could convince Margaret to retire. Joyce hadn't come down the aisles and it was nearing nine o'clock. She was either late or in her office, too busy to take her daily eight-thirty stroll. There was plenty of work for me to do, so I got my mind off Joyce and began working on my list of things to do.

Joyce

I loathed Mondays, especially this one. I'd made the mistake of letting my young tenderoni stay the entire weekend. We drank and had sex so much over the course of two days that this morning I slept through my alarm clock and woke with a minor hangover. Now I was poking around my house like I didn't have a job. My intention was to be there first thing this morning to pick up the surveys and give Faulkner the disk for the MSCOT review, but it took me damn near fifteen minutes just to get out of bed and another twenty-five to get showered and dressed. That alone made me realize I was going to be late, but I'd known that when I was being flipped over in my king-sized bed as the young man licked the palm of his hand and slapped my behind last night, well past midnight. He'd left an hour ago, chipper and walking on clouds. I'd already let him break my number-one rule, never let the man stay over on a work night. I blamed it on the cognac this time and promised myself to never let it happen again.

By the time I was headed out the door, the small hand on my antique wall clock was resting haphazardly atop the eight and the long hand was seconds away from the six. I lived exactly forty-five minutes from the office, pending traffic and weather. I couldn't predict the traffic, but it was the end of April and the weather couldn't have been better. I could make it there by a few minutes after nine if I hurried. I grabbed my purse and briefcase that coordinated with the mustard-yellow Donna Karan two-piece suit I was wearing. With a push of a button on my key ring, the BMW that sat idle in my garage started up. Minutes later, I was pulling out and on my way.

I lived in Plano, Texas. It's a predominantly middle- to upper-middle-class suburb on the far north side of Dallas. Other than the fact that it had a high rate of teen drug use, Plano was safe, clean, and nowhere near the inner city. That was my main reason for moving out here. Sure, it had its bad points. The police were ridiculous and a few times I'd had to confront the chief about being an African-American woman who drove a BMW. I was pulled over three times in two months when I first purchased my car, and the excuse given was "random halting of vehicles," which the police claimed the right to do, but I knew racial profiling when I saw it. I supported the city council, paid taxes, and participated in the Neighborhood Watch program, and I knew rich white people weren't the only ones who drove expensive automobiles. Nevertheless, I hadn't been pulled over for anything since. The police, I thought, should be worried about the heroin floating around the school halls instead of concerning themselves with an adult woman who had earned every single thing she owned.

When I pulled into the parking garage, Simeon, the security guard, stopped me as usual to scan my parking sticker. I considered him valuable. He was a tan-colored man, older than seventy and weighing less than 130 soaking wet. Simeon was hardly security material.

"Good morning, Ms. Armstrong."

"Simeon," I said with my magnetic smile. "How are you?"

He waved his hand and nodded his head, letting me know he was doing well. The skin on his face was like leather. He'd been here as long as I could remember. Sometimes I felt sorry for the old man. Who in his right mind would sit in a parking booth smiling all day long at people coming and going? He didn't have a gun and even if he had, the man was just too ancient to be taken seriously.

"I made sure no one got your spot this morning," he said as he pointed to the empty space.

I slid a ten-dollar bill into his hand. "Wonderful, and thank you so much. You always take good care of me, Sim." I winked at him.

He tipped his cap to me as I drove by. I didn't have a parking spot with my name on it like the executives did, even though I felt I deserved one, but I paid Simeon to make sure no one got the spot that was adjacent to where the executives parked. My emerald-green, five-series BMW was the missing complement to the other expensive, foreign cars parked near the building entrance that belonged to the execs. Fred had already promised to make sure I became an executive. He'd been grooming me for the job, and I was more than ready to accept the challenge. I could already see myself in a top financial magazine like *Black Enterprise, Business Week,* or even *Forbes*.

I went to my office and got the disk to give to Faulkner. I cruised the floor just to let the team know I was in the office, like a queen bee looking over her drones. Everyone was in place except for Margaret Eddye. I double-checked to be sure she wasn't anywhere in the area, making a mental note to add another strike to her already diminishing attendance record. It was the fourth day this month she'd been either absent or late. When I got to Faulkner's cube, she was busy assisting the intern, James Hardy. For the first time, I noticed how nice he was, dressed in brown slacks and a cream shirt.

I interrupted. "Ms. Lorraine, here's the disk for the MSCOT review."

They both looked up at me. James offered the smile of someone who didn't want to rock my boat on a Monday morning. Faulkner smirked briefly, looked at her watch, and took the disk. "Thanks."

Before I could retreat and get back to business she asked me over to the empty cube. I hated standing inside the small, boxlike area. A cube space wasn't big enough for a pig to survive in, let alone a person. There was no privacy to be had.

"What is it, dear?" I asked.

"It's about Margaret."

I placed my hand on my hip. "Yes, what about Margaret?"

"Joyce, I want you to talk to her and get her to see that she needs to retire."

James stepped out of the other cube to give us additional privacy. The look on his face told us he didn't want to witness the conversation.

I shifted my weight. Faulkner was soft on the old woman. Margaret had been sick for some time, in and out of the hospital due to diabetes and hypertension; I was aware of that, but all of it was due to Margaret not exercising and spending too much time living for others and not herself. When Faulkner first started working here, Margaret took her in, trained her, mothered her, and created a close union. They shared a bond outside the job and now, Miss Thing was trying to get me to sympathize. But she didn't know how much I did not like Margaret Eddye. I knew a different Margaret Eddye. As she had with Faulkner, she had taken me in too, taught me everything, and watched me move up. But after my first real promotion, Margaret separated herself from me and left me out to dry and I suffered for it. Tell the truth, I couldn't stand her then and I couldn't stand her now.

"I don't see that as a necessary measure, Ms. Lorraine. Margaret is aware of what she needs to do. It's evident she wants to work and I have no control over her decision to do so. Why don't you talk to her? You seem to have more influence on her than me."

"She won't listen to me; besides, I know that you two go back. You've known Margaret a lot longer than I have. Maybe you can say something different to her."

"Different like what? Ms. Lorraine, the fact that Margaret and I have worked together for some years doesn't mean anything. I don't have anything mind-altering to say to her that will make her decide to finally care about her health."

"But Joyce, she's sick and this job is stressful. I know

if you talked to her she'd listen. Margaret's given thirty-three years of service to this company. How can you stand there and be so callous? Margaret taught you and me what we know. The least you could do is see what she's doing to herself, especially as her boss. Don't you even care?"

"You're overstepping your boundaries, Ms. Lorraine. I told you where I stand—no further discussion." I looked around. Margaret's cube was still empty. "Is Margaret in today?"

Faulkner hesitated, proving my point of why I didn't want to address Margaret. She wasn't even dependable anymore. "No. She went to the doctor's office. She'll be in tomorrow."

"Yet another missed day that we can't afford," I replied. "I can't convince Margaret Eddye to take something she doesn't want, and business can't cease because she's not here. We're still on company time, so I think we both need to get back to work."

I attempted to walk past her, but Faulkner put her hand on my arm to keep me from getting by. I stared at her as if her hands had no business on my clothes. Her face softened, losing its straightforwardness. "Joyce, I'm begging you."

"Dear, I will not use my time, *my work time,* trying to sell the idea of retirement to a woman who seems bent on working herself to death. Margaret, by her own will, has become perishable, do you understand that?"

"What I don't understand is how a woman can watch her former friend kill herself."

Faulkner's eyes told me that all she wanted from me was a yes answer. She was right—Margaret and I were former friends, with a lot of things to say to each other, though not necessarily good things. I could easily use this as my chance to get some things off my chest with

Margaret Eddye. By the time I would be finished with her, she'd quit on the spot.

"Okay, I'll talk to her." With that I pushed past Faulkner and left the cube.

I took the elevator to the fifth floor and knocked on Ella Parnell's door. She was on the phone but waved for me to come in. I placed a file in her hand and she smiled, giving me the thumbs-up. Ella was head of financing for the customer relations department and oversaw the fiscal operations for the Dallas division. She and I were friends and went way back—attended grade school together and furthered our education together. We were graduates of Wiley College and pledged the same sorority as line sisters. I sat and watched her handle business. When she got off the phone she smiled and rose from behind her desk to hug me.

"Joyce, girl. I barely got to see you last week. I hope this week won't be the same. We have to find time to do lunch."

We embraced. Ella's brawny arms covered me. She wasn't always so overweight, but having a child, a husband, and a knack for fried foods kept her out of the gym and in the kitchen. Pictures of her family adorned her desk and bookshelf, along with all types of elephant statues. She still kept the one I gave her on her desk. It was a porcelain, hand-painted elephant I'd bought when I visited Venezuela. Cost me quite a bit, but Ella, given her friendship over the years, more than deserved it. Besides, she was still active in the sorority and was excited whenever she got a gift in relation to the commitment she'd made when we were undergraduates.

"Girl, this job is about to drive my ass up the wall," I said. I tipped my feet out of my shoes and leaned cozily in the leather guest chair. "Requisitions, line closings, account adjustments, the drama never ceases."

"I know what you mean," she responded. "I just wish

they would send me some people who know what they are doing. Out of the thirty staff members I have, only ten of them really have a good grasp on what accounting is. Schools just don't teach them accounting like they used to. I still have people trying to get certified when what they need to do is go back to school and try this all over again."

"Just try to show people how to do business. Especially young, know-it-all black folk."

"It can't be worse than these I have."

"Don't get me started. I just had one of my little employees tell me what I needed to do about Margaret. I've been here forever and a day, am about to be an executive, but she tells me what *I need* to do about Margaret Eddye."

"Bless her heart. But you know how stubborn Margaret can be, Joyce. Maybe you should talk to her."

"I don't know why the good Lord doesn't just take her and put her out of her misery." I laughed. "I didn't mean that, but I don't have time for some woman with barely enough real experience to be advising me on the status of another employee."

Ella paused then smirked, taking her eyes off me for a second. The next time she looked at me, her eyes were probing. "Let me guess, Faulkner is the one pushing you to get Margaret to take retirement."

"Exactly, and I'm sick and tired of her trying to tell me what to do about Margaret. I know she's sick. I know she needs to be at home getting rest and relaxation."

Ella laughed.

"What is wrong with you? I didn't hear a damned thing funny."

"You and Faulkner. Y'all go back and forth, back and forth, you pull, she pushes. You go left, she goes to the right. You're too much alike."

"Like hell we are," I belted out. "That obsessive,

overachieving, Similac baby is going to make me show her a thing or two if she keeps trying to be the Red Cross instead of doing her job."

"Joyce, you come in here complaining about Faulkner at least twice a month, but each time, you're making issues out of the same things Margaret used to complain about when she was training you." Ella fiddled with the pen she held between her fingers and changed the subject before I could get my two cents in. Her face calmed. "Do you envy the relationship Faulkner has with Margaret?"

"Hell, no. I don't care one way or the other what kind of relationship they have. Margaret and I were closer than she and Faulkner will ever be."

"Eunice Joyce Armstrong, you're being callous."

I hadn't heard my full name in ages. I looked around to make sure no one was coming into the office. "I told Faulkner I would and I intend to talk to Margaret."

"Maybe you should see if Mr. Price will talk to Margaret instead. At least that will keep you from having to do it since you don't really want to."

"Honey, Fred isn't capable of dealing with this. He's so far removed from MSCOT and what we do that I'd have to fill him in on Margaret's entire health history. I'd rather talk to her myself."

"You know he came to my office last week asking me a million questions about Faulkner."

"Questions like what?"

"Does she get her work in to me on time, what was her attitude like, did I know anything about what areas in the company she might be interested in working in if she were to be promoted."

"What did you tell him?"

"I answered the questions as best I could. I think he's been impressed with her work ethic. Has he come to observe her any?"

I adjusted in my seat, crossed my legs, and flexed my hose-covered toes as I changed the subject.

"I haven't seen him. He came down about two months ago, but he rarely goes past my office. I wonder if that bastard is going to try and promote her before me. There's a junior executive position coming up. It hasn't been posted yet, but I heard about it."

"You're not jealous or upset about it, are you?"

"That's the last thing I'm worried about. Faulkner is hardly ready to deal with people like Fred, but I'd be pissed if she were moved up before me."

Ella relaxed in her chair. "Looks like somebody in here isn't being totally true with herself."

"Ella, that is the truth."

She held up her hands in retreat. "Okay, okay. I'll leave it alone but you know that Faulkner is just doing her job and if she's anything at all like you tell me, then it's possible that you have met your match."

"I'll fire her before I let her take the job I've worked hard to get."

"Just be sure that's what she wants before you go getting into something that could easily backfire."

I got up and fixed my clothes. "Faulkner isn't that clever. Honey, let me get back to my office before my crew falls apart."

Ella rose and walked me to the door. Before I stepped out she touched me on the shoulder. "Joyce, are you okay? I mean, is everything good in your world?"

"Why are you asking?"

"I just don't see you like I used to. You don't come to the house anymore. I know you got the new house out in Plano, but I'm hoping it hasn't made you a stranger."

"Ella, stop. What you're saying is totally preposterous. I've just been busy, that's all." I let out half a laugh that wasn't convincing.

My friend put her hand on her hip. "Look, I know

you and I know when things aren't right. We grew up together. I may not know you like your mother knew you, but I knew you back when we sat in that three-room wooden school in Calvert, Texas, you hear me?"

I cringed at the memory and then broke into laughter. "Ella, please, you're hurting me, girl."

She shook her head. "Hmm, see you be trying to act all high-society with me. You can pull that off on those employees of yours, but you can't pull it off on Ms. Prudential."

We laughed and sang together, "Solid! Solid as a rock!" It felt good to revisit old times with Ella. She really did understand me, more than I knew at times. However, she had issues. From family to personal, Ella wasn't on the same page with me. Her caliber was different. She didn't get manicures, didn't shop at Lord & Taylor's, had somewhat of a lazy husband, and, worst of all, she didn't think anything was wrong with her situation when I saw flaws galore. She looked the same age as Margaret, who was riding close to sixty. The shoes Ella wore reminded me of the same ones cafeteria workers wore, and I hated those therapeutically designed shoes. Ella was old-fashioned and I wasn't. She was a homebody. I was a somebody.

I headed back to the fourth floor thinking about the days I'd left behind. They were distant memories until I thought about them, then it seemed as if I'd just left them behind. I'd think of something I'd done or someplace I'd visited and it would seem like yesterday. Then, there were the things I'd just plain forgotten. Things that I'd locked away that were only revealed in my dreams. I could usually clear those with a drink before bed. When Ella mentioned Calvert, I almost hit the floor. I hadn't been back there since I'd graduated high school. I didn't know if my relatives still lived down there or not. I hadn't even returned for my mother's funeral, leaving my younger brother to take care of everything. He was six-teen at the time and I was partying my grief off in college, too mad at my mother for not being the woman I thought she should have been. Her decisions forced me to go through things I didn't deserve at such a young age. My brother, Jimmy Roy, sent me a letter, cursing me and calling me every bad name under the sun for not coming home to bury Mama. The letter had turned a dreary brown, lost somewhere in the pages of Mama's Bible that was sent with the letter. Now I didn't know where my brother was. I didn't know if he was alive or dead. He always talked of moving up east and joining a jazz band. He could play some sticks. Naturally gifted is what Nan Ruth called him; she was Mama's sister. The woman I wanted to be like all of my life. She wasn't run down like Mama. Nan Ruth whored, gambled, and drank like a Florida crocodile, but she was lively and that's what I ad-mired about her the most. Energy dripped from her skin and lit up our house each time she visited. She'd bring me fancy materials to make dresses with, photos and hair ribbons. She told me stories about her travels that made me long to get out and see the world. She'd been to New York, Chicago, Detroit, and Kansas City, where she'd met a lot of interesting and sometimes famous people. She was exuberant, and I always thought men loved her, until she told a man, who wanted her to stay with him, she wasn't letting any man confine her and he killed her. Her head was laying on Mama's porch early one Sunday morning. Mama screamed until her voice left her body. I realized that big, open minds couldn't survive in small, closed towns and that being a woman meant nothing to a man with a hard penis and no self-esteem. That was half the men in Calvert, Texas, back then. I couldn't imagine it being much different now—still the country, as Mama used to call it. No large buildings, few paved roads, and only one main road attaching it to the rest of the world. Growing up, I had dreamed of going to places like Rockdale or Bryan to shop or see new faces, but we did most of our shopping in nearby Hearne, which wasn't much bigger or much more exciting than Calvert. The church homecoming was the one thing we looked forward to each year, aside from pea-picking season, when you might make company with a hungry deer in the early morning hours, which were the best time to pick. That's probably why Nan Ruth hated it so much, because it was a town too small for her grand heart. I wondered, if my situation had been different, would I still be in Calvert? Probably not, but I longed for the peace of the country. I liked being in the middle of Mother Nature and someday hoped to have a home built away from this concrete jungle called the city when I retired.

When I stepped off the elevator, my mood had totally changed. Thinking about Mama and Nan Ruth depressed me. I longed to be in their company again, Mama telling me what good girls don't do, while Nan Ruth argued that good girls do it all. Then I thought about Ella Parnell and her life. I didn't have a husband nor did I have any kids. I didn't cook homemade apple pies or tea cakes, and, frankly, I didn't want to. Those things were bothersome, and the thought of submitting my life to a man irritated me. Having his kids, only to have him decide one day he didn't want to work anymore or, worse yet, he didn't want to come home wasn't my cup of chamomile. If anyone was going to be doing the playing, it was going to be me. My past would not end like my mother's or Nan Ruth, both dying at the hands of a man. I wasn't having it.

Faulkner crossed my mind, and I began to think about the junior executive job. I wondered if she knew about it. I wondered if she had any intentions, aside from accepting the job she'd applied for. I wondered.

Faulkner

Even though I had got out of Joyce what I wanted, she still pissed me off. I don't know what I would have done if she had stuck to her original decision not to talk to Margaret.

I teamed Brenda and James to formulate a report for MSCOT. If Joyce thought I was going to keep doing her work for her, she had me confused with someone who didn't mind being her scapegoat. I pulled up our company's website and read through the newsletter. Several employee birthdays were listed, as well as which couples were announcing new additions to their families. Aside from national news and a few other announcements about the phone company's accomplishments and community endeavors, there wasn't anything of interest to read. Perfume trailed up my nostrils. I turned around and Joyce was standing behind me. I couldn't read her face. Her face was expressionless. "Ms. Lorraine, I need to see you in my office for a second."

I'm sure she would have noticed I wasn't doing any work if she hadn't appeared so spaced out, but her words were as quick as her presence. She was halfway to her office by the time I'd processed what she'd said and got up to follow her. When I stepped into her office, she was already sitting down, her hands locked in front of her and elbows placed flat on the desk. I sat in the burgundy chair across from her.

"Lorraine, I just want you to know that you are a valuable asset to this phone company. In the twenty-seven years that I've been here, I've never come across a more steadfast and sharp young woman."

I sat without moving. My value to this company was something I didn't need to be schooled in. As a matter of fact, Mr. Price had sent me an e-mail congratulating me, once again, on making stats. MSCOT had consistently met its numbers due to my hard work and commitment. But Joyce's face showed everything but sincerity. She was up to something.

"It's very important for me to find a person to fill the management position who is dependable, flexible, a born leader, as well as extremely tractable concerning the regulations and edicts that govern how we operate as a team."

I wondered what she was getting at. I'd been nothing but diligent, flexible, and obedient. I knew this, didn't need her to reiterate what I knew. I wanted her to get to the point.

"I haven't made a decision yet because I'm trying to assess where you are."

I felt my chest tighten. Was Joyce telling me this because she felt like I wasn't dependable, flexible, or tractable? "What do you mean?"

"I'm letting you know that I need to be sure you want this job bad enough. I need to know that you know what it means to run a large operation."

"But you yourself said that I was a top candidate for the position. Joyce, you know my work ethic. You've witnessed it for the past four Fridays. I think that if you can't choose me for the promotion, it's because you don't want to. You know I want the job. I want the job more than anything."

Joyce's eyes fixed on me like I'd killed her favorite pet.

"Ms. Lorraine, I don't appreciate you telling me how to handle my job."

I squared eyes with Joyce, tired of letting her dog me. She needed to know that I could stand up to her. "This is about Margaret. You're going to renege, aren't you? That's what this is about. To keep from giving me the job, your exchange is talking to Margaret."

Joyce sat silent long enough to infuriate me. I stood as words spewed from her lips. "That's not what this is about. I asked you in here to see where your head was. This was business, but since you're convinced I'm out to ruin Margaret Eddye and you can't leave that alone, I do realize that your inability to keep your personal decisions away from professional ones lets me know that it's just not your time to move up. I need to know that you can make sound business decisions instead of emotional ones. You've allowed your personal relationship with her to affect your ability to see what's best for Southwest Meridian, and quite frankly, it appalls me to see such a bright, intelligent woman *waste* her time on people who aren't thinking about themselves enough to show some initiative. What are you going to do when it really boils down to you not having a choice?"

"I will always have a choice. It's what I've been trying to get you to see. You can choose at any moment to approach Margaret as her friend instead of her boss."

"And you think it's that easy, do you?"

"If it weren't for Margaret's choices, you wouldn't be sitting behind this desk. Her inability to be selfish is what got you to this point, this much I know." My intentions were not to raise my voice but it wasn't easy. I was in defense mode, ready to crack at any moment, grab Joyce, pull her sharp-dressed ass across the desk, and beat her down.

She unfolded her hands. "This job is about ability, Faulkner. It's about having the ability to cut your peripheral vision in half. You either will rise to the top, float in the middle, or sink. It seems to me that you find comfort floating in the middle, and those who float usually end up sinking."

"Floating in the middle? Ms. Armstrong, this isn't a lifeboat. We're not in the center of the ocean drifting away from shore. There are people here, and I'm concerned about those people as employees of this company. You think MSCOT has been performing well because all I concern myself with are line closings, input charts, and making sure there is equal representation at company parties? No. It's because I have the ability to make those people out there realize what they mean to me so that they don't mind doing what needs to be done for the company's sake. I'm concerned about each of their well-being. It's what sets good leaders apart from the rest."

"And I'm telling you that if you want to move up, then you need to be more concerned about yourself. Unfortunately, Faulkner, this *is* an ocean and you're on a lifeboat with a distance from land that you can't calculate until you jump in the water and try to get there. People jump in and swim the best they can every day. I've been swimming in it long enough and I finally made it to land. I advise you to look at it more closely before telling me what this is and what this is not."

Silence wafted between us. Joyce had made her point and made it clearly. She wasn't concerned about Margaret or anyone else, for that matter, and as long as I was trying to bring people up in the ranks that she didn't care for, she would do what was necessary to keep me from moving up. I walked toward the door. "So that's how it's going to be?"

Joyce turned one of her diamond rings back to the upright position as she half-smiled my way. "Dear, that is how it *is*."

"Fine." I looked at Joyce one last time. "No matter what happens from here, I still expect you to talk to Margaret. I'm holding you to that."

Joyce almost smiled. "Lorraine, do you call yourself making some attempt at a threat?"

I kept a straight face. "Yes." With that said, I left Joyce sitting at her desk, staring at me with venom in her eyes.

Margaret

I slid on my robe and a pair of socks. Despite the irritating limp I now had, I was determined to find out what Lisa had going on across the hall. I opened my door as softly as I could and made my way into the hall, standing within earshot of the room across from me. Lisa and her gentleman visitor could be heard talking through the door, the man's voice much clearer than Lisa's.

"Damn, girl, you been hiding all this from me?"

Her fake, dainty laugh made my flesh crawl. "I can't just give it all to you at once, otherwise you have no reason to come around."

There was silence, then more laughter. Give him what? I thought. My mind was telling me they were doing something they should not have been doing in the room Lisa shared with her daughters. I reached up to knock on the door out of habit, before grabbing the knob and forcing the door open. As I suspected, Lisa was on top of some man, gyrating like a dog in heat, as he lay naked under her. I was beside myself with anger.

"Lisa Jeanette, get this man out of my house!"

The man quickly pushed Lisa off him. I'd never seen him before, but I could tell he was shocked at my presence. He had on the biggest silver chain I'd ever seen. Dangling from the chain was the number 87 with diamonds all around it. As he moved to cover himself, I could see big rings on his fingers. His black skin shined in the grayness of the room. He grabbed his pants and slid them on. Lisa looked at me, her face red with embarrassment and rage.

"What are you doing in here, Margaret?"

"This is my house, I got a right to be in here. I live here and I pay the bills here. That's my bed you feel so inclined to lay naked in with some stranger and that's my carpet your bare feet are on. This is *my* house. The question should be what in God's name are you doing?"

"You don't have a right, busting in here like that!" By now, Lisa had slid on a T-shirt and shorts. "I invited my friend over to talk."

"Girl, shut up that lying!"

Her male friend slid on his shoes and grabbed his shirt. "Ma'am, I apologize for disturbing you." With that, he grabbed his keys and walked past me. "Lisa, call me later."

I stared him down, taking in everything from the lines cut into his hair all the way to the expensive necklace and rings he wore. He looked like a man who had money but made it illegally.

I hollered after him, "She'll be calling you from a pay phone."

"Okay, baby," Lisa said under her breath. The look in her eyes showed that I was the last person she wanted to talk to. She stomped past me, forcing me into the wall with her shoulder and narrow hips. I leaned against the wall to catch my bearings. I heard the front door open so I walked as best I could to the living room and watched out the front door. Lisa stood talking to the man as he slid his dark hands under her shirt, caressing her breasts. I yelled at the top of my lungs, "Get out of my driveway with that mess!" They were embarrassing. Lisa gave me the evil eye again, but she pulled away from the man as he got into his truck and backed out. I waited for Lisa. She came in and walked right by me.

"Girl, don't you walk by me like I'm not here," I demanded. "You've lost your mind, bringing a stranger into this house and getting it on like it ain't nothing. I sure hope you were using protection because there are diseases out there, and I know you don't need another baby."

She flung herself around. "You had no right doing that to me. You can't control me or my life."

"And you had no right leaving this house last night and coming back acting like some floozy."

"I have a life, Margaret, I still have a desire to go out and have fun. You can't expect me to just sit around here bored to death. Just because I have kids doesn't mean my life ends. You're a woman, you should be able to sympathize with what I'm saying."

I placed my weight on my good leg. "Don't make me slap you into kingdom come, girl, because I will do it. When did your social life come before your responsibility to your girls? You are an adult, not a child."

"That's why I didn't bring Derrick over until they were gone. I'm responsible. Shylanda and Nikki have never seen me with a man in that way."

"Lisa, they hardly *ever* see you, that's the problem. You don't spend quality time with them, and as soon as some smooth-talking man comes around, you abandon them for your own personal gain. You need to get your act together."

"I take care of my children. Don't you dare tell me I don't take care of my children! I was there when they were born, not their daddy. I fed them! I kept them clean, bought their clothes, and when it was all said and done, I didn't leave them with their father, they came with me."

"Then where were you the day Nicole got sick at school and Lester had to pick her up? Where were you the day Shylanda asked what a tampon was? Where were you then? Where were you when all the girls wanted to do was spend a few hours at the park two weeks ago? Where were you? Because I was at the park watching them, not you. I need to know where you've been lately."

"I've been trying to find a job and get in school."

"Lisa, shut up. I know you didn't enroll in school. You haven't so much as called to see if you could enroll."

Lisa sucked her teeth and walked down the hall. "If y'all would stay off my back, then maybe I could find a job. I can't do a job hunt worth anything with you and Daddy always pressuring me. That's why I don't do well in my interviews."

"Girl, you haven't been on an interview since mutt was a pup, don't try to get over on me with that sad tale because I've heard it before, and it's pathetic. As a matter of fact, Lisa, I've heard all your little excuses, but you never fail to have some man following behind you sprinkling you with jewelry and dinner, while your daughters eat hot dogs *with matching buns*. What kind of mother would do that?"

"Margaret, I'm doing the best I can with my girls. How dare you think I'm not thinking about them or what's best for them. I'm out because I want their lives to be better than mine. I'm out because of them!"

"Then find you a job, get you a place to live, and stop

chasing men who don't care nothing about you. If you want to make their lives better, teach them to be independent."

"Oh, like you, I suppose? Working until they can't walk on their own swollen feet, only to come home to a man that doesn't even appreciate them. Daddy will starve before he goes into that kitchen and cooks his own meal. When was the last time he even took you out? Is that what you mean by independent? I don't think so."

"It's honest living, honey. I've never had to sneak your daddy inside somebody else's house, that's for sure, and he would have taken me out the other night had you been here to watch your own children. As a matter of fact, Lester took me out Saturday when you had the girls God knows where. I don't have to prove myself to you."

Lisa held her hand up and dropped it as if giving up. "Whatever." She walked down the hallway.

"You can act like you don't hear me if you want to, but I mean it this time. I'm not going to have no foolishness going on under my roof. Me and your daddy work too hard building what little we got, and nobody is going to come in here and dismantle it like it ain't nothing. You hear me?" A sharp pain ran from my back up to my neck. I stiffened, waiting to see if it would come back, but it didn't. I could feel my heart pounding in my body like a million drums against my chest. My blood pressure had probably gone high enough for me to faint at any minute. I went to my room and slammed the door. As I took my medicine, I heard Lisa come out of her room and go down the hallway. I checked my window and saw her walk across the front yard and down the sidewalk. She didn't even have the decency to shower and change clothes. I'd threatened to send her on her way the last time she stayed out all night, but I knew she didn't have anywhere to go. I wasn't good at making threats because I hardly ever kept my end of the threat. If Lester knew about what just took place, she'd be gone for sure, and I kept wishing she'd straighten her act up and fly right before he got a hold of her. There wasn't anything wrong with Lisa except she depended on her looks to carry her, which they did for now. Her raffia-colored skin and long wavy hair, not to mention those green eyes, kept men swarming around her, leaving her with no reason to think that her looks *couldn't* carry her.

It was times like these I was glad she wasn't my biological child or I'd have killed her by now, but as her stepmother, I'd never put my hands on her. I never felt like it was my place to, even though Lester had given me full authority. In my opinion, she was too old to get whippings by the time she moved to Dallas. Lester was good at disciplining her, punishing her by taking away privileges. He even took a belt to her once, but because she was a girl, the majority of her time had been spent with me, and I spent time trying to instill virtue and honesty in her. I see now that was about as useful as skiing in Africa, because Lisa was already who she was going to be.

It was also times like this I wished I'd been able to have children of my own, but for whatever reasons, God just didn't design me that way. The doctor told me when I was sixteen that I only had one ovary and it was underdeveloped. It didn't mean anything to me until my second year of college, when I met Henry Waters, a senior education major. He was the most brilliant man I'd met and he was sweet on me. Unfortunately, Henry wanted a big family, and he wanted it enough that he left me when he found out I couldn't have any kids. I became so depressed, I withdrew from school and never went back. I also didn't date much for fear of the same kind of disappointment, until I met Lester, who already had a child and wasn't interested in having any more. We dated all of seven months before heading to City Hall and exchanging wedding vows. Now, here I sat wondering if marrying a man with a kid had been the right thing for me. Did I mind? No. If I had been more secure with the fact that I wanted a child but couldn't have one, would I have chosen differently? I thought so.

By the time I was dressed and headed to the bus stop, it was close to eleven o'clock. It wouldn't take me long to get to the hospital. My bus would arrive in a matter of minutes and I'd be on my way. I would have been at work, under normal circumstances, dealing with customers and chatting away with my coworkers, which is what I preferred because it took me away from this. Faulkner was concerned that my working was stressful, but I didn't see it that way. What I did at the phone company was something I could walk away from each day. The irate customers, the deadlines, even Joyce, all had nothing to do with me. It was my home life that kept my blood high. I liked work.

Thoughts of work made me smile, but I was feeling that maybe it was time for me to let it go. I was tired, more tired than I'd been in a long time, but there I was trying to stay on until Faulkner got her promotion because I believed in her and what she could do, given the chance. Joyce didn't want the young, ambitious woman to move up because Joyce wasn't sure what kind of woman Faulkner really was. Joyce needed her to be a certain way. Joyce desired Faulkner to be like her, and I was sure she would try to get to know where Faulkner stood before promoting her. But Joyce knew that I would not stand by and let her overlook Faulkner. No person should work as hard as Faulkner, know more about the company she worked for, be able to do her job blindfolded, and not be rewarded for her hard work. She should have had the job months ago.

But Joyce was being pushed by her own ill will to control Faulkner, and if she didn't come to terms with her ugly ways, Faulkner would get hurt in the process. I didn't want to interfere, because I didn't agree with forcing a person to do right, but that's just how God worked. Sometimes you had to put the mirror on the devil to make the devil see the devil.

The bus pulled up and I stepped on slowly and ran my pass through the machine. Yes, if the Lord saw fit, I'd get to see Joyce do something right, for once in her life.

Faulkner

As soon as I stepped out of Joyce's office, the main floor felt like a foreign land. I didn't want to be there. The only thing on my mind was getting my shit and leaving. The voices of operators could be heard with a few sprouts of laughter coming from across the large room. The area where I worked was now quiet. The only voice I could hear was that of Carmen Estrada speaking Spanish in quick, aggressive tones, and I could tell she was handling a difficult customer. Brenda and James were now in James's cube, leaning over paperwork, smiling at each other. It made me glad they were getting along. Work would get done better and faster that way. Gail was nowhere to be found and her phone was ringing. I stepped in her cube and pressed her wrap-up button, which forced the call into the waiting cue. She was probably somewhere running her mouth with her friends from the fourth floor. I went to my cube to get the call. Before I knew it, I was back in the swing of things, but feeling as if being in the swing of things at Southwest Meridian was no longer a part of me.

"Southwest Meridian, how can I help you?"

"You can help me by turning my phone back on." It was Jonnie Coleman, the last person I wanted to hear.

"Ma'am, can I have your phone number?"

"Oh, shut up, you know my account number just like you know who this is! Don't play these games with me! Which one of you is this? Sounds like Faulkner."

"Yes, ma'am." I really wasn't in the mood to entertain Mrs. Coleman, but it wasn't in me to take my frustrations out on her and be rude. I still considered myself to be a professional.

"Lorraine. Yeah, I knew it. I spoke to Gail Perez and Brenda Jones today and I haven't heard back from them and they promised to have my phone service back on. I want to talk to your manager."

I sat for all of five seconds before putting Mrs. Coleman on hold, knowing that no such promises had been made to her. As much as I resented my job right now, I never saw myself going out as a half-assed employee and I wasn't going to send her to a manager. I could handle this. I wasn't weak, nor was I a quitter. No one would ever be able to say that about me. I pressed the button connecting me back to the customer. "Mrs. Coleman, this is Faulkner Lorraine and I am in charge. Until we obtain proof that the previous bill has been paid, your service will not be activated."

"This is a disgrace! I'm a poor, working-class black woman and y'all just tryin' to keep a sista down, you hear what I'm saying? Jobs can't call me if I ain't got no phone. That bill was paid!"

"We have no record of that."

"You don't have no record of how many childrens

I have, but that don't mean I don't have any, now does it?"

"Mrs. Coleman, I don't want to disconnect this call with you and I'm not here to argue. I would like to get this resolved and I would like for you to have your service reactivated."

"Then reactivate the mothafucka! Ain't nothing to it but to do it, right? I mean, you prolly sitting up in your nice, air-conditioned office with your fancy, two-hundred-dollar suit on, and getting a nice fat-ass check to pay your bills every month while your own people suffer on these hot streets, dying and hustling just to make it through the day."

"There are jobs out there, Mrs. Coleman."

"And I can't get one if I ain't got no phone, Faulkner Lorraine. See, it's people like you who make me sick. You can control whether my phone gets turned on and you won't help a sister out. I remember back in the day when there was love in the black community because the people who worked at the big jobs came home every night to the 'hood and shared what they had. They gave back and they weren't afraid to hook one another up. With you new black businessfolk, there is no love. None at all."

"Excuse me, Mrs. Coleman, but we all work here, and I think that you are being critical about something you don't know about."

"Is you disrespecting me?"

I said nothing, pressed the mute button, released a breath loud enough to shake the heavens, and pressed the button again, deactivating the mute function.

Mrs. Coleman kept ranting. "I'll report you to the Better Business Bureau and have your job like that. Don't you disrespect me! I'm a customer and I have rights!"

I tried to get back to the matter at hand. "Mrs. Coleman, do you realize we can turn this account over to a collection agency and it will damage your credit?"

"Credit? Credit!" Mrs. Coleman exploded in laughter, sounding like an old bird. The cackling forced my frown into a smirk. She actually was amused and it was the first time I'd ever heard her laugh. This woman had found real humor in my comment.

I kept my composure. "Mrs. Coleman, if we turn your account over, this will affect your credit rating."

Mrs. Coleman was still laughing. I could hear cars going by in the background along with people talking loudly to each other. She was on a pay phone somewhere. I was tempted to repeat myself, but decided to wait until she stopped laughing. That never happened. After a few thuds, as if the phone had been dropped, I could hear Mrs. Coleman talking to someone. Evidently, she'd put the phone down and was holding a conversation.

"Newt! Newt! This bitch said if I don't pay my bill, she gon' report it to the credit people."

I heard more laughter this time, not just Mrs. Coleman's but from other people in the background.

The voice I assumed to be Newt's responded, "You tell her you ain't got no credit, Jonnie! Tell 'em to go on and report you, then they won't ever get what they askin' for."

I could hear Mrs. Coleman's laughter again. This time mixed with coughing and wheezing, but the laughter stayed intact. I sat waiting for her to get back on the line, but the laughter eventually subsided and Jonnie Coleman's voice began to fade as if she were walking away. The next thing I heard was the phone rattle and then the line went dead. The green light on my phone that glowed when I was on a call was now gone. Carmen could still be heard from her cube. I thought about Mrs. Coleman and how easy her life must be, with no responsibilities other than making sure she called here and harassed us daily. I sat back in my chair and sighed once again. I didn't care anymore.

Joyce

After the tiff with Faulkner, I spent no time deciding to leave early and get some exercise to release some energy and forget how I was now feeling. My hangover was still wearing off and I was no longer in work mode.

As soon as I got home, I changed out of my clothes and put on a pair of black spandex tights, a black spandex halter top, a cutoff, ocean-blue sweatshirt, socks, and running shoes, and headed out to run around the neighborhood. I kept trying to disassociate myself from thinking about Faulkner and her concerns, but the incident with her had my adrenaline flowing. I didn't foresee her putting in her two weeks' notice on a whim and for such a weak argument. However, I was about to find out who this woman was, and if she really had what it took to play with the big boys.

It wasn't as if Faulkner were being asked to strip for the company picnic. I didn't want her to quit, but I'd be damned if I was going to sit there and try to make her see reason. I didn't do that with anyone. She could be replaced easily and effortlessly. Brenda Jones would make an excellent manager, and I could depend on her to do what I wanted her to do and not go against anything I asked of her, even though I didn't like the fact that she wasn't one of my own, meaning a black woman. It was just as important to me, as it was to Faulkner, to bring black people up in the ranks, but they had to be quality black people. They had to be black people who understood the art of playing corporate politics. They had to be black people who had a universal frame of mind, who wouldn't get so caught up in race and sex that they couldn't function effectively on the high end. Faulkner would just lose out and be another prime example to the white world that black people were too petty and emotional to handle business, if she chose to quit.

When I stepped outside, spring sun warmed my body. I made a mental note to do my arm weights when I returned, if I wasn't too tired. My body had withstood some hard times, so the run I was about to do was nothing. I stepped from my porch and began an easy jog down the sidewalk. The energy I was using helped me think. I thought about my life, my job, and my past, especially my past. Mostly, I thought about my marriage and my betrayal by my mother.

Raymond, my first and only husband, was the reason I'd never seriously dated after I left home. He was six years older than I was, and we'd married for all the wrong reasons. I wanted to get out of the house, and he, I would soon find out, wanted a human punching bag. I wasn't even out of high school when Mama gave us permission to marry. Raymond pursued me and I liked it. He was my ticket away from the misery of being in my mother's house, dealing with her own weakness for men. My father had died when I was ten. After that, my mother tried to fill the void with men who didn't work, but seemed to hit her for a living. But, soon as Raymond and I were settled in his two-bedroom home, located on seven acres of land on the Old Franklin road, the trouble started. I never thought he'd be as abusive as he was. The first time he laid his hands on me, I was stepping out of the tub. He crashed into the bathroom, drunk, smelling of reefer, and demanding his dinner. Of course it was there, covered and warming in the oven, but I soon realized that the beatings never had anything to do with my ability or inability to have things the way he wanted them to be. I supposed beating me was like his drug and alcohol habits; his body begged to have the desire to be abusive filled until he would just snap. If the house was cleaned, it was too clean and he couldn't find anything, and if it was dirty, then he still couldn't find what he was looking for, and both reasons resulted in blows to the face, arms, legs, and whatever else he could bruise.

At sixteen years old, I learned that Raymond Reed beat women because he didn't know how not to beat them. His father had beat his mother until she was forced to flee her home and her children. His uncles abused their wives. His grandfather sexually molested Raymond's sisters, and his great-grandfather, after killing his wife by hitting her with an iron, had fathered two stillborn children with his own daughter. Ray's life was made up of the kind of stuff you see today on talk shows. All the men in the family were abusive, but I didn't know this until I was well into our marriage and had come to know the women in his family. They only talked when they got together and got loaded full of liquor. Then, it seemed it didn't hurt so much when they talked about the men. In two years I went to three Reed family funerals, all of them being for women who'd died because of being "too clumsy." And even though she unintentionally tried to, my mama didn't succeed in raising a fool. Thanks to Nan Ruth, I didn't stay with Raymond long enough for him to kill me. I ran to her whenever she was in town, after I'd gotten pushed, slapped, hit, or kicked, and each time, she'd fix my face up, comb my hair, put me in fresh clothes, keep my secret, and send me right back over there to him. Her advice to me was always, "Eunice, a man is only naturally compatible with the heart he grows up with." I'd take her advice and try to make it make sense, but each time was a repeat of the time before.

The last time Raymond jumped on me was a month before I was to graduate high school, just two weeks after Nan Ruth's head was found on Mama's porch. He'd been real good to me for a few days, bringing in a few gifts, making love to me, and giving me the quiet I needed to study for my tests. Therefore, this particular beating came as a surprise and I still considered it the worst one I'd ever gotten. I remembered being excited about getting the clearance that I would graduate. I wanted to celebrate, so I planned on making a big dinner when I got home. Thoughts of smothered, fried pork chops, baked yams, mashed potatoes, cornbread, and ice cream for dessert ran through my head. I'd walked three miles home from school after waiting an hour for him to pick me up. I wasn't in the door five seconds when I felt his hot, sweaty hands around my neck, constricting the flow of air from my head to my chest. He dragged me to the back room and closed the door as he ranted and raved about where I'd been. He yelled that I wasn't in front of the school, where he'd been waiting the past three hours. I couldn't get a word in due to his hands restricting my flow of oxygen, so I immediately began bracing myself. Even as I tried to focus and listen to him, all I could think about was dying.

Raymond swung me into the vanity he'd bought me for my birthday. The mirror cracked and speckled glass cut me, burning into the side of my face and neck. I became light-headed when he pulled me up, beginning to flash in and out of consciousness. I saw one of my teeth laying lackluster on the floor near the leg of the vanity. I closed my eyes and relaxed my body, because Raymond's fist met my rib cage, knocking the air completely out of me, and then his blows came like bullets. In my mind I was begging for God to let me black out, anything to dull the pain. I could feel my lips pursing together to just say, "Please," when Ray's hands covered them. He wavered over me like death. Sweat was dripping from his face and neck onto my forehead and into my eyes, burning them. My legs kicked and I imagined myself appearing like a dying fish beneath his six-five, 220-pound body. Raymond slurred insults as he demanded that I learn to obey him. His words triggered something in me. All at once, the bloodied head on Mama's porch, the words Nan Ruth always sent me home with, and Raymond's words blended.

"Eunice, a man is only naturally compatible with the heart he grows up with. That's where he left her, Eunice. Nan Ruth's head was right there. Next time I come looking for you, BE WHERE YOU ARE SUPPOSED TO BE! DO YOU HEAR ME?"

I heard all the words loud and clear, and I finally understood. My heart was just as much of a coward as my husband's. I'd been refractory and negligent to myself. Up until that moment, I'd been a natural fool, just like the man I'd married. I'd been too scared and impatient to deal with the harsher side of life. Too lofty-minded to walk away from Raymond and admit he was a mistake after the first time he ever laid his hands on me.

After the beating, he left me lying in the disaster that used to be our bedroom. He scratched his penis through his dingy jeans and strolled out into the afternoon. As soon as I could gather my senses, I grabbed a pillowcase and stuffed it with as many of my things as I could find, including the dress I had planned to wear at graduation. I slipped out the back door and headed to my teacher's house, fifteen miles away on the north end of town. She was a single woman who lived in a four-bedroom house.

By the time I got there, my ankles felt like bricks. Ms. Patterson took me in, no questions asked; she'd seen me on more than one occasion come to her class with a black eye or busted lip. When she saw me now, she cried. I attempted to comfort her by letting her know I was better than I looked. She wanted me to go to the police, but I balked, not wanting Raymond to find out where I was. I was scared and just wanted to graduate and get out of Calvert. She let me stay at her house and that's where I took my tests, did my final assignments, and had my own, private graduation ceremony without my husband, mother, or brother. Letting anyone know where I was would have put my life in jeopardy, and Ms. Patterson agreed to protect me at all costs. She saved my life. Better yet, she helped me save my own. Two years after I left and went to college, I received a letter from my former teacher informing me that Raymond had died, apparently from eating rat poison. The police ruled the death accidental.

Sweat rolled from my neck as I paced myself. Running always made me remember those times, left me wondering how I ever made it through and making me glad that I had lived, in spite of the violent episodes. These were the things I kept hidden, and they were still painful.

I checked my stopwatch. I had another forty minutes to complete my three miles. I drifted from my past and began to sift through the present. I couldn't help going back to my thoughts concerning Faulkner. She did deserve the promotion. She deserved it so much, I didn't want to post the job listing, but it was company policy. I was hoping in the meeting with her today that she would show me that she could lay her issue with Margaret Eddye aside, show me that she knew what the promotion meant. I was hoping Faulkner would see that, but things had to be her way or no way.

She was pigheaded and she asserted herself when it

was unnecessary. That's what I absolutely couldn't tolerate from her, because I was her boss. No matter what I tried to do for her, she was always opposing me, fighting me tooth and nail to prove that she had a better view of things. She didn't respect authority, in my opinion. I'd been there longer, knew more, and had the control.

The next few days would reveal much. I decided if Lorraine quit, I would offer Brenda Jones the position, even if I felt like she was too concerned with having babies and raising a family. That's why I'd put so much time and energy into Faulkner. She had a great work ethic, she was single, and she was effective. Faulkner wasn't the average, every-day-late, worked-on-colored-peoples'-time kind of woman.

The black people I'd had the displeasure of supervising over the years had all been that way, and I knew how the white people viewed them. People like Fred never let me forget it. He was always using slang with me, as if I knew what he was saying, or stereotyping me like I was some former welfare recipient. This made me more determined to master how rich white people did business. In order to get the things I desired, I had to. I learned the language, the poker face, the schmoozing. I wasn't ashamed to do it because the rewards were always sweet, even if I didn't like having to do it any more than the average person. Survival was survival, and I wasn't going to go back to those days when beans and cornbread were Thanksgiving dinner.

Faulkner wasn't afraid of losing her job, but she was afraid to use people as stepping-stones. She didn't understand that the Gail Perezes, Brenda Joneses, and Margaret Eddyes of the world were just props in her one-woman show. Why couldn't she just drop the socially conscious routine and do her job?

By the time I'd finished running, I was soaked in sweat and too tired to do arm weights. I practically peeled the spandex from my body before I got into the tub. The lukewarm bathwater spiced with mango-scented salts was just what I needed. I mixed my favorite Harvard cocktail, put on a Nina Simone CD, and slid into the water. From head to toenails, I felt myself relax. Nina's voice had always been my pièce de résistance when it came to relaxing music. The way she sang, deeply, made the hairs on my arms stand on end. Her singing seemed familiar, like every song was performed for me. Some days, it was like she was talking directly about something I'd gone through or was going through. No matter what, her voice was exemplary of my life. We even shared the same first name, Eunice, which was symbolic to me. My name was Eunice Joyce Armstrong and she was Nina Simone, born as Eunice Kathleen Waymon. I think the heavens saw we were both named Eunice because we both knew suffering, but we also knew strength. Our connection was spiritual.

I sank down into the water, feeling the suds on my chin, letting my mind wander. For the second time, I went back to thoughts of my girlhood, where I was called Eunice and I was the wife to a wimp of a man. Raymond never even knew my middle name was Joyce. He never cared enough to ask. I could still hear his voice and how he called my name. He'd yell no matter how he said it, and it always sounded like the coming of a bad thunderstorm. I could hear it loud and clear: "Eunice!" My arm jumped beneath the water then relaxed. There was never a question in Raymond's voice. Never that soft, deep, loving call of a man who appreciates the way his woman walks, smells, or the way she does for him. Raymond lacked a lot of things, consideration being only one. The music wafted as I felt myself slip deeper into my thoughts. I sensed a hand reaching out for me, but couldn't open my eyes. The touch was cold and firm. Pain grilled through my shoulders.

"Push her under!" the male voice yelled. It was Raymond, and his dirty hands held my feet. I felt my ankles trying to run but couldn't. The oil from his hands dirtied my bathwater.

"Eunice! Eunice!" another voice called out. "I got you this time!" I looked up above me and Faulkner was there. She had fangs and her dark hands were clawed and covered with meshed fur. She was pushing my head down into the water as I struggled.

"PUSH HER!" Raymond's voice was yelling now. "SHE CAN'T SWIM! PUSH! PUSH EUNICE DOWN!"

Faulkner's furry hands pressed against my head and I could see the yellow in her eyes and smell the garbage on her breath. She took on the form of a large rodent. Fur, dirt, and oil floated in the water. A scream lingered in my throat, but I was losing the battle. Before I could get out a cry for help, I'd slid under the water. The warmth woke me, and I came up quickly with my mouth open, gasping for breath and fighting the suds that were around me. When I realized there was no one at the end of the tub holding my feet, I turned swiftly to make sure no one was behind me and put my hand near my neck because I could still feel the hands on me. My heart was pounding in my chest. I wasn't concerned that my hair was drenched. I jumped out of the tub and slid into my robe, staring down at the suds moving rhythmically atop the water. My legs were rubber and my hands were shaking. It'd been years since I'd had a dream about Raymond. I flipped the Nina Simone CD off and looked in my nightstand drawer for the revolver I'd purchased years ago. I walked around the house and made sure I was the only person there. The dream had felt too real. I still sensed the pressure of the claws on my forehead. I shivered and went back to my room, closing and locking the door behind me. It took me a few minutes to feel comfortable, but I eventually placed the gun beneath the mattress. I dried my hair and oiled my body before sliding under the covers. Four cocktails and three hours later, I was finally able to sleep.

Margaret

The bus was off schedule all day. After I left the doctor's office I went to the grocery store and then home. Lester was outside working on his truck. Lisa and the girls were nowhere to be seen. I looked at my husband working underneath the hood and wished, for the thousandth time, he would have chosen to cook dinner instead.

"Hey, there," I said as I limped past him, trying to get my load of groceries into the house.

Lester looked up and smiled. He wiped his hands. "Hey." He watched me walk up the steps and stand at the door. He let the hood down and dropped the cloth before he hustled over to open the door for me. "Baby, we got the house to ourselves tonight."

I met his smile with a casual glance. "Is that right?"

Lester patted me on my behind. "Yeah, baby, that's right." He put his body against mine, wrapping his arms around me, smelling of oil and dirt. I grimaced as Lester placed his lips near my ear. "I want you to cook us a good meal tonight and after that, I'm going to have something for you." Lester kissed my ear. He knew that was my weak spot. I smiled.

As much as I knew I wasn't in the mood for Lester or

preparing dinner, I still blushed at the thought of us having time alone. "Where are Lisa and the girls?"

"Lisa's new man took them out."

"It's a school night. Those babies need to be in the
bed." I moved around the kitchen putting up groceries
with Lester sitting at the table watching me.

"That's Lisa's problem."

"And knowing Lisa, she'll spend the night with this
total stranger, and Lord knows what kind of condition
those girls will be in."

Lester slammed his fist on the table. "Damn, Margaret! I'm trying to spend some time with you and all
you're worried about is Lisa and the girls. They'll be fine
and tomorrow they'll be back in this house keeping you
busy. Can't a man enjoy one nice, quiet evening with his
wife?"

I turned and looked at Lester, not sure what I was
going to say to him. "Lester, it's not always about you. I
come home from a long day at the doctor's office, getting on and off buses with my arms full of groceries and
my knee big as a grapefruit, only to find that my grandbabies are out with their mama and some stranger.
Then, my loving husband wants me to cook him a meal
so he can reward me by having sex with me."

"Margaret, you're turning my intentions around and
making it seem like they're bad. You're misunderstand-
ing me. We've both had a long day and I think all we
both need is a little relaxation."

"You're right, Lester, but there is a bigger picture
here."

Lester stood and walked over, grabbing me around
my waist. I could no longer smell the dirt and oil as
much. I leaned my head away from his lips this time, but
he was persistent. Lester pulled me close and began
dancing.

"It had to be you . . ." Lester sang. It was one of our favorite songs.

I smiled. "Lester, stop, I have to get dinner ready."

He continued singing and dancing me around the kitchen. "I looked around, and finally found, somebody who, could make me be true . . ."

"Lester Eddye, you keep fooling around and you're going to wind up in bed on an empty stomach."

My husband kept singing and swaying me until I could feel his nature rising against my plump midsection. "Lester Eddye, you ought to be ashamed of yourself," I said, giggling.

He leaned in and kissed my neck. Chills showered my body and I felt my own excitement begin to develop between my legs. I squirmed in his arms as he kissed and licked me in places I thought he'd forgotten about. "How are you feeling today? Is your knee okay?"

"It's fine," I lied as I gave in to the moment. "I went to the doctor's office just to be sure. It's bruised, but the swelling should go down within the week if I keep ice on it."

"Why didn't you call me? I would have come and taken you."

"You were supposed to be home for lunch. When you didn't come, I figured you were too busy."

"Yeah, but I would've come home if you had called."

"All that doesn't matter now. I'm fine and there's nothing to worry about."

"That's good," Lester whispered. His hand moved from the middle of my spine down to my behind. "I love you, you know that."

I pulled back to look Lester in his eyes. "Sometimes you don't act like it," I teased.

Lester smiled and went back to kissing on me. If I'd had the strength to climb on the kitchen table right then, I'd have been ready to give him dinner. Lester danced me out of the kitchen and down the hallway to our bedroom as he kissed, sucked, rubbed, and sang. I unzipped his pants as he squeezed my butt. I stimulated his penis. It felt good in my hands and reminded me of the days when we were home alone all the time. Lester kissed my breasts. They hung like pendulums from my sagging skin. Lester was humping me against the wall when we heard keys in the door and the voices enter. Nicole's voice was the loudest.

"Well, shit!" Lester quickly stepped away from me and zipped his pants. "I can't have a damned moment to myself no more."

"Lester, watch your language," I said as I pulled my bra around my breasts, slid my skirt on, and buttoned my blouse. He went to the bathroom, slamming the door behind him. I patted my hair to make sure it looked okay, counted to ten, and left the room. Nicole met me in the hallway.

"Big Mama!" She ran to me and hugged my waist. I was happy to see them, knowing they were safe. Lisa walked by me with Shylanda sleeping in her arms. Once she got her in the bed and calmed Nicole down long enough to get her pajamas on, Lisa had her climb in next to her sister. Lisa then strutted down the hall past me with her purse still on her shoulders. She did one last check in the mirror. "Margaret, Carl and I are going for drinks."

I walked to the end of the hall and saw a man sitting on the couch. He wasn't the same bald, dark-colored man that I'd seen in bed with her this morning. This man wasn't as broad in the shoulders and he had hair on his head that was loose and curly. He was obviously some new guy she'd managed to fool.

"Lisa, don't you have parent conference in the morning?" I asked, trying to get a good look at the man before Lisa set foot out the door. "Shylanda is having behavior problems in her science class."

She ignored me as she whizzed past and grabbed her friend's hand. "Thanks, Margaret. I appreciate you for watching the girls tonight. I'll be back in an hour." They were out the door and in the car before I could protest against watching Nicole and Shylanda. I locked the door and went to the girls' room. The night-light beamed from under the door. Shylanda was still in her clothes. Lisa had merely taken the barrettes from her hair and removed her shoes and socks. Nicole lay next to her sister, eyes wide open, with her thumb in her mouth. I sat on the edge of the bed. "Big girls don't suck their thumbs," I said.

Nicole removed her thumb and giggled. "Big Mama, we went to the zoo."

"Oh, you did? What did you see?"

"Monkeys and birds and bugs."

"That's an eye's full you saw."

Nicole shook her head and smiled. "We had fun with Uncle Carl and Mama. He bought us ice cream and he took us to McDonald's."

"He did? Well, that was nice of him. Did you tell him thank you?"

"Yes. Mama said we will have a new house soon with Uncle Carl."

I looked at my grandbaby, wishing she could see through her mother the way I did, but God didn't design children that way. They didn't have total insight or the experience to know how people's actions were more important than their words. It would be some time before Nicole saw the woman in her mother that I saw. Nicole and Shylanda didn't know that their mother wasn't working or that she never did what was in their best interest, and I knew they didn't need to, so I, Big Mama,

was taking up the slack for a woman who was still trying to find herself through instant gratification.

"That's nice, sweetheart. Now I think it's time for you
to close those eyes and go to sleep." I leaned over and
kissed my granddaughter. She still smelled salty from
being out all day, but I was glad to be able to smell that
smell because it meant she was somewhere safe and loving. I turned the night-light off and closed the door behind me.

I crossed the hall and stuck my head into Lester's and
my bedroom. "Lester, you still want something to eat?
I'm going to fix me something."

Lester was sitting on the bed with his back to me. He
didn't even turn to acknowledge that I was standing
there. "Nah, I'll just make me a sandwich."

My feelings fell. I still wanted to snuggle and have my
husband hold me close, but his mood was gone and I
knew Lester Eddye wasn't going to attempt to be romantic again tonight. I closed the door and went to the
kitchen to make me a cup of tea. It was important to me
that Lester be happy, but he and I had reached an im-
passe concerning our grandchildren. Maybe if I would
have let the groceries wait until tomorrow, I could have
been home earlier and Lester and I would have had all
the time we needed to do what we wanted to do. I still
liked being with him and feeling him on me, but there
was just so much going on around the house that, lately,
time didn't allow for us to be randomly getting it on. I
needed to be home more for him. I needed to be home
more for my grandbabies too. As much as I enjoyed
working and being around my coworkers, my family
needed me just as much at home.

Lester came into the kitchen and began rambling
through the fridge. He had showered and now smelled
fresh.

"Where's Lisa?" he asked.

"Out."

Lester didn't respond. He placed a leftover pork chop between two slices of bread. As he grabbed a glass from the cabinet, I walked over and rubbed his back with deep strokes.

"Baby, not now." Lester walked away from me to pour himself a glass of orange juice. "I got some things on my mind."

"You want to talk about it?" I asked. Normally when either of us had something pressing going on, no matter what it was, we ran it over with the other to get additional thoughts.

"No, it's roofing stuff," he responded. "I have to figure this out on my own." Lester picked up his sandwich and went into the den, leaving me in the kitchen feeling disregarded. I felt like it was my doing that his mood was in a funk. Lester and I were usually happy-go-lucky, but lately it had been happy-to-go and lucky-to-get-some.

I knew I couldn't spend all night fussing with myself about making my husband happy. I had work tomorrow, and there would be a lot of catch-up to do because I'd missed a day. I finished my tea and went to bed, knowing that it was time I made a decision.

Faulkner

Stepping into my apartment seemed to be the best thing I'd done all day. First, I took off my clothes. Getting out of my silk blouse, panty hose, shoes, and slacks added to my already solitary mood. I called Teresa but got her voicemail. I knew once she knew what had occurred, she'd have my back, no questions asked, and I needed her support. Any minute I expected my phone to ring with her on the line, ready for an earful.

Once I was comfortable, I took my laptop into the den and set it up on the coffee table, poured myself a glass of wine, and sat on the floor to compose my thoughts. I was going to type a resignation letter, but I also contemplated typing a complaint against Joyce.

I picked up the remote to my stereo and flipped it on. Nina Simone's low, shaky voice drifted from the speakers. I nodded my head in agreement that her voice was what I needed to accompany my mood. I looked at the computer screen. The blue background had my eyes transfixed as I hesitated. All of a sudden, I didn't feel like doing my resignation letter. I pulled up the word-processing application and began typing. I wanted to type how I was feeling and how I'd gotten to this point, so I did. I typed about Joyce, Margaret, and the others. I typed about their personalities and how we all had to make things work as a unit. I even mentioned Mr. Price and the story Gail told me about him. It was something that I wasn't comfortable knowing. By the time my phone rang, I'd typed ten pages.

When Teresa heard my voice, she responded without hesitation. "What's the matter? You don't sound like yourself."

I wondered where to begin. "I'm not. You won't believe what happened today."

"Bad day?"

"The worst."

"What happened?"

"Joyce and I had some words and I'm resigning. I finally got fed up."

"Lord, Faulk, I didn't know you had that kind of

news. You didn't go off on her or nothing like that, did you?"

"If you're asking did I hit her, then the answer is no. If you're asking did my neck roll as I yelled at levels that make a person nervous, then the answer is no. I didn't make a scene."

"That's not what I meant and you know it." I could hear the smile in her voice. "I just know that you like your job, and letting Joyce finally get to you is something I didn't expect, so when you told me I envisioned it getting close to physical. Good for you."

"Teresa, I would never go out like that. Granted, Joyce could make the dead want to rise and stomp a pothole in her ass, but I kept my cool. Today was just the icing on the cake."

"You don't have to convince me. You felt you had a serious decision to make and you made it and I'm proud of you for standing up to Joyce. She's a bitch anyway."

"Quitting is not what I would ever want to do. I don't look at myself as a quitter, but there's only so much I was going to take."

"I know."

"I really had no choice. I mean, Joyce wasn't trying to listen to me in regards to Margaret, she was wearing out her welcome with keeping me late on Fridays, and in so many words, she told me that I didn't kiss ass good enough for her to promote me."

"She said that to you? You can sue her and the company. If you decide to do that I will write the story. Girl, I'll have it on the news so fast, you'll be vacationing in the Bahamas by June."

"Teresa, stop playing."

"It's a possibility, Faulkner. That's discrimination."

"I'm not taking Joyce or the phone company to court, Reesa."

"So, what's your plan, Faulk? How do you plan to deal with this?"

I shrugged as if Teresa could see me. "I have a little money saved up to get me through this."

"Are you going to finish the full two weeks?"

"I was thinking of taking a leave of absence first and then resigning when that was up. I could pull in more money that way to buy me some time."

I heard Teresa take in a breath and release it slowly.

"What is it?" I asked.

"I don't know," Teresa responded. "I know I clown you all the time about how much you go back and forth with Joyce and how you should find something else to do, but are you sure quitting is best?"

"After what happened today, I'm positive. Teresa, don't turn your back on me now, I need some support."

Teresa laughed. "Girl, you're the strongest person I know. You can handle anything. I'm going to support you, but I need to make sure I'm being real with you."

"Then why are you tripping as if I'm going through a phase? This is not a phase."

"Because you love your job, girl. That's all you ever talk about, that job and the people you work with. Mrs. Eddye is practically your second mother, Gail Perez is like your baby sister, Carmen and Brenda are like sisters to you too. They're family to you and I know you talk about getting that promotion so you can help them. You're too close to quit now, and I'd be a fool to support you without including the fact that you really love that job. I can already see you moping around, missing what you had."

I frowned. "Joyce told me she wasn't going to hire me for the manager position. She said it to my face. You should have been there and witnessed it, then you'd know why I have to leave."

Teresa fell silent. She was thinking. "Maybe Joyce is

testing you. Maybe keeping you on Fridays is just a test. She's a control freak, Faulkner. A well-dressed, weave-wearing bunch of hype. What if all she's doing is seeing if you can make the grade? You may stay there and you two end up being friends."

"I don't have time for that childish shit like being *tested*. I'm a grown woman. I'm there to work, not to be tested by Joyce, and best friends we'll never be."

"I know and I don't blame you for how you feel. I can't say that I would be trying to make my situation make sense if I were in your shoes. But, Faulkner, I know what the people at your job mean to you and I wouldn't be your friend if I didn't try to at least make you see both sides of this. Joyce could have never called you into the office to talk about that position, so why did she do it?"

I laid my head back on the chair and thought.

"I simply want you to understand that you can't win the war if you stop fighting the battles, girl. It's probably right up Joyce's alley that you are sitting here talking about turning in your resignation. You could be giving her what she wants. Imagine how weak she thinks you are now. She successfully dogged you until you caved in and let up the white flag."

"I see what you're saying, but on the other hand, I'm not to be played with like that. If Joyce wants to have a lab rat as Tech Lead she can hire someone else."

"Well, a few things are now evident. The people who depended on you will no longer have you to depend on." Teresa laughed.

I sighed. "But it's about me." I elaborated on my comment as soon as I said it because it reminded me of the type of thing Joyce would say. "Not in the selfish sense, but, Reesa, I felt alone in her office. The feeling was so overwhelming I just wanted to be out of there."

"Girl, you don't think Malcolm X felt alone when he

walked across that stage at the Audubon Ballroom the day he was killed? He knew it was about him. It's okay to be emotional and it's okay to act on those emotions; I'm not saying you can't do that. You're a woman. Telling you not to be emotional would be like telling Mike Tyson not to act a fool. But there comes a time when you have to evaluate a situation without the emotional element. You have to be brave when being brave is not the thing you want to do."

"I understand what you're saying."

"Faulkner, whatever you do, I will support you. *Whatever*, and I mean that. But you reacted on emotions today and I don't want you looking back on this and regretting it later. You have a giving spirit and I know this isn't the end for you. I've never known you to abandon something you believe in."

"Maybe I no longer care about the job, because that promotion meant a lot to me."

"Then if that's the case, you will walk out of there and never look back."

I thought a minute about work. I'd started as an intern and worked hard to get where I was. "You think I'll regret quitting?" I asked.

"Hell, yeah, but I can also see you quitting. Either way, you'll be okay and I got your back, girl."

My best friend's words struck a nerve inside me. I felt one hundred times better. I wanted to change the subject, talk about something lighter. "Have you talked to Phil?"

"Yes, which reminds me, did a guy named Greg call you?"

"Greg? Who is Greg?"

"Phil's friend, remember? I was trying to tell you this the last time we talked, but you hung up in my face like I had the plague. I gave Phil's friend your phone number and told him to call you. He said he would."

"You did *what*?"

"Girl, don't worry, he was nice. Besides, it's time for you to stop working so much and get you some dick in your life." Teresa started singing to me. "You need dick in your life! Dick in your life!"

"Shut up, girl," I hollered with amusement. "You shouldn't give strangers my phone number, Teresa. I would never do that to you."

"Yeah, but you've done worse. Remember Donald Deberry?"

I laughed loud. "Now, why did you have to go there?"

"You left me in the car for one hour and twenty-seven minutes while you and him had sex in his mama's house. Left me in the car with no keys. I couldn't even listen to the radio."

"Dang, you are not going to let me live that one down. That was in college."

"Hell, no, I'm not going to let you forget."

My phone clicked. "Teresa, hold on while I get the other line."

"Uh-oh, that might be Greg," she squealed. "Put me on hold and see if it's him!"

"I'll call you back. It's probably my mom because I called and left her a message before I left work."

"Click over and see." The phone clicked again and I clicked over, leaving Teresa on the line by herself.

"Hello?"

"Yes, may I speak to Faulkner?" a male voice asked.

"This is she. Who's calling?" I asked while looking at my Caller ID box. The name read, "G. Alston."

"I'm Greg. Greg Alston. Your friend Teresa gave me your number, and I hope you don't mind me calling."

It was the guy Teresa wanted to hook me up with, and if he looked and acted as nice as he sounded, then I was definitely interested. I never clicked back over to Teresa. She eventually hung up.

Joyce

I had dark circles under my bloodshot eyes when I peered into the mirror this morning, a sure sign that I wasn't going in today. I felt pitiful, like I was the only one who understood me. I went to the kitchen, filled a small glass with ice, and poured the best gin I had in my liquor cabinet over it. I dragged myself upstairs to my home office and dialed into the Meridian network via my laptop. The clock on my desk read five-thirty.

I scanned my e-mails. One was from Ella inviting me to her husband's surprise birthday party. I politely declined. The thought of having my Beamer parked on her street in her neighborhood didn't sit well with me. I sent Faulkner correspondence on what I needed her to do and then sent an e-mail to Fred informing him that I would not be in today. Before I sent the e-mail, I reopened it and added I'd be absent the next two days as well. I would work from home and come in after hours to take care of things until Friday.

I left my home office and went back down to my room and climbed under the covers. I wanted some company, but the young gentleman I was seeing needed the job he had and I wanted to respect that. I wasn't one to let my personal life hinder me from taking care of business, but I needed some sex to help me dodge these blues that hung over me. As I lay in bed thinking about the last time we were together, I picked up my cell phone and dialed his number, hoping I could get a quickie from him before he left for work. When he answered, I could hear loud music blaring in the background.

"Yeah."

"This is Joyce and that is no way to answer a telephone."

"What's up, baby doll? I was thinking about you last night."

"Do you mind turning that music down first?" I sighed. When the music was gone, I rested easier on my pillows.

"Is that better?" he asked.

"Much."

"So what's up, baby doll? I know you didn't call me just to tell me to turn my music down. You must want to see me."

"Why else would I be calling?"

"It would be nice for a brother to think that you just wanted to talk or that you were just thinking about me and wanted me to know."

"I *am* thinking about you, that's why I'm calling."

"You know what I mean, Joyce. This is a booty-call."

"I don't make booty-calls."

"Oh, let me correct myself. This is a request-for-sex call." He chuckled after saying what I preferred he called these types of phone calls.

"And? Is there something wrong with a woman who calls to let a man know what she wants?"

"Nah, ain't nothing wrong with that, I guess, you're being real with it. I'd like to think we're deeper than that, but it doesn't have to be that way. If you want sex, then I can give that to you."

"Oh, I see. You want to be more than what I make you. You want to stroll around in public places and meet the relatives. I'm almost thirty years your senior. What would that look like?"

"You *are* thirty years my senior. Thirty-two, to be precise, and it would look like two people who care about each other spending time together. Anything other than hiding out on your side of town or sitting up in my apartment with take-out would be nice. Six months is a long time to have just a sexual relationship with someone."

I let out a small chuckle. "Didn't I make it plain in the beginning that this was an arrangement? I never said that I was interested in anything other than a physical relationship with you."

"Yeah, but whenever Joyce has problems and wants to talk until she's gotten it all out, she calls me. Whenever Joyce needs her cleaning picked up, she calls me. Whenever Joyce is horny and needs sex, she calls me, but what do I get?"

"You get me, dear. You get Joyce Armstrong. That's prize enough."

"You're flattering yourself. That's not cool."

"Hmph."

"When I called you at work, you didn't even accept my call. You dissed me. What's up with that?"

"My job is not the place for personal business. I've told you that a thousand times. So, you can either get with the program or move on."

He paused. "I like spending time with you. That's all I'm saying. I'm not about the age difference and I'm not a trinket you will be able to use for the rest of your life. That's not what I'm about. I know there's more to you than your money and the nice things you own. You keep hiding behind this fake-ass persona of yours, and I personally think you're a better person under all that hiding. Maybe I do need to move around."

I sat up against the pillows. I didn't like feeling as if someone had put me in my place. If any place-putting was going to be done, it was going to be done by me. Of course, a thirty-two-year age difference would make any true adult leery about being out in public, and so what if I had nice things? Hell, I worked long and hard for them. Dennis was mistaking my not being ashamed to show people what I had with hiding, and I didn't have to sit here and listen to this. "I told you in the beginning where I stood."

"Okay, then, I'll holla at you later."

I held on to the phone. "Why would you wait until I call you and really need you, then you decide to get political on me?"

"This is not political, Joyce. I'm a man. I care about you and you're trying to play me."

"Play you?"

"Yeah, you're trying to play me like Tiger Woods, when all I'm asking of you is the same considerations I give you. It seems like there's no room for compromise here. You're an amazing woman with business sense out the ass, Joyce. I'm not trying to take that from you, but you're always playing defense with me. I would be lying if I said I didn't like what you bring to the table. I like getting to know you, but I need some reciprocity."

"I think I reciprocate. That stereo you blast and the cell phone you have complete with intercom capability and unlimited minutes anywhere in the country are hardly signs of me being nonreciprocal. And what about that expensive car alarm?"

"Joyce, you know what I mean. Stop fighting me. I am not a battle you can win or lose. We are not a battle."

I didn't respond. I couldn't.

"Don't get quiet on me now. You treat Daddy so mean."

I giggled, even though I was too old to be giggling on the phone with anybody. I called him Daddy whenever he went down on me. That was my pet name for Dennis and he loved it. "I see you haven't strayed from what this call is really about."

"If that's the only way I can make you smile then I won't stray from it. I guess I have to admit it to myself that you're just about getting down."

"What does that mean?"

"You're a freak."

"I don't hear you complaining about me being a freak."

"Nah, you don't. I'd be a simpleton to admit I don't like your bedside manner."

"So that means I'll see you this morning before you head off to work?"

"Nope. It's already close to seven and I have a twenty-minute ride ahead of me. I'd be late if I came way out to Plano and then tried to make it."

"Tonight, then?"

He sighed. "Sure."

"One other thing," I said, using my sweet voice. "Don't come in my neighborhood blasting that car stereo like you did last time. Half the street complained about that."

"They lived, didn't they? A little music has never hurt anybody. I don't know why you moved out there anyway. Move closer to downtown. Take a chance for once in your life."

"I'm dating you, aren't I? That's chance enough."

"Sometimes I think the only reason you put up with me is because I ain't afraid to let the thug in me out. I'm not like those refined men your age, all caught up in money and younger women. I don't need the ego boost. You like the nigga in me, and the sad part is, that's just an inkling of who I am. I'm college-educated, come from good peeps, and I'm making decent money for an intern, with the best yet to come. The only thing you can see is that I like to get down and dirty every now and then." He laughed. "I'm the shit and you *can't* see that."

"Don't flatter yourself. I deal with you because you're

obedient. My name is not Stella and there is no groove for me to get back. I got the groove, always had it, always will."

"Yeah, between those soft thighs of yours, that's where the groove is. You know, you amazed me that first time we slept together. I thought I was going to be limited with you, but you showed me something."

"I showed you a few *somethings,* didn't I?"

"Like I said, you're an amazing woman."

"I am." I could hear him shifting the phone. I assumed he was gathering his things to go to work.

"Daddy will be over tonight and I'll take that fight out of you. Before I go, I want to hear you say Daddy's name."

As much as I hated his arrogance, it made me want him more. I paused, playing stubborn.

"What's Dennis's name? C'mon, be a good girl and call out my name."

I closed my eyes and remembered me and him on the patio, my breasts up against the glass doors with him behind me. "Daddy," I admitted.

Faulkner

I got in early this morning as usual, but I was dog tired. Greg and I had stayed on the phone until three A.M., talking and getting to know each other. I hadn't had so much fun talking on the phone since I was in high school. He was a nice guy and Teresa was right about our love for jazz music. We were both big fans. As a matter of fact, Greg's parents were well-known musicians, and I owned two of their early recordings. They're collector's items. At any rate, we couldn't get enough of each other and agreed to meet for lunch. I would be able to put a face with the man I now considered intriguing.

Tuesdays were usually fast paced, but this was the beginning of the quarter, so everyone would be in cruise mode, only handling calls, which meant there was room for slacking, and I wanted to make sure the team members didn't get too comfortable. It just wouldn't look good if the team started slacking while I was in the process of leaving the company. However, they were used to this time of the company cycle and it showed. Carmen had already called in late, James had requested to leave early for a dentist appointment, Gail was playing solitaire on the computer as she talked to a customer, and Brenda was working on a knitting project. The only person I knew I could depend on to work a solid day was Margaret, and she hadn't made it into the office yet.

Gail closed her call. She spoke, apparently having gotten over my forcing her to apologize to Brenda yesterday. "Good morning, early bird." She continued playing the game on the computer.

"Hey, Gail," I said. "How are you?"

"Fine, girlfriend. Miguel wanted to fool around before the kids got up." She laughed loudly. "Almost got caught. Little Sederrick came in the room when my behind was in the air."

I giggled. "Did he see anything?"

"No. We were under the sheets. Once we got dressed, he told his sister that Mommy and Daddy built a tent in the bed. Girl, I almost fell out right there on the floor."

"Isn't that something how kids see differently from adults? Thank goodness he didn't see you two out in the open."

"Yeah, 'cause we ain't fine like we used to be and I know if my son had seen all this hanging out, he woulda gone into a coma. Can you imagine a five-year-old in a coma because he seen his parents' asses?"

We both laughed.

Gail got situated and turned the volume up on her small radio. I didn't mind her having the radio, but Joyce didn't like it, so we were always on watch when she had it on. I stood up and leaned on the wall that divided us. "You never told me how the family outing went."

She asked, "The one at Six Flags? Girlfriend, it was off the hook, do you hear me? Those people who work with Miguel acted like they'd never been anywhere. Somebody's kid took a bite out of Bugs Bunny in Looney Tunes Land, Miguel's supervisor got drunk, slipped, and sprung his ankle, then to top it off, an entire family got removed from the park for jumping line. It was drama all day."

"Did the kids have a good time?"

"They had a ball. My daughter cried all the way home 'cause she wanted to stay and play with Bugs Bunny. I was like, 'Child, you better c'mon here and stop all that nonsense.' "

"That's what matters at places like that. Kids can't get enough of those cartoon characters. I'm glad they had fun."

Gail closed the game and turned the tuner dial on her radio, looking for something interesting. Suddenly, she rose to her feet. "Ooh, this used to be my jam! I haven't heard this song in a while." She looked around to see if the coast was clear, then turned the radio up enough for both of us to hear. "They played this song in the club last week." Gail pushed her chair under her desk to make more room and she started to groove to the music.

I watched her as I bobbed my head to the beat. I'd

heard the song a few times, but didn't really dig the lyrics, which told me to back my ass up and drop it like it was hot. However, the beat of the song forced you to move something.

"C'mon, girl!" Gail waved at me. "I know you ain't scared to show your stuff."

I actually was scared. Well, I used to be. Now, I had nothing to lose, I'd be gone soon anyway, so I joined Gail.

Gail turned and began dancing with more effort. She put her arms in front of her and moved them around. I considered myself a more suave dancer than she was. I dipped my shoulders a little and then rotated my hips like I had stiff joints. Gail let out a wild laugh, dropped to the floor, and put her hands on her knees. Then she looked around at her butt as if she was trying to see how it was moving. I dipped to the right then to the left and back to the right. I puckered my lips then closed my eyes. I was in the groove now. I turned and bent down, joining Gail in her booty dance.

"I see you! I see you, girl!" Gail said as she jerked her shoulders and rotated her hips. "Go, Faulkner! It's ya birthday! Go, Faulkner! It's ya birthday!"

I smiled and shook my shimmy harder. It felt good, even though we were risking a lot, acting like it was Friday night at club Lose Your Job This Way. I came up and gyrated my upper torso, then broke it down with a dance I used to do in high school. Gail let out a resounding "Ooo-oo!" I threw my hands up and let her have the floor. Gail did a nice little turn, popped her hips to each side, and flung her head in the opposite direction. I called out to her, "Heeey now! Aaaaw sookie sookie, Gail Perez! Do your thang!" I joined her and we did the same dance, as if we were on a *Soul Train* stage. We turned with our backs to the aisle, risking it all, but having fun and not caring. When we turned back around, I almost fainted when I saw who was standing there. Gail jumped and immediately turned off the radio. We'd both been caught red-handed.

The woman walked over and lit into Gail and me. "Now, I know your mamas taught you better than to be up in here acting like monkeys loose from the zoo. This ain't no juke joint and we can't lose you two on account of no foolishness."

I smiled. It was Margaret Eddye and she was leaning against Gail's cube, pointing her finger with a grin on her face as wide as the Atlantic. "Scared you, didn't I?"

I ran over to her and hugged her. "Oh, are you a sight for sore eyes! Margaret, how are you doing?"

Gail embraced Margaret after I did. It already felt good to have her at work, and Teresa was right, I was regretting having to leave such wonderful people.

"I'm fine, fine, fine. Looks like you two were having a party without me, honey. You know I don't like that. I don't get to do the old Camel Walk at home."

We walked Margaret to her cube. That's when I noticed her slight limp, but I decided not to comment on it. Something told me it was the reason she had called in yesterday. She stood and looked around for a moment. "I sure didn't miss this little box called a workspace. What do we have to do today?"

I pulled her chair out for her. "Margaret, you got all day to worry about that. Relax for a while. I know your doctor doesn't want you working too hard anyway."

Margaret looked at me. "Was you there? No. Well, then, hush up."

Gail immediately began probing. "So, tell me for real, Margaret. What did your doctor say?"

"A whole lot of nothing. Told me to take my pills, get some rest, and to not ignore the dizzy spells and heart flutters."

I leaned forward. "Dizzy spells? Heart flutters? Margaret, you never told me about that before."

Margaret shook her head. "It's nothing. Just doctor talk is all. I'm fine."

I had to pull back. I knew Margaret had health concerns with her blood pressure, but not with her heart. "Is that a sign that you're doing fine?" I asked, pointing to her wrapped knee.

"This is from a bump I got from rushing. I was moving around too fast and bumped my knee."

Gail looked at Margaret's leg and then at Margaret. "Are your spells the result of your diabetes?"

She took in a long breath. "Yeah. That and a stroke I had a long time ago made my heart weak, but I haven't had another since then, and I didn't think these new issues with my body had anything to do with my current spells. Stress is all it was, but now it's nothing. They're just spells that don't last long at all. I told my doctor about the spells."

"But, Margaret, you should make sure you keep track of when you have those spells."

"For real," Gail added. "My cousin Pumpkin had those heart flutters and she is good for calling her doctor."

"Really, now?" Margaret asked. "How old is she?"

Gail thought for a moment. "Thirty-five or thirty-six, somewhere up in there."

I frowned. "That's young. Was it menopause? Oprah did a show on that."

"Girl, Oprah ain't in touch with the 'hood no mo. Pumpkin's issues were drama- and health-related," Gail said. "She has six kids and ever since that last one, her body just shut down on her. But I think it was those two abortions she had back in the day because after that second one, she started having clotting issues with her legs and chest. Something just wasn't right. I told her to keep her legs closed, and with Royal in and out of jail it's just too much stress."

"Royal is her husband?" I asked.

"Father of three of her kids. The other three are from this other situation she had."

"Lord, that's drama," Margaret said. "She needs to get rid of that man and start eating right."

"She ain't trying to do neither one of those. Pumpkin eats greasy food and lots of leftovers. She smokes weed to keep her calm but it makes her paranoid and that makes her blood pressure go up. I keep telling her she needs to get right with God, but she won't listen to me. Bad food, bad kids, and bad men are going to be the death of her, but one thing I will say in her defense is, Pumpkin *will* go to the doctor. Can't no one keep that woman out of the hospital."

I looked at Gail and wondered if she had any shame about anything before focusing back on Margaret. "Did you get a second opinion?"

She chuckled. "Child, I may be too young to be having heart flutters, but I'm too old to be getting a second opinion." She waved her hands at Gail and me. "Go back to your seats. The phones will be ringing soon and I'm ready to get back to work."

I patted Margaret's shoulder and kissed her cheek. "Take it easy over here and if you feel sick, let me know and I'll let you go home. I'll even take you myself."

Margaret picked up her headset and put it on. "I'm letting you know now, Faulkner, retirement is starting to look good to me."

I smiled, happy to hear those words coming from her. I wasn't going to tell Margaret about yesterday's run-in with Joyce. Now wasn't the time. I rubbed her shoulder again. "Okay, Margaret." I headed back to my cube. Before I sat down, I saw James and Brenda walking back onto the main floor. A funny feeling hit me and I realized

I'd missed something with them. Brenda's arm was entwined with James's and they were both smiling big about something. Brenda looked over and waved at me. I returned the favor. James walked Brenda to her cube, said something to her, made her blush, and then retreated to his own cube.

Like a prairie dog peeping from its hole, Gail's head popped up in front of me, her *I Dream of Jeannie* hairdo plastered to her head. "You think something is going on between them?"

I stared at Gail without saying anything.

She used her hands to make her point. "Well, it ain't like they can't be involved. I mean, look at them, girlfriend. It's obvious."

I shook my head. "Gail, don't let your lips write a check your behind can't cash. Brenda and James are working on a project and the only thing you need to be concerned about is Gail's work."

"Hmm, whatever." Gail sat back down. She rustled through some things, then I heard her bite into a chip. "I've seen it on television a million times. Two people working together and before you know it, they bumpin' uglies in the stockroom."

Ignoring Gail, I checked my watch and looked around for Carmen. She was late again. I hoped she would get in before Joyce strolled through. I hadn't had the thought two minutes before Carmen came rushing in. She waved, smiled, and went straight to her desk.

"The bus was late," she explained to me.

Gail popped up again. "Girl, you can't depend on DART for nothing. My cousin Jackie, she's filing a lawsuit 'cause they never get her to work on time."

Carmen shook her head. "I know the feeling, but the route I'm on isn't so bad. Jesse, the driver, has four kids and he isn't always in the best mood when he's doing the route."

"But you are still a customer. He should have thought about that when he had them kids," Gail said. "That's a lot of kids anyway. He sounds like my cousin Pumpkin."

I let Gail and Carmen continue their conversation without me. I sat down and checked my e-mail. Joyce had sent me one marked with red letters, which meant it was urgent. I clicked on the small envelope icon and read the e-mail. Joyce wasn't going to be in today or the next two days. I relaxed in my seat, glad not to have the pressure of her presence around me. On one hand, this was a good thing. I could work stress-free, but on the other hand, I was still dealing with the questions Teresa had put in my head: Was Joyce up to something? Was she testing me? I replied quickly, letting her know I would take care of everything and that the phone stats and line closings would be on her desk when she came in. She didn't respond, so I assumed all was okay. I slid on my headset and began my workday with Greg Alston on my mind.

Margaret

I spent the morning handling on-site business dispatches and by noon, I was ready for lunch. I could always tell when it was time to put a little something in my stomach because my mood would change from whatever to depression. It was funny how my high blood pressure and diabetes seemed to choose depression when I needed sugar or food or rest. Sometimes it went from depression to depression times two, which meant it was time for my medicine.

I stayed at my desk and pulled out a dry turkey sandwich, bottled water, an orange, and a peppermint, plus Faulkner would bring me a salad. I liked eating lunch at my desk, for one, because it kept me from having to walk to the elevator, and, two, I could turn my radio to my favorite gospel station and listen to some good music while I ate. All of the team members were gone, so I welcomed the peace of being alone in the cube area. I peeled the fresh-looking orange, but when I bit into it, the taste was bitter. It tasted like tired lemonade. I trashed what was left of it and attempted to eat my sandwich, but it wasn't much better. I trashed it too and decided to wait for my salad. I searched around my purse for my medication. My hands had started to shake. I wasn't used to the feeling hitting me so fast. As I looked into my purse, objects blurred. I squinted through my glasses, but the view didn't change. My arms began to feel hot, as if the sun were shining directly on them. I sat back, closed my eyes, and counted to ten, trying to relax the rising panic inside me. Now was not the time for one of my spells, but I felt it coming. Just as my vision began to fail me more, my hand curled around the pill bottle, gripping it until my fingertips were white. I released the bottle and struggled to reach for my water, knocking it over and watching it roll to the floor. My arms and hands tingled and then went numb. The things on my desk swayed as my body rocked, until my head hit the desk and I stared motionless at a photo of my grandbabies. I felt captured inside the heaviness of my being. The warmth was now making its way to my stomach and down to my knees. I closed my eyes and tried to count to ten.

I woke to find myself at a desk with a typewriter, a normal twelve-dial telephone, a small plant, a pencil holder, and a photo of me and Ms. Patterson, from my high school graduation. I looked around and noticed the office was a wide, open space with several other desks that looked like mine, with different women seated at each one. There were no cloth-covered walls separating us. I recognized the faces, and a few of the names I knew. This was my office from some time ago.

Mary Culligan, my first trainer, walked past and waved at me. "Congratulations," she beamed. Her hair was feather-cut with huge, bouncy brown curls. I smiled back nervously, not sure why she was congratulating me. I lifted my hand to wave and it seemed to float more than be taking commands from my brain. I did notice that my arm, both my arms, were thin and had definition to them. I looked down and saw that my chair could be seen because my legs didn't cover the entire seat. I knew what I felt like on the inside, but my outside had changed.

"Margaret, are we still on for drinks after work? I really need to get away and rid myself of some of this tension."

I looked up and Joyce was standing over me. She was thinner than I was. Almost bone thin.

"Joyce Armstrong?"

"Who else? Honey, what is wrong with you? You don't look so hot." Joyce sat her thin frame on the edge of my desk. A few of the other operators looked at her. One of them was Carrie Greene, a white girl who sat at the desk across from me. Her husband was a truck driver and an alcoholic. They had two children. Two boys. Carrie stared at us as she talked to a customer. Joyce's eyes met Carrie's, then Joyce flipped her hand at her. "Find you some business, Carrie Greene," she said, loud enough for the entire office to glance our way. A few of the ladies let their mouths fall open in disbelief, while others shook their heads, and talked to each other in lowered voices. The sound of typewriter keys being tapped and telephone rings filled the air, confusing me. Joyce shifted on the desk, not caring that her brown plaid skirt rose high enough for her thighs and part of her panties to be seen. She wore flesh-toned panty hose over them, but it was still an unladylike way to behave. Her blouse was white and it matched the leather platforms she wore. "How about the Green Parrot again? I could sure eat some enchiladas."

I looked at Joyce like I didn't know her.

"Margaret, what in the hell is wrong with you? If I didn't know better, I'd swear you'd gotten your hands on some bad Mary Jane."

I finally opened my mouth to speak. "The Green Parrot? Didn't they close it down?"

"What?" Joyce leaned over and placed her palm across my forehead. "We were just at the Green Parrot last night celebrating your birthday and your promotion. If being thirty-one makes you senile then I don't want no part of it." Joyce slapped my shoulder as her laughter brought attention to us once again. She was acting like a monkey out of its cage, as my mother used to say.

Did Joyce just say I celebrated my thirty-first birthday? I looked at myself again. I was wearing a blue-jean jumpsuit with a red belt across my waist, which wasn't the bulky sack of skin I was used to. I grabbed a mirror from my desk drawer and looked at my face. There was green eye shadow on my eyelids, my lips were covered with glossy burgundy lipstick, and my hair was pressed with full curls framing my face, which contained no dark circles around my eyes and no sagging skin for cheeks. I was thirty-one and I remembered the woman who was staring back at me in the mirror. I broke out in laughter. Joyce looked in the drawer and removed a box of unopened Cracker Jacks. I looked on my desk calendar for today's date: October 28, 1974. That's when it dawned on me that I was at my job at the phone company twenty-seven years ago. I looked at Joyce again to give her the once-over. Her hair was neatly Afroed and her makeup was as sharp and perfectly blended as always. Some things never change. She pulled a catalog from my desk and leafed through it.

"When are you going to stop selling this Tupperware shit? You can't make real money doing this."

I was still chuckling. "Eventually," I said as I simultaneously remembered saying it.

Joyce put the catalog back. "Margaret, you sure that stuff we smoked yesterday wasn't bad, because you are acting funny today."

"No, Joyce, I'm fine. Just excited about being thirty-one, I guess."

"I'm not looking forward to it," she groaned. "If it were left up to me, I'd be twenty-six forever, you dig? Keep my figure, my nice Afro, my varicose-vein-free long legs, and my vitality. I'm going to grow old with grace, class, and style. All I need is the right man and the right plan, you understand?" Joyce held out her hand and I slapped her five. I'd almost forgotten how cool Joyce thought she was.

"You're in for a surprise," I said, smiling.

"What is that supposed to mean? Are you saying I'm not going to marry Isaac Hayes and live happily ever after? Shit."

I put the mirror back, still smiling.

"So is it the Green Parrot or not?"

I shrugged. "Sure, I can dig that." This time I giggled uncontrollably. "I can dig it."

"Margaret, hush before you get us in trouble. You know Jack is in his office."

Things began coming to me quick. Jack Loomis was our boss and it was no secret that he and Joyce were involved. That was one of the reasons she could sit in the office all day and do absolutely nothing without getting fired. I also knew that Joyce and I were the only two women of color in the office, so we hung tight.

"I'm sorry," I said, as I controlled my amusement.

An office door across from us opened and Mr. Loomis stepped out. Joyce slid off my desk and leaned over my shoulder as if we were talking business. Before him, another man came out, turned around, and shook his hand. I couldn't place the face, but I knew that I knew him. As the man left, Mr. Loomis looked across at Joyce and me. He motioned for me to come to his office. Joyce walked to her desk and sat down, keeping her eyes on Mr. Loomis the entire time. I walked over and entered the office. Mr. Loomis stepped in behind me and closed the door.

When I sat down in the chair alongside Mr. Loomis's desk, a wave of dizziness swept over me. It was as if I had stepped into a portal and everything from seeing Joyce to the overabundance of Old Spice cologne Mr. Loomis wore overwhelmed me. He sat and looked at me. I always liked Mr. Loomis. He was a nice man and a good boss. He always told the women in the office that we came first.

I looked around his office, remembering all the little things I'd forgotten, like the photo of his wife, Donna. She always made cookies at Christmas and sent them to the office. Then there were all the management books he had on the bookshelves that lined the walls of his office. I would borrow them every so often, take them home, and read them. That's part of the reason I'd gotten the promotion. My self-motivation had paid off. I'd forgotten about the papier-mâché turtle his daughter had made that sat on his desk.

"Margaret, I want to reiterate to you that you are being named office manager because you have the strongest

character out of all the women there. I know you're concerned about leading and being in management with no
degree, but you won't have to worry about that. I will do
all I can to make sure you feel comfortable in the position."

I smiled as the day became more familiar. I remembered the feeling of joy I was now having and the sense
of accomplishment. I even remembered feeling good
about being thirty-one and still having my sanity because so much was going on in the world. Nixon and
Watergate, the Black Panthers, Duke Ellington's death,
there was so much.

"You women have proven to be hard workers and it
wasn't easy for me to make this decision, so you must
know that a lot was riding on my choice regarding to
whom I would give the promotion. I'm going to need
you to dig your fingers into the dirt and make me not regret that I chose you."

I shook my head, but my joy was fading into skepti-
cism. I was feeling weird all of a sudden. My memory
began coming to me again, yet I couldn't think ahead
fast enough.

"Presentation is everything too, Margaret. I know this
is the phone company, but I try to be liberal with you
ladies when it comes to how I want us to be perceived by
clients. Don't get me wrong. How you look is fine. As a
matter of fact, you're a very beautiful woman. Did I ever
tell you that you remind me of Cicely Tyson, who I think
is absolutely stunning?"

"Yes, sir." Too many times, truth be told, I thought.
If I looked like Cicely Tyson, then Lena Horne looked like
Eartha Kitt.

"While I was vacationing in Africa two years ago, I
saw a picture of an African princess in Senegal. She was
something to see, but all I kept thinking was that she reminded me of my little office worker, Margaret Willis."

"Thank you, Mr. Loomis."

"And that is what I want to see more of. I want to see more of that naked beauty I know you have. Don't be afraid to wear a higher skirt or lower neckline. It helps to beautify the office and that impresses our clients. Besides, I'm not so much of a crocodile when I come in and see beauty." Mr. Loomis placed his hand on my leg and squeezed.

I stood, or more like jumped, from the chair.

Mr. Loomis smiled. "Your desk will be moved next week. You will be right outside my office door. You will be my personal assistant."

I finally opened my mouth. "Mr. Loomis, I'm doing business accounts now, not secretarial work."

"You will not be doing secretarial work. You are the office manager, which not only pays more but allows you to work closer with me, to learn more about the inner workings of upper management. This is a step up for you, Margaret."

I stared at Mr. Loomis, looking for some sign that the touch on the leg was what I sensed it to be.

Mr. Loomis rose and reached out his hand for me to shake. When I placed my hand inside his, he rubbed too long, shook too soft, turning a business handshake into something secretive and intimate. When I turned to leave, he placed his hand on my back and rubbed until his hand was on my butt, squeezing and massaging. I stopped in my tracks. Now I remembered this moment. I wasn't going to be office manager and this incident would change my relationship with Joyce. This was why to this day she and I didn't get along. I turned to Mr. Loomis and stared directly into his baby browns. "Mr. Loomis, I cannot accept your offer to be office manager at this time. Unfortunately, I don't feel qualified to fill the position as you would have me do."

Mr. Loomis looked at me and smiled as if things were

still going his way. "Very well, I can respect your inability to have faith in yourself, Ms. Willis. I will notify human resources that your salary will remain the same. That is contingent upon this conversation staying where it is."

I didn't respond. I didn't have to. Defeat and agreement were on my face. I exited the office and returned to my desk. This was a bad déjà vu trip. The phone rang and I picked up.

"Customer service, may I help you?"

"What'd he say in there?"

I looked across the office. Joyce was staring at me, holding the receiver close to her mouth. She flipped her hand at me, motioning for me to give up the information.

"Nothing. I told him that I would not be able to be office manager."

"What? Margaret, do you know how much money you turned down? You could have gotten that Plymouth Duster you've been ranting about. Why did you renege?"

I shrugged. "He explained to me the job would be demanding and you know I'm trying to go back to school to get my business degree. I just can't risk my education. I'll apply when another position becomes available."

"Shit, that was the opportunity of a lifetime. I could only dream of being office manager and making that kind of money. I'd be the coldest chick since Pam Grier, ya hear?"

"Yeah," I mumbled. I wanted to tell Joyce about what really happened, but I needed this job. I wasn't degreed like Joyce. If I lost this job, I'd end up sweeping halls at some school. Besides, men were always reaching out to touch a woman's behind. That didn't mean they wanted to have sex with her. They did it all the time at the club. Mr. Loomis wasn't any different. He didn't come right out and attack me, and as a black woman, I knew that trying to take my white boss to court would mean spending big dollars that I didn't have, not to mention the public embarrassment.

Joyce was still talking. "You know, women don't make as much as men and it isn't often they want us for anything outside of being homemakers and hookers. I can't wait for my chance to be in management, because nothing is stopping me. Then I'll get the respect I'm due from these white girls around here. They're always looking for some excuse to write me up or get me put on probation, but they just don't know. I'm Joyce Armstrong, you dig? Mr. Loomis already told me I have potential."

"Joyce, I have to finish logging these phone orders. Can we finish this tonight at the Parrot?"

"Yeah, girl, it's cool. I'll see you after work."

I hung up and tried to finish my work, the entire time feeling sick to my stomach. Each time Mr. Loomis's door creaked open my stomach became an ocean. He never looked at me again, that day or any other day. When he passed by me a few times, he never acknowledged that I was there. Years later it would dawn on me that he treated Carrie Greene and two other ladies in the office the same way.

That night, Joyce never made it to the club. She stood me up. I remembered getting to work the next day to discover that she was the new office manager, naked African beauty and all. With her new position came the division in our relationship. She treated me the same way Mr. Loomis did, every day after that, until Mr. Loomis moved on to other things. I remembered being at the Green Parrot waiting for Joyce to show up, but I'd met my future husband instead, Lester Eddye. We shared enchiladas and danced the night away to Rufus and Chaka Khan, Stevie Wonder, the Temptations, and the O'Jays.

My muscles jumped and I felt my own breath. The feeling was back in my hands and I struggled to bring myself out of the spell. My head felt like a ton of bricks. Spittle oozed from my mouth and down my cheek as I lifted my head from the desk. My neck ached and I could barely turn it to the left. It had cramped up. Once I steadied myself, I opened my pill bottle and swallowed the tiny green pill. I picked up the water bottle from the floor and chased the pill with water. Something had happened to me that had never happened before. I'd had a spell at work. Evidently, nobody had noticed, but I couldn't be upset because it had happened during lunch and the office was a desert during lunch. I looked at the clock on my desk. I'd been out for about thirty minutes.

I tried to recall what had happened. Much of it was still clear. I saw Joyce's young face and her thin frame. I saw the blue-jean jumper I had worn and Joyce's plaid skirt. I then went through present information. My name was Margaret Diane Willis Eddye and I was fifty-seven years old. My husband was Lester Eddye and our daughter was Lisa Jeanette Eddye. I had two grandbabies, Nicole and . . . and . . . I couldn't remember! She was older than Nicole, I knew that much, and she was good in science and math. I clenched my fist as pain rose in my chest. I attempted to pace my breathing but it wasn't working. I was upset. I was losing the battle with my health. My body was no longer willing to make concessions for the stress. I tried to call for help but my breath felt short. The only thing I could do was look up and pray because I didn't want to die this way.

Faulkner

For lunch, Greg and I agreed to meet at Café Brazil in Deep Ellum, just northeast of downtown. Colorfully decorated and with an old-Texas ambiance mixed with a contemporary touch, Café Brazil was the perfect spot for conversation against an urban backdrop. I couldn't wait to get there to finally put a face to Greg's handsome voice and attractive personality. I peeked at my watch: five minutes before I had to leave to make the restaurant on time. I stood and stretched, seeing who was already gone for lunch and who wasn't. Most of the team was gone except for Carmen and Gail. Carmen was getting ready to leave, but Gail's head was resting in her hands and her eyes were closed even though she still wore her headset. I thought she was sleeping until she nodded and tried to get a word in to whoever was on the other end of the line, possibly Jonnie Coleman. The look of anguish on her face told me she tolerated irate customers more than she wanted to. She noticed me looking at her. I smiled and gave her the thumbs-up; she responded by sticking out her tongue and closing her eyes again, but not before smiling too. I looked across the aisle to see if Margaret was in her cube and there she was, pulling items out of her lunch container. I started to go over and check on her but I was too excited about meeting Greg, and she looked as if everything was fine.

When I walked into the café, it was busy. The Deep

Ellum contingent during lunch consisted mostly of self-made businesspeople, tattooed bikers, kids working their way through college, and any kind of artist imaginable. It was a place for the avant-garde types. I immediately knew Greg when I saw him. Dressed in khakis and a navy-blue Polo shirt, he was the only black man in the place standing idle at the bar, looking around each time someone walked through the door. Teresa was right: he was good-looking, not too tall, not too short, and when he smiled, something inside me let me know he was happy with what he was seeing too. I could tell my cocoa tone, medium-length locks, and my five-foot-five, 120-pound frame was something he could get with.

"Faulkner, we finally meet." He smiled.

I took his hand and shook it. "I know," I cooed. "I'm excited to be here."

A waitress led us over to a table by the window that looked out onto Elm Street. Once she got us seated and took our drink orders, we were able to talk and take in the fact that we were meeting in person.

"How is work today?" Greg's eyes were focused on me. Our vibe was on point.

"Work is work is work." I grinned. "Busy as usual, but I can't complain."

"Sleepy?" Greg sipped his water and smirked at me.

"Not really, even though we talked on the phone last night like we didn't have jobs to go to."

"Yeah, but it felt good."

The waitress returned with our drinks. She took our food orders. As soon as she was gone, we were like teenagers again, talking, laughing, and making great eye contact with each other. The flirting was intense.

"Your friend Teresa and my friend Phil have been kicking it strong since they met."

"I know. She loves her some him."

We laughed.

Greg's face took on a more serious expression. "I know you told me that you sometimes work long hours at the phone company on Fridays, but I have tickets to see Joe Sample and Laylah Hathaway in Fort Worth this coming Friday. Would you be interested?"

"I saw that in the paper. They're going to be at the Caravan of Dreams, right? The last show before they close the place down. You can't just say Joe Sample and Laylah Hathaway in the same sentence like it's nothing. I would love to go."

"Do you want me to pick you up or should we meet each other there?"

"No, you can pick me up. I'll e-mail directions to you when I get back to the office."

The waitress came with our food. Greg had ordered the veggie sandwich with chips and I had a large salad that looked like Mardi Gras on lettuce. We looked at each other's plates and agreed to taste-test from each. We talked, ate, and laughed until I was half an hour over my scheduled lunchtime, but I didn't rush to get back. After leaving a nice tip and treating for lunch, Greg walked me to my car.

"It was a great lunch." He smiled.

"Thanks for making it great," I replied.

"I'll call you later this week to solidify plans for Friday."

"Sounds good."

Greg and I shook hands again. He waited long enough for me to get in the car and watch me drive off before heading to his car. I was impressed with him. He was a genuine guy whom I wanted to get to know better.

As I took Elm back into downtown, I had Greg on the brain. I wanted to spend as much time as I could with him and find out how many more things we had in common. I hadn't dated seriously in three years and for the first time, this was a man I was wholeheartedly interested in.

Margaret

As quickly as the second spell had come it was gone. My forehead was damp and I could feel the moisture on the armpits of my dress. Now, my chest felt light as a feather, minus the earlier constricting pain from being pressed against the desk. My mouth had dried to a miserable state. I was thankful nothing worse had happened. I could hear a few people talking and carrying on, and wondered where Faulkner was. She normally checked on me before she went to lunch, and I don't know why in the world she didn't come over here today because I brought a sad lunch with me and could have used something with some seasoning in it.

I steadied myself before attempting to stand up. Once I got my bearings, I felt the blood rushing to areas that had been restricted when I was passed out. Hunger was on me and I needed to get something into my system before I got sick from taking the medicine with nothing on my stomach. The last thing I needed was for someone to discover me laid out on the floor. Faulkner's desk was empty. I looked at my watch. She'd been gone over an hour and I needed her. I looked over and saw Gail. She was munching on a bag of chips and drinking a Coke. I walked over.

"Gail, is Faulkner in the building?"

Gail looked up. She brushed crumbs from her hands. "No, she's at lunch." Gail looked at her watch. "She should be walking in here at any minute, though, because it's about time for her to be back."

I headed to the cafeteria and got me something anyway, because I couldn't wait on Faulkner to bring the salad. Lord only knew when she'd be returning. The cafeteria was still buzzing with people even though the regular lunchtime rush was over. I bought a side of fruit and a small order of mashed potatoes with brown gravy.

The episode I'd had was still heavy on my mind and I couldn't help but feel confused about where I stood now. As much as I conceded that the Lord gives and the Lord takes away, I wasn't sure if I was ready for him to take *me* away. I knew the good thing was that I'd been faithful to the Word and I'd lived a faithful life. I had wonderful friends and people around me who were honestly concerned about me, but this brush with death had put a new twist on things. When I'd had my stroke, I was out and couldn't remember anything, but the spell had taken me somewhere. I'd seen things and heard voices. Up until today, it had been easy for me to say that I was ready whenever God was willing to take me, but now that I'd had a brush with death that allowed me to revisit my life, I wasn't so ready to keep myself open like that. I knew that if I passed tomorrow, I wouldn't be satisfied. Death was a concrete thing; I'd never looked at it that way until now. It had always been some event to me, where I could see myself in a casket with all my people around me grieving, but I never thought about all the other things that fade with death, like memories. This scared me and frustrated me all at once.

When I stepped off the elevator, Faulkner was just getting seated at her cubicle. I walked over, food in hand. She looked at me and smiled, but I needed more.

"Hey, Margaret, I'm sorry I didn't check on you like I usually do, but I had a lunch date."

"A lunch date? With a man?"

"Yes, with a man." She smiled as her eyes beamed.

She reminded me of Nicole when she first learned how to play "Twinkle, Twinkle, Little Star" on her violin. Faulkner busied herself at her desk. I got the hint that her mind was on other things, but I wasn't budging so easy. All of a sudden, I felt put off by her casual disregard of checking on me before she left for lunch. She'd done it every day for years. Faulkner was starting to act like Lisa, forgetting what was more important.

"Tell me about him."

"Not much to tell. Teresa hooked us up, but we officially met today. I talked to him on the phone for hours last night and we're going to a concert Friday night."

"Already going out and you just met him? Moving kind of fast, don't you think?"

Faulkner hesitated. "No. I think he's a great guy."

"Foot. You young women don't know the first thing about dating. You sleep with the first thing that comes along. You're not interested in substance or values. All you want to know is how much money he's making or what kind of car he drives."

"Wait a minute, Margaret, that's not true. What would make you say that?"

"It is true. First you'll sleep with him and then he'll do you wrong. Then you'll come running to me, crying and looking to be consoled, and you assume I'm going to be there for you, you take it for granted that I will. He's on your brain and everything else is getting ignored."

Faulkner's mouth opened and closed from shock. She closed her eyes and shook her head like she was in a bad dream. "Margaret, are you okay?"

"Why do you want to know?"

"Because you're talking to me like I've done something wrong. I have a life just like everyone else. Nothing is going ignored."

"A man comes along and all of a sudden you gain a life—well, whoop-de-doo. You've never taken an hour-

and-thirty-minute lunch. You've never forgotten to check on me before you went to lunch, and you've never come back here without a salad for me. Whatever life you had outside of work just wasn't worth the extra time and lack of consideration until now, was it?"

Faulkner put one hand up as if to stop wind from hitting her. "I'm going to finish my work before this conversation leads to some things being said that would be regretted later on. I did think about you before I left. I looked over and you seemed to be fine. As far as the salad, I forgot, and I apologize, Margaret, but that doesn't mean I was ignoring you."

"Faulkner, I always thought you were smarter than the rest of the young women around here. I pegged you differently. You were the one woman I thought I could look at—and know she had her priorities straight."

"My priorities *are* straight, Margaret, and I don't think anything is wrong with me meeting a man and taking a little time out of my daily schedule to eat lunch with him. All I do is work. That's all you've ever seen me do." Faulkner's voice was shaking. I didn't want her feelings to be hurt, but I was hurting because of her.

I let her words drift into nowhere as I walked back to my desk and ate my food even though I was no longer hungry. Faulkner came and stood at my cube in silence. I couldn't even look up at her. She'd never understand what it was like to feel all the things I was feeling. I sat stubbornly ignoring her.

"Margaret, I'm sorry if not checking on you before I went to lunch upset you. Can I make it up to you somehow?" I could tell Faulkner was trying, but I wasn't interested in her making it up to me any more than I was interested in knowing she now had something else to occupy her time. She stood over me for a few minutes before resigning herself. "Fine. Have it your way," she said and stepped out of the cube.

Faulkner

I didn't know what had gotten into Margaret, but I couldn't take her attitude toward me to heart, although it felt that way. When I walked away from her cube, I didn't know how or what to feel, really, except bad. Sure, I usually checked on her and brought her a salad back, but she had to know that I was still a person with a life. If she depended on me it was because she chose to. It was like having my mother, grandmother, and friend mad at me at the same time. Of course, I knew this would pass, but when and why had it happened in the first place?

Gail was waiting for me when I returned to my cube. She'd sat quietly at her desk the entire time Margaret and I were going back and forth, so I knew she'd heard everything. "I think Margaret might be losing herself."

"What do you mean?"

"Right before my husband's father died, he became the meanest old man I knew. He was a diabetic too and never took his insulin like he should have. When it finally caught up with him, it was too late. But, I distinctly remember the way he acted. He snapped at Miguel, cursed him, and accused him of being ungrateful. Girlfriend, it got so bad that we stopped going over to see him because he did it in front of the kids. He'd lost himself."

I thought about what Gail was saying, but Margaret

told me she took her medicine and I believed her. "No, Gail, that's not it. I disappointed her and she's just trying to deal with it the best way she can."

"I think we need to check and make sure she's taking her medication just to be safe, because I know when diabetics don't take their medicine, they get depressed and angry."

"Margaret is a grown woman and if she says she's taking her medicine, then she's taking it," I snapped. "Just leave it alone, okay?"

Gail's eyes widened then softened. "Okay, but don't say I didn't tell you."

I turned my attention back to the work I was doing. I hoped Gail realized that I wasn't in much of a mood to try and figure out what Margaret's problem was. I loved Margaret, but I was not her keeper. I checked on her because I appreciated all the things she did for me and I wanted to always show her that, but if she was going to let one day of me *not* showing her determine that we could not be friends, then so be it. I didn't want to have that attitude, but it felt safe. I'd tried to apologize and she wasn't hearing me.

I needed to set a date for a staff meeting. I looked to see who was here and saw everyone except James. I figured he'd already left for his dentist appointment. I decided to have the meeting Friday, since he was out, Joyce was out today, tomorrow, and Thursday, and Margaret was in a bad mood. I set the appointment up in "Outlook," and sent the reminder to my boss and the team.

I picked up the phone to call Teresa, but hung up before she could answer. I felt like she needed to know about what had happened with Greg and with Margaret, but I didn't feel like telling her. I felt like Teresa could say something to me that would make it all make sense, but she'd also probably get on me about my letting my interest in Greg make me lose sight of my relationship with Margaret, and I wasn't up for hearing that. I felt guilty enough. Margaret had never talked to me like that before and it really upset me more than I cared to admit. I was worried about her, but I refused to take her hostility.

I busied myself pulling up the call statistics and noticed we hadn't even done our usual seven hundred calls. We were only at four hundred and twenty. I could hear Gail on a personal call. I tapped on the wall between us and politely asked her to wrap up her call and take care of some reports that needed to be done. I then e-mailed Brenda and asked her to see me before she left for the day. I wanted to talk to her about ACIS training, which she needed. I was expecting her to e-mail me back, but was surprised to see her at my cube in a matter of seconds after I'd sent the e-mail.

"Brenda, you didn't have to come over, I just needed to know when you'd be available for training."

"I didn't get it yet. I was actually coming over to share some great news with you."

I leaned back in my seat, ready to hear what Brenda had to say. "Go for it."

"I'm pregnant."

My eyes widened and my mouth fell open. I rose from my seat and embraced her. "Oh, my goodness! Congratulations."

Brenda and her husband had been trying to have a baby since they'd been married, but were having all kinds of problems. He had a low sperm count and she'd had an abortion from college, irregular periods, and one miscarriage to add to their drama. Brenda's face went crimson and her eyes watered. I stood back and looked at her, still sharing the excitement.

"I'm so happy for you."

Brenda wiped the tears from her face. "I'm sorry for crying, it's just that each time I think about having a

child inside of me, I get so emotional. Babies do that."
The tears began again.

"So do menstrual cycles," I joked.

Brenda's smile remained.

"So, how far along are you?"

"Four months." She nodded, reassuring herself that
she was correct. "I woke up one morning and wanted
some peach cobbler and green beans. It was the weirdest
thing, you know? So Craig goes to the fridge and brings
me cookies and leftover corn because that was really all
we had that remotely sounded like peach cobbler and
green beans. As soon as he sat it in front of me I got so
sick, I didn't make it to the bathroom. That's when I
knew. I stopped by my doctor's office the same day and
got tested."

"That's fantastic!"

"Thanks." Brenda rubbed her belly, still too small to
be noticed. "The doctor said we're not out of the woods.
He's putting me on bed rest for the duration of the pregnancy, so I was actually coming over to tell you that I'll
be leaving."

"You can take the leave for as long as you need,
Brenda."

Brenda shook her head. "No, I'm leaving the phone
company. Craig and I have been saving for this. We have
enough money for me to be a stay-at-home mommy."

"Whoa, then we have reason to celebrate *and* be sad.
I'm going to hate losing you but I can't be mad, because
you are doing this for your family and that's more important."

The tears welled again in Brenda's eyes. "Oh,
Faulkner, I was hoping you'd make me feel better about
having to make this decision."

"No, no, Brenda, I'm happy for you, it's just that you
will be missed. I'm really going to miss you." Tears

spilled from my eyes. Brenda's joy had made my afternoon.

We hugged again.

"Monday will be my last day. I'm sorry I can't give two weeks' notice. The doctor said I'm already at risk by making the sixty-mile round-trip commute every day."

"I understand. It shouldn't be a problem."

"When I told James he was a little bitter. He said he was just getting to know me and hated to see me go. He's a great kid; I'll miss working with him."

I'd forgotten about the project I had them working on. "Yeah, he's on his way." I brushed an invisible piece of lint from my blouse, senselessly giving my hands something to do. "We'll have to send you off with a blast."

"I'll be here. Craig is bringing me in to get the rest of my things."

Brenda went back to her desk. She was in her early thirties and wanted a child more than anything. She was an essential asset to MSCOT and would be hard to replace, but I was glad that she was getting what she wanted.

I sent a message to the team and a few of the people from other floors who knew Brenda that we would get together Monday and have a farewell party during the lunch hour. I called and placed a cake order and began thinking about the perfect going-away gift for her. After work, I would go by Pottery Barn, a moderately expensive home furnishings store, to get her something. The rest of the day went by quietly. By four-thirty, I was tired of being there, so I decided to leave early.

"Gail, I'm leaving for the day. Can you close up shop for me and put your call orders on my desk before you leave?"

Gail mumbled something that sounded like "Sure." I blew it off like I had Margaret. As long as Gail did what I asked her to do, then in my eyes, we didn't have a problem.

Margaret

I saw Faulkner leaving for the day and felt relieved. I was relieved because I had thought about what happened and felt bad. Seeing her over there all afternoon did nothing but make me regret ignoring her during her last attempt to apologize to me. I knew she was disappointed with me because she normally didn't leave the office without saying good-bye, and I deserved it. I didn't know what was wrong with me, but my emotions were restless, and I took that restlessness out on Faulkner instead of taking it out on the real cause of my unhappiness. I spent the rest of the day wanting to make it up to her, but didn't. Once she was gone, I waited for five o'clock and headed home.

As soon as I stepped off the bus I sensed that the flashing blue and red lights I could see from the corner were at my house. The closer I got, I saw that I was right. There were two police cars, one on the street and one in our driveway. Four officers were standing exchanging words as one of them wrote on a pad. I started to walk in the house as if nothing was going on, but Lisa, who was sitting in the grass handcuffed and dressed in only a halter and shorts that left nothing to the imagination, began screaming my name as soon as she saw me.

"Margaret! Margaret! Could you please tell them I live here? This is my house too! See, Officer, that's my mother right there!" Lisa stuck her leg out, aiming her bare foot in my direction. "Margaret, tell them to get these stupid handcuffs off me!"

I looked Lisa in the face. Her right eye was bruised and she had whelps across her arms, shoulders, and neck. Her eyes met mine briefly and she saw that I wasn't impressed. More than that, she saw that I was tired, but kept yelling at me to tell the cops who she was.

I looked around for the girls and didn't see them. That's when I heard a different voice calling my name.

"Margaret!"

I turned and saw my neighbor from two streets over, Gloria Pickney. She hugged me and rubbed my shoulders. "The girls are at my house. They've been over all afternoon playing with my grandbabies. I can have them spend the night if you want."

I wanted to ask Gloria what was going on and why my grandchildren were at her house all afternoon instead of school, but something deep inside me simply wasn't curious enough to know. "Thank you, Gloria. I'll bring an overnight bag as soon as I get to the bottom of this and get these people out of my yard."

"No problem, sweetie. You helped me when that son of mine, Gerald, was in and out of trouble, and the Lord knows what it meant to me when you watered my plants and got my mail for me while I visited him in Huntsville. Don't seem like there's any rest for the weary around here." Gloria stepped away, unmoved by the flickering lights. I looked at the small crowd that had gathered in the yard and up the sidewalk. I never thought my house would ever be the focus of a scene like this. It made me feel exposed with my neighbors standing around staring in my direction.

I looked in the police car on the street and noticed a young woman about Lisa's age sitting in the backseat. Her hair was all over her head, but her face was calm and unbruised. Our eyes met, but she didn't know me and I didn't know her and we knew we'd probably never see each other again. The white truck I'd seen in my driveway yesterday was there again. The front window had a brick nestled inside the shattered glass, and the passenger window had been knocked completely out.

"Ma'am, is this your house?"

A small, female officer was standing near me. I hadn't noticed her until now. I nodded, letting her know that this was my property. She scribbled some things down on the pad.

"Is Lisa Eddye your daughter?"

I hesitated before I answered. I looked again at the girl in the car, still calm and unfazed, unlike Lisa, who was now yelling something about racism and police brutality. I wished Lisa would just shut up and reserve herself like the girl in the backseat. Maybe then I'd feel better about laying claim to her.

"Ma'am? Is the lady in the yard your daughter?"

I looked at the police officer. Her face was solemn. Before I could answer her, the squealing of tires made us both look away from each other and toward the street. It was Lester, and if I didn't know better, I would have sworn he jumped out of his truck before he put it in park. When he saw me, he ran over to where the officer and I were standing, giving no mind to Lisa, who was now crying and calling on her daddy.

"What the fuck is going on at my house?" he demanded more than asked.

"Lester, watch your language," I replied, half dazed from the lights and the onlookers.

The policewoman looked at Lester and attempted a friendly face. "I'm Officer Cobb and we received a disturbance call from one of your neighbors at about three-thirty. Evidently, the two young women we have in custody were fighting in your yard. When we arrived, the woman over there, who says she lives here, was tussling with the woman in the car. We need a few questions answered. The young lady in the yard says she lives here but she is claiming that she locked her keys inside her SUV. She also said the lady in the car followed her home because the woman in the yard was sleeping with her husband. We've been told that the woman in the car attacked the woman in the yard and a struggle ensued until we arrived."

"What SUV?" Lester looked around. His eyes fixed on the white truck. "That car? That's a goddamned Cadillac utility vehicle. Can't nobody that live in my house afford a car like that!"

"The car is registered to the woman in the yard. It's in the name of Lisa J. Eddye. Is that your daughter?"

It didn't take Lester any time to give an answer. "I don't know the woman in the yard. She doesn't live at this address."

"So she is not your daughter, sir?" the officer asked for clarity.

"Not today," Lester said in a tone that dared the policewoman to challenge what he was saying. "Officer Cobb, I don't know her. Do whatever you need to do with her except leave her in my yard." Lester grabbed my hand.

The policewoman motioned her partner to come over. She whispered something to him and he headed over to Lisa. Lisa let the officer pull her to her feet and waited for him to remove the cuffs. When she realized she was being led to the car, she began yelling and struggling to get away.

"Daddy! Daddy, don't let them do this to me! Daddy! Margaret, please don't let this happen! What about the girls? I have to take care of my girls! Fuck you, Margaret!" The tears flowed from her eyes and for the first time, I saw the little girl I used to know. I had to turn my back on Lisa just to keep from crying myself. She kicked and screamed until the car door was shut and all we could see were her lips moving.

Lester released my hand and walked up the driveway.

"Where are you going?" I asked.

"To call the towing company so they can come pick up this Cadillac."

I inhaled, feeling a slight pain in my chest, but ignored it. I had to pack some clothes for the girls and take the bag around to Gloria's. The police stood talking to each other only a few more minutes before loading into their vehicles and driving away to Lew Sterrett detention center. I figured if one of Lisa's boyfriends didn't come and get her from jail, then that's where she'd be.

I watched the car drive away, happy that Lester had made the decision. I had been going to allow them to let her go, in the hopes she was ready to change, but Lester knew his child much better than I did, and I knew he'd made the right decision.

When I returned from Gloria's, Lester was in the kitchen. I could hear him moving things, but was too tired to go in there to see what he was doing, especially knowing that I would have to clean up his mess. The only thing on my mind was taking a warm shower, reading my Bible, and getting a quiet night's sleep.

Before I stepped in the shower, I took a long look at my body. Even though I'd never had children, my breasts sagged and the skin around my neck was following it. I looked at the few moles and birthmarks I had, remembering a time when everything was tight and out of sight. I laughed as I thought about myself back in the day. I ran my hands over my face and around my plump midsection. I used to be a thick, fine something; all that seemed like yesterday, but I knew better. It used to be that Lester always had to have one or both of his hands somewhere on my body. Now if he touched me, it was because he was hungry or he needed a back rub. We were down to having sex about once every four months or so, and it usually wasn't romantic like I liked it, but now I seemed able to take only what I could get, because I still loved my husband more than anything.

I stepped into the shower and bathed, allowing all the day's events to stream down my neck to my stomach, past my knees, over my toes, and into the drain. Soon, I would be home every day and maybe I could finally have that garden Faulkner and I always talked about. I could even finish some crochet and knitting projects I'd started that now sat in a container in the attic. I could bake cookies for my grandbabies and tea cakes for the neighbors. I'd have more time for Bible study and fellowship, and Lester and I could finally take that trip to Vegas he'd been talking about. I could even take up a low-impact exercise class for older women and get myself back into some shape. It was time for a change and the more I thought about it, the better I liked it.

I smelled food when I stepped out of the bathroom. I put some scented lotion on that I'd never used. It was a Mother's Day gift from Faulkner and had sat in the same bag in my closet until tonight, which marked a new night for me. I was going to start smelling good every night from here on. I deserved to start treating myself better, and as soon as I turned in my resignation, I was going to get me a body massage to celebrate the new me!

I wasn't down the hallway before Lester grabbed me and pulled me into the dining room.

"Lester, what in the world are you doing?"

Lester put his finger to his lips. "Shhh." He led me to the table and sat me down. The room was lit only by two candles, which stood in the middle of the table. They were a gift from Lester. When I looked at the place settings, I nearly lost it.

"Lester, those are my candles you gave me and this is my good china!"

"Margaret, we've never ate on the dishes and you've never used the candles. You've had them for I don't know how many years and not once have I ever seen these candles or this china get some action."

"I never burned the candles because I know you paid a lot of money for them."

"Baby, I didn't pay all that money for them to become museum items. Can't you just relax and let me do something nice for a change?" Lester placed a paper towel in my lap. I'd never owned any real cloth napkins to go with my dinette set. He kissed me on the cheek. "I'm trying to create a moment here, do you mind?"

I looked at Lester, still shocked that he'd lit the only two good, expensive candles I had and had gone into my china cabinet.

"Margaret, let's enjoy our lives together, not minding all the things we can't take to the grave with us. Let's eat off these plates because we deserve to eat from fine china that was washed by your grandmother's hands, and let's burn these candles because if I want to look into your pretty eyes by candlelight, I'd rather they be forty-dollar candles because anything less would be undeserving."

Now this was the man I married! That's how Lester got me in the first place. He was a smooth talker and an even smoother romantic. He left the dining room and came back with two plates. He placed one in front of me and sat the other at his place. Each plate had fried chicken, courtesy of Kentucky Fried Chicken. The green beans and carrots were Green Giant brand. And the hot rolls were from Mrs. Baird's.

My initial reaction was to ask Lester when did he go get the food, who cooked the vegetables, why didn't he get KFC's mashed potatoes, and what did he need me to forgive him for, because he must've done something wrong to be doing all this. But I kept my peace, and suddenly I knew this was one time when Lester Eddye was doing the best he could. He'd pulled out the good china and lit the good candles for me. I did matter to this man, and that's *all* that mattered. He smiled at me from across the table.

"Margaret, I know you say I don't do this for you or that I don't do that, but I'm always thinking about you."

"I know, Lester." I exhaled. "I know you love me and, sometimes, I'm just being pushy."

Lester bit into his chicken. "How was work today?"

"Not too good. I wound up letting all my anger I had built up from home bleed over to work and I said some things to Faulkner I didn't mean."

"God bless her parents. If Lisa had an ounce of the good sense that girl has, I don't think we would have had that fiasco in the yard tonight."

"I owe her an apology."

"Yeah, but Faulkner will understand."

I placed a forkful of green beans in my mouth. They weren't seasoned at all but I didn't need the salt and butter anyway. "I had a spell at work."

"A spell? But yesterday you said the doctor gave you a clean bill of health."

"That was yesterday. This snuck up on me. Stress, I suppose, more than anything. One minute I was working, the next minute I was lifting my head from my desk. I'd just passed out right there. It scared me."

Lester put his fork down and stared at me.

"Anyway, I was feeling down, like nobody cared about me. I was having my own pity party and that probably triggered it. Come to find out, the entire time I was out, nobody noticed. Faulkner met a man and she'd rushed off to meet him for lunch."

"She didn't check on you like she usually does."

"Right, and after my scare, I was angry at her. Lester, I talked to that girl and said everything to her that should have been said to Lisa."

"Faulkner has a right to her own life too."

"I know, but I'd gotten used to the attention. I know she doesn't owe that to me."

"But you'd gotten used to it."

"I sure did." I smiled. "Thought it belonged to me." We laughed.

"But she's not ours, Margaret. We've been dealt the cards we have to play."

"Yes, and I'm going to apologize to her."

"Why don't you just call her?"

"Because it needs to be face-to-face. I'm not ashamed to admit I was wrong."

Lester looked at me admiringly, lovingly, and all the other nice emotional ways a person can look at another to get a passionate nonverbal message across.

"I have good news for you," I said.

"What's that?"

"I'm retiring from the phone company. I'm going to let them know before the week is up."

The smile that appeared on my husband's face let me know I'd said the right thing. He bit into his roll and spoke with his mouth full as he motioned to me with his fork. "Go ahead, baby, eat up! The night is still young and we have some celebrating to do!" We finished dinner and Lester cleared the table. I went to the kitchen to start washing the dishes, but Lester stopped me. "I got this, baby. I want you to go to the living room and pull out one of those dusty albums of ours. Pick out your favorite one, that 1972 O'Jays, and put it on. I'm going to clean the kitchen and shower while you relax and enjoy some good music."

We still had our cabinet component system that looked like a dresser, but instead of drawers, there were speakers on each end and the top opened up, displaying a twelve-inch record player. I had to move family photos and a plastic floral arrangement to the floor to get to it. I went to the garage and found an old crate of albums that hadn't been played in years. I picked up a stack, as much as I could carry without overdoing it, and carried them into the house. I sat on the floor in front of the component system and leafed through the albums. Gladys Knight and the Pips, Smokey Robinson, Stevie Wonder, the Delfonics, the Temptations, Nancy Wilson, and last but not least, my 1972 O'Jays. I was some crazy about Eddie Levert back then! I took the album out and blew off the dust. When I put it on the player it crackled but in no time Walter Williams, Eddie Levert (who, let me tell it, would have been my husband if I hadn't met Lester), and Bill Isles were singing "When the World's at Peace" and I was right in there with them. I surprised myself that I still knew most of the words. I pulled a pillow from the couch and lay on the floor like I was twenty-seven again. When Lester came from the back, I was crooning a serious rendition of "Listen to the Clock on the Wall." Lester invited me up from the floor. He smelled nice and it turned me on. We danced and Lester held me close. It felt good to be in his arms this way. Lester poured us each a glass of wine while I moved the needle over to my favorite song on the album, "Sunshine." Before the song was over, Lester's lips had started tickling my spot and his hands were roaming under my robe and I was butt naked in the middle of the floor in no time. I wanted him tonight. I wanted Lester like people in hell wanted ice water. He took his robe off and I realized I wasn't the only one sagging and lagging in places that once defied gravity, but Lester still looked good to me. His skin was still the same smooth brown and his chest hairs still made me want to nestle my face in them. And even though Lester had a potbelly, his magic wand didn't have a problem peeking from below. I blushed because the lamp was on and it was the first time we'd had sex with the lights on in a long time. Lester licked his lips and lay next to me. "Margaret, lady, you still got it."

"Well, let me go look for it," I joked. "I think I left it at work with one of those young girls."

"Nah, I don't need no young girl that don't know nothing about pleasing a man. I need a woman. You're just what I need."

Lester ran his hands over my flabby arms, my cottage-cheese thighs, my kangaroo sack of a stomach, and my water balloons that I sometimes called ankles and kissed each as he went down. He still made sure I came before he did and we even managed to get my legs on his shoulders. But not for too long, I almost caught a cramp, so we changed and did it in the doggie position. All in all, Lester's way of making love to me was unchanging. The way he loved me made me forget about wishing he'd cook sometimes or wishing he'd leave that truck alone. The only thing it didn't make me forget was that our love couldn't produce children. When Lester came to orgasm, he pressed his body against me, kissing my back and caressing my nipples. I felt like I was twenty again. I closed my eyes and let him enjoy his moment.

Things slowed down and when I looked up, Lester was probing more than he was caressing. He turned me around and looked at me. The look on his face validated my theory that something wasn't right.

"What is it?"

Lester didn't say anything at first. Then he took my hand. "Feel right here." He placed my hand below my left breast, between my ribs and armpit. "Have you ever felt that before?"

I felt the lump, which moved like jelly when my finger rotated around it. "No." I kept feeling the lump as if it would go away if I kept feeling it. "My Jesus."

Lester took my hand and kissed it. He grabbed my robe and I rose to put it on. He took his robe and covered up. "We'll go to the doctor in the morning," he said. "For now, let's just go to bed and dream."

The mood was gone like that, even though Lester held me most of the night, his warm breath tingling my ear, my G-spot. I felt a million miles away laying in the bed with him next to me. On the night that I decided to be better to myself, God paid me back for all the nights that I hadn't been. I guess I deserved it. By morning, all I could do was drag myself from bed, get dressed, and ride to the doctor's office with my husband.

Faulkner

Teresa came over after work. She strolled in toting a bottle of cheap wine, a few magazines, and some music. We lounged in my apartment and gossiped about everything from Michael Jordan's comeback to why in the hell a presidential intern would keep a dress in her closet with semen on it. That was the perk of having a best friend who worked in the news industry. We always had something to talk about or some issue to ponder. I was on my second glass of wine when I gave Teresa the lowdown on Margaret.

"Margaret's age is catching up with her and she don't know how to handle it. Girl, you know how old people can be. They're grumpy about everything. There's not a complaint in the world that they haven't let be known.

My granny used to swear up and down that my mama and her six brothers and sisters didn't love her one bit and that she was going to fix them because she knew they were waiting for her to die. Come to find out, she left them nothing in her will." Teresa fell against the couch laughing.

"What's so funny?"

"She left everything to her dog, Hitler, so the family had him put to sleep just to spite Granny from the grave. Girl, we don't need soap operas, real life is much better."

I smiled at my friend's story. "But Margaret has never done that to me before."

"Chalk it up to a bad day and forget about it. Come tomorrow, she'll be back to her old self. Based on what you've told me, she needs to go ahead and retire." Teresa fingered her auburn-colored curls. "You know what? She might be finally coming to grips with having to retire. It's scary for people to look at themselves as getting too old to work. I did a report once and found out that one of the common traits of people who retire is that they become afraid because they feel like they aren't needed anymore."

"Yeah, but it's not like Margaret is bent over with a walker. She's just fifty-seven. She still has a lot of life and vibrancy about her. I can't see her as the kind of woman who would be afraid of anything."

"But, Faulkner, she's fifty-seven with diabetes, high blood pressure, and she's practically raising two children under the age of ten. She's fifty-seven, but she's a worn-out fifty-seven."

"So you think it's fear of being at home and not having something to do?"

"Probably. But, girl, it could be anything with black folk because we don't really live to be retired, you know? Half of us can't stay at a job long enough to get retirement and the other half have to work past retirement age."

"My parents are both set to retire. As a matter of fact, my mother can't wait. She said the people at her school should consider themselves lucky if she comes on her last day. She doesn't care about a party, gifts, or none of that."

"Of course. Your mother is crazy just like you. Seriously, teaching is something that you hate once you get into it, but you get addicted to having summers off, so it all makes sense. Besides, teaching is guaranteed if you stick with it. By the time it becomes stressful, it's time for you to retire. Corporate America is different. There are no summers off. You don't get to spend much time with family, and when was the last time you saw any company trying to put a day care center in the facility so working mothers could be near their children? You're lucky. Your parents are doing something that we will always have a need for. That's why I'm glad my daddy is a mortician. He could have retired at forty if he wanted to because business was always constant and always will be. How many of our friends born after 1975 can say that about their parents?"

I shrugged.

"A handful, that's how many. Generation X better wise up because their parents may be living longer, but many of them won't have social security benefits or retirement because of limited job security."

I thought about the few people I knew who were younger than me. "Reesa, you might be right, but I'm not going to totally agree with you."

"You don't have to," Teresa said sarcastically. "I know I'm right."

"Margaret's had a lot of time to leave and try something else. Maybe she is going through something she can't tell me about. What if it's something that she's holding in and *won't* talk about?"

"Look, I know you care about her, but she's her own person with her own life and there is nothing going on with Margaret that isn't obvious. You have to be careful how you attach to different people, because at some point, you become faced with who you are against who they have made you out to be. You allowed Margaret to be the mother she's never been able to be and today was your wake-up call. No matter how you look at it, she put you on a pedestal in comparison with her daughter, instead of just accepting you. That's why it's good not to get so close to people at work, because you just never know what's going on behind closed doors." Teresa pointed to her head. "At the newspaper, I'm off limits to personal relationships."

"It's different with us, Teresa. The team really is a close-knit group. We care about each other and it's all sincere."

"Whatever. People are fair until the opportunity for them to be self-serving comes along and they do the fool on you. That's why as much as I hate the way you let Joyce treat you, I can't be mad at Joyce, because she's been real and up front with you about her feelings."

"Margaret isn't a hateful person."

"You can't assume Margaret doesn't have that in her, especially since you told me they used to be tight. Birds of a feather flock together. Now that you have another interest somewhere else, she's dropped you like a bad habit."

I shook my head. "Margaret isn't like that. Joyce is just being Joyce."

I sipped the wine and leaned back and thought for a minute. "You remember when we had that conversation about me putting in my two weeks' notice and you told me that me and Joyce may end up being the best of friends?"

"I was tripping, you know that. What about it?"

"You might be right."

"Yeah, and that's long, long blond hair on your head."

"Teresa, I'm serious. You're right, maybe Margaret has turned on me. My feelings are hurt, but I thought about it at work and I realized I don't know Margaret as well as I thought I did if something like this can jolt me and make me doubt who she is. But when Joyce changed, I just went with her flow. I never questioned her actions or tried to address this on a personal level."

"Faulkner, Joyce is evil. Don't go pokin' and proddin' like you're a detective. You ain't Tamara Hayle and this is not a Valerie Wilson Wesley novel."

"Teresa, I'm serious."

"I apologize. Faulkner, whatever you're thinking about Margaret and Joyce, you still have a decision to make. Margaret is entitled to have a bad day without you psychoanalyzing her. I think you're making a mountain out of a molehill. I also think that wine has you talking crazy. I didn't really mean what I said about you and Joyce being best friends. She can't have my spot."

I sat quietly, still having my own thoughts. One moment I wanted to totally excuse Margaret from her words and actions toward me, and the next minute, I wanted to put her in the same box I put Joyce, as a bitter woman who couldn't have things the ways she wanted them without upsetting someone.

Teresa poured herself another glass and used the remote to turn the CD carrier and change songs. "Let it go, Faulkner."

A rap song blared from my small stereo. I let go of my thoughts and rolled my eyes at what I was hearing. Teresa sprang from the floor and started dancing. "Hey, that's the shit right there!" She reached down and tapped me on the arm. "Come on, Faulkner, and shake ya ass, watch ya'self."

I let Teresa dance around me as I played with the new thought of reapproaching Joyce. The cheap wine had an even cheaper effect: it was making me sleepy. I yawned and rested my head on the back of the couch.

"What's this?"

When I looked at Teresa, she was sitting at my computer desk leafing through papers. I stretched my neck to see what she was talking about. "That's some stuff I was playing with. I was thinking of writing a story about all this, but it's nothing serious."

Teresa scanned a few of the pages. "I would hardly call thirty pages 'nothing serious.' Do you mind?" She waved the pages in my direction.

"Knock yourself out. I need to clean off that desk anyway." I had to go to the bathroom. I left Teresa and her rap music. When I came back, she was on the couch. She'd turned the music down and was face-deep in the papers. I went to the kitchen to start washing the few dishes that were in the sink.

She came in and scooted me over as she turned the water on and began rinsing. "Faulkner, that was good." She laughed. "You may have something."

I smiled a very tired smile. "They're just thoughts I was playing with. It's nothing, really."

"I never knew you could express yourself on paper that way. I'm actually impressed."

"Teresa, you're drunk."

"I can handle my liquor, hush. I'm not drunk and if you sleep on those thoughts you've written, I'm personally going to kick your ass." Teresa splashed me.

"You better get to personally kicking, then, because I'm not interested in doing anything with that except keeping it as a reminder."

"Then give me a copy."

"You can take the original, I have it saved on disk."

Teresa took her wet hands out of the water and hugged me. "See, I know'd you was some kind a' special!" Teresa did a corny little move as if she were tap-dancing in a minstrel show, pushing and moving me with her.

I cringed in her arms, feeling the cold wetness dampen my sweatshirt. "You're messing up my shirt."

Teresa let go and nudged me. "I swear, you act like an old-ass lady sometimes. Wash it. Wash your wet shirt in water." Teresa scowled as she hugged me tighter then let go. "It's not every day I get to hug you, my *bestest* friend."

"Well, if one of the best friends wouldn't spend so much time with her new man, maybe they would get to hug more often and go to the movies on Tuesday nights like they used to."

"You make me sick, you know that? Always got something smart to say, but speaking of new men, you never got back with me on whether or not Greg called you."

"He called."

"And?"

"And it was great. He's a great guy. The vibe was there. We had lunch today, and Friday we're going to see Joe Sample and Laylah Hathaway at the Caravan of Dreams."

"You cow. You couldn't call and tell me? So I take it you like him. I can't believe you finally found you somebody that can deal with your difficult ass. You haven't had a man in over three years. You think Greg might be the one?"

"The one for what? So far, all I know is we have great conversations."

"What kind of conversations? What did you talk about? Has he been married before? Does he come from a dysfunctional home? Any brothers or sisters? What kind of car does he drive? You have to tell me more."

"Can I get my date in before I go yapping my business to you?"

Teresa looked at me. She knew I was being slick. "I'll keep my mouth shut for now because you know I want to know everything. I'll let it rest until next time, and I'm bringing a fat bottle of wine and plenty of chips because I know you got some info."

"I thank you for your kindness." I smiled.

"Are you still thinking about leaving the phone company? You know a man isn't going to stand a woman sitting at home."

"Yes, I'm still thinking of leaving. And if Greg doesn't like it then too bad for him, because I'm not expecting him to carry me while I'm unemployed. I have my own money."

"I hear what you're saying. Be independent, girl."

"I'm going to enjoy my time off. Maybe travel or do some volunteer work."

"So when is the last day?"

I stalled. "I haven't turned in my notice."

"Then you're not serious, Faulkner. See, that's what I keep trying to tell you about yourself. You're all talk, no action. Everything has to be by the book. You're nothing like me because I would have walked out on those mo-fos in a New York second. I bet you're going to work the full two weeks after you write the notice and leave with a small party, including parting gifts. I told you that you had too much emotionally invested in that job."

"I *am* leaving. I'm just trying to do the thinking you *advised* I do. If I'm not mistaken it was you who brought up the fact that I'd set some goals there and if I left, those goals would never be accomplished."

"Yeah, but I didn't think you really heard me. When did you start listening to me?"

"I needed time to run it over in my mind, that's all. You said some things that stuck."

Teresa turned the water off and dried her hands. "You're scared. You're scared of leaving the money. You're scared of what people will think of you. You'll miss the security, right? You're scared that something better isn't waiting for you on the other side of quitting, and you're afraid to walk away from unfinished business. You've always been that way."

"I have bills, of course I'd be a little reluctant about leaving. You act like working is as simple as blinking."

"No, but there are other jobs out there. There are a billion jobs out there."

"I've been at the phone company for five years. I have time and money invested."

"And every day is a day toward rebuilding. Five years is nothing compared to a lifetime of fulfillment based on one leap of faith."

"I'm leading some wonderful people and they support me. We all work well together. Why dismantle that?"

"They have lives of their own too. You all act like a bunch of codependents."

"Teresa, there are billions of women like me, young, black, and professional, doing well and making the money. We get up and dress in clothes that aren't comfortable and that we can't afford in order to represent what we do. We go to lunch for exactly an hour, we attend company parties, we shuck and jive with each other at work until it's time for us to retire—so what? I'm not the only one."

"And my question to you is why? Why would you fake your way through life so you can finally get to be who you are in your old age? I don't know who in the hell thought of retirement, but they should really be congratulated."

"What do you mean?"

"Exactly what I'm saying. You tire yourself out working decades for motherfuckers you don't know, only to be tired again trying to live off the few pennies they give you for all those years of service. It's re*tire*ment, all right."

I smiled. "It's just the way it is."

"Not for me," Teresa boasted. "If Ed, my program director, so much as grits his teeth at me the wrong way, I'm out of there. Now, a coworker is a different story because they're on the same level as you, but when your boss threatens your peace, that's cause for getting the fuck out."

I looked at my best friend. "Sometimes I really don't like you."

"It ain't the first time I've been told that." She looked at me and gave me a crazy face, eyes crossed, tongue sticking out, and nose flared.

I broke into laughter. It was nice having a friend who knew you and loved you in spite of what she knew about you.

Margaret

Dr. Charlotte Kipfer was my doctor and had been for six years now. She was a Jewish woman a few years younger than me. As soon as Lester and I arrived, I was escorted to a small examination room, asked to remove my top and wait for her. Five minutes later, Charlotte was walking in.

"Margaret, it's good to see you. What's it been? Two days?" She smiled.

I wondered why it always seemed that all doctors had the same, nonchalant behavior. They never strayed far from the safe areas when dealing with patients. I'd known Charlotte long enough for her to come running in here ready to get down to business, but her face held a look that wasn't telling me anything except that she was at work doing what doctors do. A frown or furrowed eyebrows would help me get a sense of what she was thinking. Even when I spoke to her on the phone about the lump, her voice kept its same bland tone. "I suppose." I smiled. "How are you today?"

"That's the question I should be asking you. I know discovering the lump in your breast was probably the last thing you needed to happen, but don't worry, I'm confident we can get you the answers you need."

"It would be my luck to have breast cancer on top of everything else. I guess the Lord is trying to tell me something. I never figured I would end up with cancer."

"This is about your body speaking to you, Margaret. Besides, most lumps aren't cancerous, so let's not be so quick to say cancer."

"Yeah, but I've read pamphlets about it and I know the chances of older women getting breast cancer is different than that of younger ones."

Charlotte opened my file as she continued talking to me. "Well, it's becoming the same across the board. More and more young women are having lumps that are cancerous, the same way older women are having lumps that are benign." She skimmed over my file and set it on a small table. She walked to me and looked at my face. "How have you been feeling? Any discomfort?"

I took in some air and released it, ventured a smile. "Tired, I guess. Energy isn't the same."

"Pains in your chest?"

"Yeah, but it felt like gas."

"Okay." She listened to my heart. I looked for some sign in her face that would indicate she'd come across something that wasn't normal. Her expression remained constant. "Lay back and let's see about this lump."

I laid back and waited nervously.

"Margaret, I want you to relax."

I relaxed as best I could under the circumstances while the doctor felt my breasts. I wondered, did she feel the same thing I felt? Was the lump still soft but firm, like old Jell-O? When she checked the breast where the lump was, chills ran up my back.

"I feel it," she said as she continued to roll her fingers where the knot was. "It's palpable."

"What kind of cancer is that?" I asked, worry shaking my voice.

"Palpable means that the lump can be touched through the skin."

"Oh." I smiled, thankful she didn't say palpable meant cancerous. Charlotte probably thought I was as dumb as they came, but I'd never concerned myself with breast cancer. I figured whatever I didn't have by the time I turned fifty, then I wouldn't get it.

"The pains, were they in your breast or more internal?"

"Well, I thought they were internal pains, but now that I think about it, some of them have been in my breast. Sharp, quick pains that come and go."

Her chilly hands continued probing in circular motions. "I'm checking for symmetry. There's no discoloration or swelling, which is a good sign. No skin-reaction symptoms."

"What do you mean by skin reaction? You mean to tell me that my skin will break out from this?"

The doctor removed her hand from my breast. "No. In some cases, the skin will have a dimpling or orange-peel look on the skin, kind of like how cellulite makes the buttocks and thighs look." She wrote something in my file before coming back over to the exam table. "How often do you do self-examinations?"

I twisted my lips. I had a breast exam reminder hanging in my shower, but I never looked at it. "I guess about every three months or so," I lied. It was far less often than that, if at all.

"Once a month is what is recommended."

"I figured you checking them when I come in for my yearly physical was enough."

"That was in June, Margaret, which means this lump could have developed at any time between now and last July." She completed her exam. "Put your top on and I'll be back to let you know what the next step will be." She left the office so I could get dressed. As I put my blouse on I went back in my mind to how early this could have been detected. If I had followed my doctor's orders by giving myself monthly breast exams, I could have caught this within days of it appearing. Now I wished I had checked. I couldn't sit here now wishing and regretting what I could have or should have been doing. Now I would just have to move on from here and deal with the consequences, but I still wished I wasn't sitting in the office, two days after having a spell, having my breasts checked because I'd come across lumps in them. Charlotte returned just as I situated myself in an extra chair that was in the exam room. She sat in a chair, across from me.

"You do have one lump at the three o'clock area of your left breast. It's palpable but not mobile. That means it's in one place."

I looked at her, trying to keep up with her explanations. It sounded like she was speaking another language that simply used English words.

"There is no detection in your left breast other than the lump, which means there is no discoloration, discharge, or irritation."

"So it's not cancer?" I asked, not knowing what else to ask. As much as I wanted it not to be, there was an overwhelming feeling that I would be diagnosed with the disease.

Charlotte didn't smile this time. "I won't know until we run some tests. "I see from your records that you have no history of breast cancer in your family?"

"Not that I know of."

"What about the men in your family? Any prostate cancer?"

I didn't know exactly what prostate cancer was, although I was almost sure that's what Gloria Pickney's husband had. "No."

She wrote some more things down in my file. "I need you to come in Saturday for testing. I have room for you. We'll do an ultrasound and breast biopsy, neither of which is painful, but you will experience discomfort because the machines are cold. Don't eat a full breakfast. Half a glass of juice and a slice of dry toast will be fine. The receptionist will give you a card with the appointment time."

"I'll be here bright-eyed and bushy-tailed."

"Sounds great. I'll see you on Saturday."

I walked down the hall with my mind already set. I was going to lose one of my breasts, my hair, and my life to these lumps. I felt heavy. I had enough burdens without having to add this to my list of ailments. I walked into the waiting room, where Lester was. His face had all the same questions I still had.

He pulled me in and kissed me on the forehead. "You okay?"

I let his arm remain around me. "Yes. I have to come back Saturday for testing."

"Okay."

I took the card from the receptionist, who was seated behind a sliding glass window, and handed it to my husband. He looked at it and slid it into his shirt pocket. We headed to the truck with few words between us. I put on my seat belt as Lester made it to his side of the truck.

He climbed in and buckled up. "Where to?" he asked. "Work?"

"Home," I said. The word heated my chest, and I cried all the way home.

Faulkner

The next two days came easy for me. No Joyce. No Margaret. I received a call from Margaret's husband informing me that she would be out until Monday due to her not feeling well. Even though I was concerned, I kept it diplomatic, tried to sound busy, and thanked him for the call. When I disconnected, I said a small prayer to myself that Margaret would be okay and tried to assure myself that her absence had nothing to do with our fall-out. Without her and Joyce in the office, it took the pressure off me of having to clear the air between us, allowing me to get ahead with work.

Thursday, I focused on the decision that was ahead of me. With the comfort of working totally stress-free, it was hard for me to decide to resign. But I still knew that

Joyce wasn't going to promote me, and I wasn't willing to sit around any longer to find that out for sure. The thought crossed my mind to try and talk to her one more time before throwing in the towel; that way, I wouldn't have all the doubts I was now having.

I got up to do a walk-through to see how everyone was doing and to take a think break. Carmen and Brenda were both on the phones taking calls. Gail was working on first-quarter line closings, but James was sitting at his desk staring at nothing in particular. He wasn't his normal, jovial self. I tapped my fingers lightly on the cube wall's metal frame.

"James, how's everything going?"

"It's not," he said, even though there was plenty of work on his desk to be done.

"Want to talk about it?"

"It's not job-related."

I smiled. "My ears are pretty versatile, you'd be surprised. Maybe I can help."

He stared at me for a moment, probably weighing the costs of opening up to me. His chocolate skin shined under the lights. If I'd been seven years younger, I'd have been all over him like white on rice. He was good-looking, had a great personality, and he was in our Young Managers Program, so as soon as he graduated college, he'd be making nice money, more than he was now making as an intern. He let out a sigh. "Why are women so trifling?"

"Excuse me?"

"Women. They're trifling. They use men, that's all they do."

I raised my hand. "Uh, pardon me, but I'm a woman and I'm about to get offended. Not all women *use* men."

"Okay, *some* women. I expect a woman to be open and up front about whatever is going on."

I waved my hand. "Back up, James. You've lost me."

"A'ight, a'ight, my apologies for going off like a loose cannon, but I'm a little upset. I thought I had something with this woman I'm dating, but it's just a surface relationship."

"Sorry to hear that."

"Not as sorry as me. I work hard, I'm in school, I'm faithful, and I don't dog women like they say we do. My father was like that, couldn't stay with one woman and took my mother through hell. Can't a brother be rewarded for being different? Can't this woman see that I'm trying to be with her?"

"James, making mistakes in love is what gets you closer to the real thing. Don't take this girl's action against you personally. She's doing what she feels she has to do to make things right in her life. Move on. The next one will be twice as good, I bet."

"She's a woman, Ms. Lorraine, and I can't just be pacified like that. It's not that simple. I have feelings for her and that should count for something. I don't want to meet anyone new and have to go through the same motions. When is your birthday? What's your sign? What school did you go to? Do you have any children? Getting to know someone gets old really fast, especially when you're single. I'm fed up with that. I need to know what I need to do to make her see that I'm serious."

James was right, the dating scene *was* old, but it was also a necessary evil, in my opinion. You had to get out to meet a person, then spend time with him or her to know if that person was for you. I thought of a response to his question.

He was still venting. "When a woman has a good man, she isn't ready for him. Women don't know the first thing about treating a good man well."

"You *mean* the woman you had wasn't ready for you."

"Right."

I patted him on the shoulder. "My advice to you is to give her room, don't be pushy, and maybe she'll come around." Another thing came to mind. "If it's any consolation, I'm glad you're a good man and I hope this doesn't discourage you from staying that way."

James smiled. "It won't." He swiveled the chair around. "But next time, a woman who wants to be with me is going to have some work ahead of her. I'm not going to be so giving and understanding."

"Okay, sounds good to me. Wanna hear a joke?"

"Give it your best shot."

"How many psychiatrists does it take to change a lightbulb?"

James thought for a minute. "How many?"

"One, but the lightbulb has to want to change." I laughed.

James smirked and barely clapped his hands. "Ha, ha."

"Oh, you got something better?" I challenged. "I dare you to come up with something funnier than that."

James cleared his throat. "Here goes. What's the last thing to go through a bug's mind as he hits the windshield?"

"What?" I was already not smiling, determined not to laugh at whatever the answer was going to be.

"His ass." James laughed.

I tried to hold in my amusement but couldn't. "That was funny."

"Yeah, that's what I thought." James put his headset on. "Thanks for talking to me, Ms. Lorraine. I feel better."

"No problem." I patted James's shoulder. "I'll bill you later."

I headed back to my cube feeling good inside. I picked up the phone and called a local soul-food café that catered. I'd decided to treat the team to lunch. When I sent the e-mail, letting everyone know, they all responded, happy that they didn't have to spend money or eat what they'd brought. Gail stood and looked at me from her cube.

"When the wolf's away the sheep will play."

I looked up at her. "What do you mean?"

She shrugged slightly. "Nothing, really. It just seems to me that since Joyce has taken a vacation, you have been more relaxed. You've barely been working."

"And your point is?"

"You've been real comfortable giving us more work to do."

"Gail, we're a team. We all have responsibilities. I still have the bulk of the work on this floor and I still have to check what you all do."

"I'm not trying to start nothing with you, Faulkner. I'm just making a comment. Don't get upset."

"I'm not upset, but I feel like you're insinuating that I'm on some kind of power trip in Joyce's absence."

"No, I'm just verbalizing what I see."

"Gail, don't make today a bad one. Why can't you just enjoy not having Joyce here? Why does it have to be me being on a power trip?"

"Faulkner, you're my girl. I love you like a sister, but I know you want to be promoted and I know you're trying to impress Joyce by doing all of her work. I just think you need to think about that and realize that you're not doing it. You're giving it to us and, personally, I don't think it's fair."

"You know what, Gail? The work has to get done regardless of who does it."

"Then why don't you do it? You put me on this project with Brenda and James and I know this is something we shouldn't even be seeing."

I was quiet. Gail was right, but she still didn't understand. "Do you want to be taken off the project, Gail? Is that what you want?"

Her lips pursed. "Yes, I do. But I also think you should make Joyce do her own work." Gail walked from her cube toward the bathroom.

I wasn't sure how to feel or what to say. I called Brenda and James over, and I asked Brenda if she had a problem working on the project. She reassured me that she understood chain of command and had no objections with what I'd asked them to do. James agreed. But it didn't matter, guilt had already set in. I told them to give me what they had and I'd finish the report.

When Gail came back to her cube, I thanked her for voicing her issue with me and I let her know how I'd resolved it.

"Like I said, Faulkner, I know we have responsibility, but you can't keep letting Joyce dog you and then expecting us to have your back. Not everyone here will stand for that," she said as we hugged and got back to work.

I spent the rest of the day working on the report. I'm sure Gail would have been happier had I given it back to Joyce and forced her to panic over it, but the ball was in motion and I didn't mind doing it. What Gail failed to realize was that the chain of command was simply an exchange of power. Joyce had given me power when she asked me to do the report. If I wanted to, I could call Mr. Price right now and discuss the report with him, knowing the damaging outcome that would have for Joyce, but it wasn't in me to be that way. However, knowing what Joyce needed to be doing gave me the power to backstab her at any time, which, now that I was thinking about it, seemed like a good idea. I was glad for the wake-up call I'd gotten from Gail.

Joyce

Dennis met me Thursday for an early dinner, and then we went back to my house for some tension-relieving sex, which turned out to be a marathon event. After our nap, I woke him and saw him off. Even though I had already let myself relax more with him, it was still important that I maintain control over this relationship. This time, he gave me no argument.

It was after eight o'clock when I showered and dressed to go to the office to play catch-up before Friday. I slipped on a pair of sandals with a matching designer outfit and headed out the door.

The main-floor lights were dimmed and the work area where the operators sat was quiet. Sometimes the silence spooked me, but most of the time I welcomed it. I went into my office and closed the door behind me. I helped myself to a glass of bourbon and began working. It took me a while to get comfortable, but once the drink kicked in, I was in my zone. By the time I left here, I would be ahead on my work. As I typed, I heard a knock on my door that startled me more than anything. No one knew I was here and no one had any business on this floor at this hour. I looked at my watch. It was after ten and I was three glasses deep in bourbon. I rose from my desk and called out to see who was at my door.

"Who's there?"

"Fred," the voice responded from the other side. "You have a minute, Joyce?"

"Oh, Fred." I hurriedly put a peppermint in my mouth to deaden the heavy liquor odor before opening the door. He was on the other side, casually dressed in a burgundy golf shirt and khaki pants. He smiled at me as he walked past and helped himself to a seat. "Joyce, it's good to see you this evening. I got your e-mail and was hoping that nothing of a pressing matter had happened. I was leaving when I saw your car and decided that I would come up to see if everything was okay."

"Fred, everything is fine. I'm just making sure I stay two steps ahead."

"I like initiative. If Faulkner Lorraine is anything like you when she becomes manager, this group will be unstoppable."

I feigned a smile upon hearing Faulkner's name. "My initiative is a small price to pay. I would hope that I'm pulling people up who represent the same ideals." Fred picked up on my overdone attempt not to slur my words. He was a lush himself, so the least of my worries was that he'd complain. "You mentioned Faulkner Lorraine being moved to management. Are you overstepping my power to make the decision?"

Fred smiled. "Yes, that's exactly what I'm doing. She'll be just what management needs."

"Consider it done, then." The last word wasn't out of my mouth before my heart rate increased. I was pissed off at Fred. How dare he come in here abusing his power over me.

"How's the report coming along that I gave you? I need it Monday."

"Don't you worry, Fred, I will have that report on your desk Sunday evening."

"Good. At any rate, as I said, I saw your car and wanted to come up and see if everything is okay."

"You know, the night is too nice for you to be here checking in on me."

I remained seated at my desk. My attention on Fred was relaxed and unguarded. He stared at me for a moment as if to say something. I looked at him and smiled, trying to remain pleasant despite the fact that he was fucking up my buzz. He had a potbelly, not to mention the hair that grew from his ears made my insides turn. I hated to see hairs growing wild and unkempt from a man's ears, but he was my boss and his appearance took a backseat to his superiority and my motives.

"I was talking to the other executives yesterday and your name came up. They wanted to know when I was going to turn in my vote on making you executive."

"Oh?"

"We all agree that you are the top candidate. Your work at this company is indisputable. You're professional not to mention you add a little flavor to our less-than-diverse team."

My face remained unchanged, even though I felt insulted.

"The job is as good as yours once I turn in my vote."

This time my smile exposed some teeth. I knew I deserved to be an executive and Fred had proven himself a man of his word. All I needed to know was where did I sign the dotted line and when did I get to move up to my new executive suite. I rose to shake his hand. "Thank you, Fred. It pleases me to know that my hard work did not go unnoticed."

He took my hand and firmly held it in his. After we shook, he picked up the glass I'd been drinking from. "Do you mind?" He held the glass up and waited for my go-ahead.

"Sure, be my guest."

He put the glass to his lips and downed the remaining liquor, watching me the entire time he drank. He walked over to my hidden liquor cabinet and helped himself to a second drink.

"Joyce, I think you're ready to take the helm as executive."

"Thank you," I said for the second time. I took a breath. "I am capable, Fred. The more challenging the work the better I perform." I smiled. "Only the strong survive in this fast-paced, technology-driven world. It's my job to make sure MSCOT is at the top of the telecommunications game. We win where I work."

"How soon do you think you'll be ready to take your position? The sooner I know, the sooner I can vote you in." Fred downed the half-filled glass in one swallow. His breath had to be on fire by now.

"Immediately."

Fred walked over and stood behind me. Having him near me almost made me up my bourbon on the carpet, but this was familiar territory. I knew how this was about to play out. When he wouldn't leave after repeating that he'd come in here to check on me, I knew what he wanted, but I had to be sure I was getting something out of it and I was.

He leaned over and licked me in my ear. I stood, my breasts moving evenly up and down as I focused on my breathing and the final outcome of this.

"What do I get for voting you in, Joyce?"

"What is it you need?"

Even though I was breathing deeply, the air felt thick. Fred slid his hand under my shirt and around my breasts. I turned with my back to him so that he could get a good feel and I didn't have to look at his drooping face. He squeezed my breasts roughly. I was depending on my buzz to hang around long enough for me to get through this. He picked up the glass he'd been drinking out of and poured the remaining cognac down my neck, soaking my two-hundred-dollar silk shirt. I didn't budge, keeping my eyes closed, knowing that this was probably going to be rough.

He turned me around. I opened my eyes and looked around the office while Fred groped and ran his wet tongue over my body. The degrees, awards, and accolades all hung quietly. They seemed to be looking at me and reminding me that it didn't matter how hard I had studied or how much I knew, my ass and breasts were worth all the knowledge and hard work in the world. The executive position would be something I would still have to battle for. I would be the only black woman in a group of seven, where only one other woman existed. Hell, what bitch would let another bitch come into a domain it had taken her years to establish?

Fred had my panties down and me pushed over the desk before I could ask him to wait so I could find something to keep me from scuffing my thighs. I closed my eyes again, thinking about my new office, the new title, and the money that was coming along with it. I moaned because the thoughts of new power turned me on. Those thoughts comforted me the same way they did when I'd had to let Mr. Loomis touch and lick and grope. Those thoughts didn't make this seem so wrong. We were cutting a deal, plain and simple.

Fred's clumsy tongue licking me made me desire nothing other than to bathe. He slid his fingers into my moistness and wiggled them like a sixteen-year-old boy who'd read too many dirty magazines. The truth was, I felt sorry for this man's wife. Poor thing was probably at home watching *Entertainment Tonight,* waiting for him to walk in the door at any minute.

The feeling of a condom-covered penis jolted me out of my thoughts. I tensed then relaxed. My pelvis bumped the edge of the desk, sending pains down my hips. I prayed that my thighs didn't bruise. Fred grunted as he thrust himself in and out like a beat with no rhythm, randomly slapping my ass like I was some farm animal. There was nothing sensual about this except my thoughts of the money.

"Talk to me," he panted.

"What?"

At first I didn't hear him, but it took him no time to say it again, and follow it with a loud, aching slap to my ass.

"Shit," I moaned.

"That's it, Joyce, baby, talk to me. Talk dirty to me."

I sighed, returning to my thoughts of money. "Fuck me, Fred. Joyce has been a bad girl, she needs you to make her a good girl."

"That's it," he moaned. "Keep it coming."

I said a few other things as he moaned and knocked me into the desk. My thighs were two seconds from giving in when he shook and thrust and shook and thrust, the rhythm so awkward I couldn't do anything but lean in and let him handle his business. He growled, leaned into my back, and bit me as he came. I screamed in pain as I felt the warm sensation of blood oozing from my back. He let his tired face fall against me and I could feel his wet, scraggly comb-over stick to my skin. "You play the game well, Joyce," he said between breaths. "A natural. You always have been."

I said nothing. I shifted enough to force him off me without appearing to be rude. The game was over and it was time to clear the field. I pulled my clothes back on and brushed myself off. I grabbed a clean glass from the cabinet and poured myself another stiff drink. The musty funk of us turned my stomach, but I kept my poker face.

Fred removed the condom and stared at the semen inside. He smiled at it like it was the cure for cancer, then dropped it in a small bag and placed the bag in my trash can. "I will be in touch with you about the position," he said as he zipped his pants and fixed the collar on his shirt. "And make sure you get that report in on time. I'm counting on you." He patted me lightly on the hand, ran his finger across my lips, and left.

As soon as he was gone, I grabbed my purse and turned off my computer. I checked the hallway to make sure he was nowhere nearby and I skittered down to the elevator. I was shaking by the time I got to my car. I dropped my keys twice before I was able to unlock the door. I couldn't get home fast enough as I moved through the nighttime traffic. Sickness seemed to be building a home in the pit of my stomach. My thighs burned, my back was sore, and all the bathing in the world would not remove the stench of the encounter.

As I drove home, I knew that sleeping with Fred was no longer fun, but more like a waste of my time. I no longer wanted his hands on me and I could no longer find a zone to go to when he came to me for sex. It, along with a heap of other things, had turned me into a borderline alcoholic. When I was in my late twenties, there had been something wonderfully thrilling about sleeping with my boss. Fred was the second boss that I'd slept with, and at one point, we'd had an understanding that allowed us to enjoy the experience. But lately I was becoming more and more irritated with his antics. He'd been promising me that executive job for I didn't know how long, and still I hadn't been promoted. So why was I letting this man abuse me? Why did I keep allowing myself to be a sucker for him? I didn't know, but tomorrow, he'd see that I wasn't playing about my job. I would make Faulkner quit.

Brenda and Faulkner were the only two in the office when I came in Friday morning. Since the foot traffic going by my door was light, I kept it open. Having it that way made me feel safer as well. My trash had been emptied, the glasses washed and placed back in the cabinet, and the carpet had been vacuumed. The only thing that reminded me of last night was my own recollection. Even though my office was now in order, I was still aware of Fred's clammy hands, wet tongue, clumsy finger, and too-eager penis.

"Joyce?"

I turned around and Faulkner was at my door. She was appropriately dressed in a long olive skirt, matching pumps, and a fitted, long-sleeved blouse with speckles of blue in it. The colors looked nice against her dark skin.

"Faulkner, come in. How are you?"

"Fine." She stepped into the office. "I was actually just coming by to see how you were." There was hesitation in her voice. "I know we never just shoot the breeze, but I thought maybe it was time."

"Did you get the e-mail I sent regarding the report?"

"Yes. I'll have it to you by Monday."

I relaxed in my seat. "So, what were you saying about us shooting the breeze?" My mind was still on last night. Whatever Faulkner was trying to say or do, I didn't have time to pay it much attention.

"You. I want to talk about you, Joyce. You know, get to see you on a different level than just work. I was thinking we could do lunch today."

"For what? I'm your boss, not your lunch buddy."

She folded her hands in her lap. "I was simply trying to clear the air between us. I have close relationships with each of the team members, except you."

"I see." I meticulously turned an ink pen around in my fingers. "What do you think you'll learn in forty-five minutes that you don't already know?"

"There's plenty to know. We can spend most of that time talking about growing up or our hobbies. I don't care, Joyce. We can talk about whatever you want to talk about. You can talk about how it feels to be you."

I got defensive because I wasn't in the mood for small talk about emotions and feelings. "Why now?"

Her eyes widened then calmed. "Joyce, I thought you and I could try to be more civil to each other. I thought maybe your behavior toward me may be symptomatic of some underlying issue that may have nothing to do with me. If nothing else, maybe just having someone at work you can talk to might change things. Make you see me and the team differently."

I lay the pen down and rested my forearms on the desk. "What makes you think you have the answers for me, huh? You don't know anything about me. I try to help you by being hard on you and you repay me by asking me to deal with something that is a waste of my time. You tell me you want to move up, but you don't really want it, Faulkner. You don't want it for a second. And for your information, my life is all right, I'm satisfied, and I don't need some overachieving milksop of an employee trying to get in it."

Faulkner stood and straightened her blouse. "I'm sorry I even came in here."

I smiled. "Make it easy on me, why don't you? Turn in your resignation."

She stepped out of the office and headed back to her desk. I got up and closed my door, intending for it to stay that way the rest of the day.

Faulkner

I had done what I could. I'd gone to my boss like a woman and tried to take the approach that I thought would make our relationship something other than what it was, and she proved to be the bitch I swore I would never call another woman. Joyce Armstrong was crazy in my book, pure and simple. She probably didn't know what a milksop was any more than I did.

After I left her office I went straight to my desk and typed my resignation.

On my way from getting the printout, I collided with Gail. Everything in her hand fell to the floor. I bent to help her.

"I got it," Gail said as she hurriedly gathered her things.

"Gail, I'm sorry," I apologized. "These aisles are like Central Expressway sometimes." I picked up the small lunch cooler that she carried every day. She was holding the sheet of paper that had fallen from my hand. Her frown dissipated and returned as she read it. "You're leaving?"

I didn't look at her. I concentrated on picking up one of her bags of chips.

Gail grabbed my arm and walked me to her cube. She put her things down and took the few items that I was holding. "As of Monday. You were just going to leave like that without giving us a chance to get used to the idea?"

"Gail, no. I was going to tell the team, but this was kind of sudden. I'm still struggling with leaving."

"Why are you leaving, Faulkner? You're my girl. The only real friend I have around here. You can't leave me up here with these crazy folk by myself."

"This is a personal move, Gail, and I'm not going into detail about it."

"Well, I know it ain't because you're unhappy. What? You found out you weren't getting the promotion? Is that it?" She was looking for my face to change and when it didn't she kept probing. "Or was it me? Oh, Faulkner, I'm sorry about yesterday. You know how I get sometimes. You just have to ignore me."

"No, Gail, it's definitely not you. It's a matter of politics and morals, really. I promise it has nothing to do with you or any of the team members."

"Hmm. Faulkner, you can't leave. I'm going to assume this is about the promotion and you have to know that Joyce can't keep you from what is yours. For the record, I heard that Mr. Price is pushing for you to be manager."

"Gail, please, no gossip. I'm really not in the mood right now."

"Daeshun told me that she overheard him on the elevator. He was talking on his cell phone, telling someone about you, and how he was going to make sure you would be a manager because he felt like you were the kind of employee he needed in management."

I stared at Gail. I wanted to ask more, but was too near tears to continue the conversation. Gail didn't mind me.

"Eventually, her old ass will have to move over. I know it's hard around here because I feel the pressure each day to conform and be something I'm not for the sake of putting food on the table for my family. I know

I'll have to change to move up, and I need you here to guide me like you've been doing. I need you to stay on me. You can't leave."

"Gail, don't assume this is about Joyce, and I think you'll be able to move up without me. You have the self-motivation to do so."

She crossed her arms and leaned her thick body on one leg. "Do me a favor, then, since you're determined to leave."

"Anything."

"Wait. Don't resign on Monday. Give it a few days."

"I can't. Joyce is waiting on it."

"You're about to leave and you're still worried about the demands Joyce puts on you. I say, just wait. Do it for me; you already said you would."

It really didn't matter to me either way, so I agreed to wait, but not before asking why.

Gail beamed and her gold tooth winked at me. She was sweet when she wanted to be. "I'm going to pray and fast because you know I don't want you to go. I know that's selfish, but your presence around here is an asset. You inspire a sista to want more. I'm going to pray for a miracle for you." Gail logged on to her phone and powered her terminal.

"A miracle. Thanks, Gail." I balled the resignation up and went back to my cube. Now I didn't know how to feel, but I was still on the road to leaving the company. I took a few deep breaths and started to work.

It was dead the rest of the day. Time dragged like a slug with no motivation. I spent most of my time in the second quad of the building training a new group, and was glad when the day finally ended. I withheld my resignation and Joyce never questioned me about it nor came looking. All I could think about was going home, taking a shower, and going to the concert with Greg. It was our first official date, my first real date in a long time.

I drafted the report Joyce needed me to do. It would take me no time to edit and print it out, so I left it on my desk, deciding I would come in Sunday evening and finish it up. I e-mailed Joyce, letting her know I would turn it in first thing Monday, and after I waited long enough to get a response from her and didn't, I shut down my computer. Teresa was out of town on assignment in New York, so the only thing I had to look forward to was my date. As I left, I didn't get the usual last-minute needs-to-be-in-before-you-leave task from Joyce. Her door never creaked open, and that was fine with me. I left the job feeling eerily liberated. It was time for me to have a life outside of work, and I was determined to have one starting tonight.

Joyce

Ask me one thing about work today and I couldn't tell you. I sat in my office with the door closed after Faulkner spoiled my morning. I took a few calls from people who were getting updates on paperwork and a few calls to set up appointments, but I didn't do any MSCOT work. They probably had a field day on the floor without me peeking in on them every so often.

As the day ended, I heard footsteps walk by my door. I sensed it was Faulkner, and I could have easily given her something to do. I looked at my watch and realized she was leaving five minutes early, something she'd never done, but I wasn't in the mood to deal with her, so I let her get away. Not long after I heard her go by, I put my purse on my shoulder and left. I didn't have any plans for tonight, but I didn't want any. All I wanted to do was be in the comfort of my home, alone.

My doorbell rang around seven-fifteen. I thought it was Dennis, so I fixed my robe to reveal cleavage. When I opened the door, Fred stood there. He was still in his suit. He looked out of place. "You ready to be an executive?" He waved the folder of documents I was to sign as he stepped past me into my home.

"Couldn't you have brought these by my office?"

"I've been in meetings all day," he said as he took a seat on my couch. "Besides, I know how much it means to you to get this over with, so I'm bringing them to you."

Resentment was rising in me as I watched him loosen his tie and put his freshly shined shoes on my glass coffee table.

He patted the empty space next to him. "Come and bring a pen with you."

I went to get a pen. When I opened the drawer to my nightstand, the handgun I owned lay there. I touched it, not sure if I should take it with me. I might need it to put a hole square in Fred's ass. As far as I was concerned, I had done what I needed to do to get the promotion. All I needed now was to sign across the dotted line. I wasn't in the mood for any more fucking for leverage. I took a pen from the nightstand and closed it.

When I returned, Fred had removed his shoes and jacket. I cut my eyes at him as he smiled at me.

"This is a nice place you have here. Must've cost you your life savings."

"What I paid on this house didn't put a dent in my life savings, thank you very much." I was irritable and the sassiness in me started to flow. I didn't know why I was trying to prove to this man that I was a black woman who was smart and savvy with her money. He wasn't listening. He didn't care. He already knew everything he needed to know where I was concerned.

He handed me the folder. "It's all yours."

I sat the file on the table and opened it. All the papers were there for me to read and sign. It almost took my breath away. My future was right here on my coffee table. As I looked over the documents and began signing, Fred placed his hand on my back and started rubbing from the back of my neck to as far as his hand would reach before having to go up again. My stomach fluttered as I let out a bothered sigh. I flipped the page and saw the salary I would be making and I could no longer feel Fred's hand. It was as if the zeros were infinite. My body froze.

"Is that enough?" he asked, referring to the number.

I smiled in disbelief. "It's perfect," I answered then laughed.

"Good." He pulled himself closer to me. "Also, I would like to schedule a meeting with Faulkner and me, can you arrange that?"

"I'll see," I responded, not really listening.

I read over the paperwork and signed each sheet that required my signature. I wasn't three seconds into signing the last sheet before Fred was all over me—his wet tongue going into my ear, and those hands, they were the coldest, clammiest hands I'd ever felt. I didn't understand how anyone could tolerate shaking his hand. He led me to the floor and didn't wait for a sign before he was pants-down and inside me. I thought about my gun. He leaned and bit my left nipple, sending heated pain through my breast down to my toes. I pushed his head lightly away but he resisted and moved it back. My head banged against the coffee table as I tried to make myself comfortable. When he withdrew and removed the con-

dom, he turned it over and let his creamy juice land on
my thighs and legs. He continued to bite and nibble on
me until his excitement wore off. As soon as he was finished, I stood and wrapped my robe tightly around my
body, refusing to let him see the fear and embarrassment
on my face. He slid on his shoes, fixed his shirt and
pants, picked up the folder, and walked out of my house
like nothing had happened.

"I'll turn this in on Monday, Joyce. I also will be looking forward to seeing Faulkner accept the offer to be in
management. Welcome to the great world of being an
executive." He smiled.

I stared at him, unmoved. The pride in my face went
unbroken. I locked my door and double-checked it before retreating upstairs. My legs and ass were aching
and my head felt bruised. I grabbed my gun from the
nightstand and brought it into the bathroom with me. I
didn't know what I was going to do with it, but I needed
to feel safer than I was feeling. I ran bathwater and
climbed in the tub slowly. One of my nipples was irritated and red. His teeth marks were all over my body. I
wanted to be anywhere but here.

I lowered myself into the tub, wishing the water could
get rid of the internal feeling of being dirty, but it didn't.
I wanted the cleansing, though. I looked over at the gun
and grabbed it. My life wasn't right and it was eating
away at me. I took the safety off and let my eyes focus
on the barrel before placing it in the small area where
my chin and neck met. I was slowly losing everything I
enjoyed. All the material things I owned no longer mattered to me but I felt like nobody without them. I closed
my eyes, and voices from all directions came at me. One
was my mother's telling me to be strong and endure, the
same words she used when I was with Raymond. "He's
a good man," I could hear her saying. "You just have to
be a good woman to him and that will keep him under

control." She knew how Raymond treated me and she'd allowed it. Then I heard Dennis's voice telling me that I only wanted one thing from a man, that I used people. He was right. Then I heard my own voice, shaking, "Let it go, Joyce. Let it go." Tears burned my eyes as my finger tightened against the trigger. The next voice startled me. It was Nan Ruth's.

"You're acting like you don't have good sense, Eunice. Put that damned gun down!" She was sitting on the toilet next to the tub, her face calm, as I remembered it. She cackled and dipped her hand into the water, closing her eyes as she took in the warmth. Then she looked at me, making me feel ashamed. I moved the gun away from my neck. "You've got more sense than this!" she fussed. "Sure, this man is using you, but why are you using yourself? Why did you tell that sweet girl that you didn't need friends? What's wrong with you? This has to stop somewhere and I'm not going to let him kill you the way he killed me."

I blinked. Nan Ruth dusted her dress off. The scent of vanilla filled my bathroom with each pat from her hands against the skirt. She always smelled of vanilla. She rose from the toilet and looked at herself in the mirror as she continued to preach to me.

"You know what it is to go without, Eunice. All this fancy stuff you have, those clothes, them shoes, that car, this house, you can do without it but you keep thinking you need it and you keep trying to validate why you need it. Now, honey, I ain't 'shame' to say it. I know my life wasn't like your mother's and you loved me more because of it, but, Eunice, you need to tap into your mother's strength at a time like this."

As she continued to talk, my tears became a river flowing from my eyes. "But Mama let Raymond beat me!" I heard myself say.

Nan Ruth put on some of my lipstick before turning

to me. "No, *you* let Raymond beat you, the same way I let Jasper kill me." She rubbed her lips together and got a second look at herself. "Now you gon' turn around and let Fred Price kill you."

My crying was uncontrollable. My voice slurred under the tears. "I can't. I can't go back."

"Then go ahead and kill yourself, Eunice, because you've forgotten where you come from and you've forgotten who you belong to." Nan Ruth put a towel on the edge of the tub and faded in the steam of the bathroom. I lay the gun on the side of the tub and pulled my knees up to my chest and cried.

I slept with my gun Friday and Saturday nights. It was Sunday evening before I felt good enough to leave the house. I headed to the office to pack up a few things so I could be prepared to move into my executive office as soon as possible.

Faulkner

Greg picked me up at exactly six. He looked nice, dressed in taupe slacks, a cream dress shirt, and tie. He smelled nice too. His Toyota 4-Runner was clean and smelling fresh as well. When he got in the car, he handed me his CD case and told me to pick the music we'd listen to on the way to Fort Worth. I leafed through the case, seeing everything from Miles Davis to Fatboy Slim. I opted for Sweetback's CD. They were Sade's original band and I knew the CD would jam. I took the CD and let Greg put it in the player.

"Good choice," Greg said.

"Actually, anything I picked from your case would have been a good choice."

"I like good music," he said as we pulled out of the parking lot of my loft.

"I wish today's soul artists would do collaborations like they used to do back in the day. Like Marvin Gaye and Tammi Terrell. Or Peabo Bryson and Roberta Flack. They used to do entire albums together. You just can't get that today."

"I agree. I think Lauryn Hill and D'Angelo should do an entire album together. That would put a whole new perspective on things."

"Or Maxwell and India Arie. It'd blow some of this other stuff out of the water."

We became quiet for a moment as we stopped for a red light.

"How was work today?" Greg asked.

"Quiet," I said as I was reminded of the drama going on between Joyce and me. I could have easily told Greg all of that, but I kept it to myself. That wouldn't be a great first impression to make on a man if I came out, the night of our first date, complaining about my job and telling him I was about to quit.

"Is that what you've always wanted to do?"

"What's that?"

"Work in telecommunications."

"Oh. No, I haven't, but I want to work in management, maybe one day get to the executive level. I'm a good manager." I looked over at him. His face was freshly shaved and clean. "What about you? Did you always know you wanted to work in the computer industry?"

"No, for a long time I wanted to be a drummer. I wanted to tour with a funk band and do concerts."

"So you didn't want to be like Roy Haynes or Philly Joe Jones and be a jazz drummer?"

"No. I mean, don't get me wrong, playing jazz is cool. Learning it in a classroom allows a person to home in on technique and theory, but I grew up developing my own sound and it was more funk-soul than it was jazz. I used to listen to Clyde Stubblefield and Nate Parker."

"They played with James Brown."

"You really know your music, Faulkner."

"I told you, I love music. Have you checked out that new soul band that's out, Common Folk? They're the first soul band of our generation that *is* a true band."

"Don't forget Mint Condition."

"Yeah, I'm not excluding Mint Condition, but Common Folk has that soul element that's being reexperienced in today's music. They're the next Sly and the Family Stone with a Marvin Gaye touch."

Greg thought for a moment. "Then I need to hear them. My friend Jamal mentioned them once or twice. They play around town, don't they?"

"Not a lot, but you can catch them every now and then. I heard they're touring in Canada now. I'll have to take you to see them next time they're here."

"Okay."

"So what happened?" I looked at Greg, ready to hear what had happened with his dreams of becoming a drummer.

"With the drumming? Oh, my mom moved away when I was eight and I just lost my love for it. I did it in high school and was on a scholarship in college, but the love of it was no longer there. I didn't enjoy it." His face took on the look of a man who had misplaced something.

"Where did she go?"

"France. She kept singing and moved to France."

"But I thought your parents were together."

"They are now." He smiled. "But for a long time they weren't."

The Gail in me wanted to come out and get the scoop on Greg's parents, but I didn't want to open a can of worms by asking. "So how did you end up working with computers?"

"College. I changed my major from music to CIS at the end of my sophomore year."

I nodded, feeling comfortable with Greg's willingness to answer my questions. "Do you like being in management?" I asked.

"It gets political sometimes, but I like it."

"Do you still play your drums?" My mind was racing, because Greg was one of the few people, outside of Teresa, Brenda, and maybe Gail, who I knew enjoyed their life outside of work.

"Sometimes I go to the garage and do a little something, but I get the most play when I visit my parents and we get together and have sessions. I figure maybe my future son will play drums."

"Or daughter," I added with a pinch of sarcasm.

"I don't know, my baby sister is pretty convinced she'll have a niece that plays saxophone."

"My bad." I laughed.

"I like the arts," Greg continued. "I can't lie. Sometimes I think about where I would be if I still had that love for drumming after my mother left. I'm still that good."

"You'll have to show me one day." I smiled. "See if you still got it." I listened to myself, hoping he wouldn't think I was flirting because that wasn't my intention. Well, not my total intention.

"Oh, yeah, I still got it." He smiled.

My body wanted him as much as my mind. I was

grateful that he couldn't read my mind. The attraction between us was real.

We ate dinner at a restaurant near the theater where the concert was. An hour later, Joe Sample and Laylah Hathaway were doing standards and originals that I considered some of my favorites. The words in each song seemed to be about me. I was especially feeling them when they did "For All We Know," which had Greg and me grinning from ear to ear.

Greg put his arm around me and I wasn't trying to stop him. I liked it. By the time the show was over, we were getting our touch-and-rub on. He'd touch me here and smile, then I'd rub him there and grin.

On the way home we talked about music, dream vacations, and played a game of Who Can Name the State Capitals. I invited him in only after he agreed that Lancaster was not the capital of Texas. I didn't want to see him leave. I just wanted to be in his presence and smell his smell and watch him. He sat on the couch and waited for me to get situated. I put my purse away and put on my slippers. I came back in and sat next to him.

"I like the way you decorate. It's nice." My album collection caught his eye. He moved to get a closer look. "Do you mind?"

I shrugged. "No, be my guest." I moved to the floor, glad that he was leafing through the albums. I could answer any question he asked me about any album I owned.

"I haven't seen a collection like this since I visited Quincy Jones back in eighty-three."

"You met Quincy Jones?" I said. Greg was the first person I'd ever met who'd actually met Quincy Jones. I shook my head. "Wow."

"Yeah, he played with my father a few times. They're good friends. Quincy has the wildest jazz collection on wax I've ever seen. He has stuff on wax that was never released."

"Yeah, I have some nice stuff too," I bragged. "They're in storage."

"You're scaring me," he joked.

"I told you I know my music now," I said with a grin on my face. "My parents listened to music all day every day when I was a child. They'd turn the television on to watch *60 Minutes* and the news, but other than that, it was jazz and soul and soul and jazz. You should meet my father. He's twice as bad as me."

"That's cool. It's good to have parents that taught you something. It's great when you can look at your parents and be glad that you were the kid in school with the coolest parents."

"Now, don't get me wrong, they tripped when I was growing up. My mama wasn't afraid to get in my butt. And if I brought home a C on my report card, my mom would tell my old man, and all he had to do was call my name and I would cry." The memory made me laugh out loud. "Yeah, I did have the coolest parents."

"I feel you," Greg said. He looked as if he felt the same way about his parents. He got up and dusted himself off. "I'm going to go so I can get up in the morning."

"What do you have planned?" I asked.

"I'm going to the gym and get some ball in, then I have to trim the hedges, mow the yard, and take care of some things around my house."

I raised my eyebrows. "Sounds like fun."

"Would you like to come over? I think I have some fish you can watch or some other hard work I'd like to see you doing."

I laughed. "I'd love to, but I have work here that needs my attention. I'll be busy through Sunday, but I have tickets to a play next Wednesday night. Soul Rep

Theatre is performing *Birdie Laughing* at the Majestic.
Can we make that a date?"

Greg hugged me. "I'll let you know Monday, but I'm
sure we can make it happen."

"Okay."

Before he left, we embraced again and held each other.
He leaned in to kiss me and I was down with that, so I
gave him a little tongue insurance to make sure he'd be
thinking about me on his way home.

Margaret

Instead of darting straight to the den to watch cartoons
and eat cereal, as they did every Saturday, the girls woke
up looking for their mother. Lisa hadn't come home
since the police incident. I called Lew Sterrett and was
informed that she'd been released the same evening of
her arrest. I assumed that boy she was seeing had come
and got her. I told the girls that their mother was out
looking for a job. God knows I didn't want to lie to
them, but they didn't deserve to have the truth rip a hole
in their exaggerated idea of their mother. I got them
dressed and ready to spend the day with Gloria Pickney.
She was taking her grandchildren to see the latest Disney
movie and then to Chuck E. Cheese for pizza. She'd
called and invited Nicole and Shylanda. Lester and I appreciated her more than generous offer, because I had to
go take my tests at the doctor's office and Lester had errands to run.

He wanted to take me to the doctor's office but I was feeling good, above average, and wanted to take the bus. My ankles weren't swollen, my sugar was steady, and I just wasn't tired and depressed like normal. Lester tried to put up a fight, but he knew that was a losing battle when my mind was set on something.

The bus ride to Presbyterian Hospital gave me time to think about some things that had been on my mind. For one, I didn't have a will and I needed to get that done. I wanted to make sure that my grandbabies were taken care of and that Lester wouldn't have any problems with my things, knowing what to do with them. I pulled out a small pad I had in my purse that I made notes on, and began writing who would get what. Since I wasn't sure exactly how my will would be laid out, I began by writing my funeral plans. Tonight I would show it to Lester and have him put it somewhere safe, even though I still expected to be here for years to come. I'd overcome so much that death had become a random thing to me, and right now I wasn't feeling as if I were dying, I simply felt like God had given me another day and would give me tomorrow because there was still much work for me to do. And with that, I chose to put some things on paper, so when that day came, for once in my life, there would be no stress. First, I wrote down what suit from my closet I wanted to be buried in. It was a lavender three-piece that my sister had given me on Easter three years back. It had a beautiful studded collar and jacket cuffs. I looked good in it, and I wanted to be buried in it. I also wanted the pastor at my church, Reverend Jameswood, to preside over the funeral. That man could lay down a prayer, and I admired him for his ability. I also wanted the ladies' chorus to sing "My Soul's Been Anchored in the Lord," and I wanted Sister Jackson's daughter Simone to lead. She had the voice of a true angel, and I always loved that song; it made me shout to glory. The church knew it was my favorite. I made sure to write down that I didn't want people giving speeches and that I didn't want a wake service, only a funeral. Lester and I had already purchased our plots over at Lincoln Cemetery, and my sisters would make sure Lester would be okay, so I really had nothing to worry about.

There were also some things I wanted my coworkers at my job to get. I wanted Faulkner to have my anniversary china and a pair of diamond earrings that had been handed down in my family for over three decades. Brenda Jones would get two afghans I'd crocheted and never did anything with, and I had a mink stole that I would leave Joyce because she was the only person I knew who would still wear fur when it wasn't so popular to do so. Animal rights activists were like hawks on chicken eggs around here and I'd stopped wearing my furs back in the mid-eighties. I smiled, thinking about the days when Joyce and I were close. Those days were good ones, and in a scary way I missed what we had back then. I decided to leave her the antique bedroom suite that was in storage. She'd take care of it, I knew that about Joyce. She'd make sure it went inside a nice room and that it never got misused. Whether I wanted to admit it or not.

Joyce was a girl from Calvert, Texas, who never thought she stood a chance in the world alone. Maybe the bed would remind her of that. Maybe if I went to Joyce and said my piece, we'd be able to at least speak and look at each other at the same time. I regretted not telling her what happened to me that day in Mr. Loomis's office. I held back and it was the main reason she and I hadn't spoken to this day. I hated Joyce for having whatever it was she had to sleep with him, because now she had money, nice things, she was together, unlike me. I was fat, making barely enough money to keep my family together, and owned more hand-me-downs than the

Salvation Army. I hated her for a long time for that. Hmph, I don't think I'd ever stopped hating her. I'd just got used to the feeling. I'd stopped putting the energy into hating her and just let it exist between us. That's why I'd stayed at the phone company, so that I could always be her reminder that she wouldn't be nothing if it weren't for me. I should have been in her position, not her.

It made it hard for me to look outside my window at passing traffic and scenery as I faced the truth, but the more I admitted it to myself, the easier things seemed. I felt light all of a sudden, light and blessed. Blessed that in spite of my bitterness, that as a Christian, I could be a woman about this and approach Joyce to apologize and be at peace with her and with Meridian Southwest phone company.

I glanced out the window just in time to see my stop coming up. I put the list in my sweater pocket and pressed the bell. I gathered my purse and stepped off the bus. All the fear I'd felt the past few days was gone. I wasn't as worried about the testing because I was now committed to treating myself better. Once I made it through this, I would be a changed woman. My mood was upbeat, I had my life ahead of me, and I was ready to grab the bull by the horns and tackle him. I'd promised myself that I would take a walk every day and cut back on all the fried foods I ate. I would also stop eating pork because Faulkner told me it had a lot to do with my blood and weight. I was determined to treat my body better. I'd already ordered the Tae Bo tapes to prove it. As I entered the building, I thought to myself that whatever the good Lord saw fit for me, I would be brave, no matter what.

Faulkner

My phone woke me out of my sleep at nine o'clock. I rolled over and picked it up, knowing it was my mother. "Hey, Mom."

"Well, if you knew it was me, why didn't you pick up on the first ring? I could have had an emergency or something."

"Is there an emergency?" I grinned.

"Well . . . no, but it could have been. Why are you still in the bed?"

"I was still asleep, the same way I am every Saturday when you call."

"Excuse me, then. I was just calling to check on you and see how your week went. No word on the promotion?"

"Nope, but it's nothing I can't handle. Where's Daddy?"

"In the garage working on the lawn mower. He was mowing the lawn last night and ran over a piece of wood big enough to finish a house. I don't know why he didn't wait like I told him."

"What is wrong with the mower?"

"The blade or something, he said. I don't know."

"Oh. What are you doing today?"

"I'm grading papers right now, but I was thinking of going to the farmers' market to get something to make a good vegetable salad with. Ms. Harvey, one of the teachers at the school, gave me a recipe and I might try it."

"Mom?"

"What?"

"When was the last time you got a checkup? How's your health?"

"Fine. I have high blood pressure, but I take my medicine because if I don't, I can't even function. The doctor told me that if I exercise and drop some of this weight, I could probably be taken off the medicine."

"So, are you going to lose weight?"

"I said I was going to start walking this summer. Me and some of the teachers are going to get together in the mornings and walk."

"Why don't you start now?"

"Faulkner, I don't have time. School keeps me so busy, I don't even have time to read like I used to. It's like the kids today are so deprived of attention at home, they come to school and take every single ounce of energy you have to give. By the time I get home, I have enough time to grade papers, eat, watch the news, and after that, I'm in the bed ready to do it all over again."

"I wish you would find the time to put in some exercise. You and dad."

"I will. I just have to wait until I *have* time. I talked to your brother this morning."

I thought about my older brother, Russell. He was a civil attorney living in Elmhurst, Illinois, a growing suburb west of Chicago. He lived there with his wife and three children. We e-mailed each other more than we talked, but our mother kept us abreast of each other's business so much that we rarely communicated. "How is he?"

"You need to call him. He closed on his new house yesterday. I'm hoping we can make the drive to see him when summer comes."

"Why would you drive all the way there when it's less stressful to fly?"

"Your daddy's been talking about buying a camper."

"A camper? If you're going to spend money on a camper, then you could give that money to me. I'll drive you wherever you need to go."

My mother laughed. "We've done our job with you. Now it's time for us to do something for us."

"Then I'm not mad at you. Do your thing."

"When are you going to check on going back to school?"

"Can we have one Saturday when you don't ask me that question?"

"No. Now, when are you going to check, Faulkner Michele?"

"Mom, I haven't even decided if I'm going back. I don't know what I want to do."

"One day you tell me you're checking on it and the next day, you don't know if that's what you want to do. You never could buckle down and make a decision. You're indecisive, just like your father. Just last week, we spent fifteen minutes in the soup aisle at the grocery store because he couldn't decide between Campbell's or Progresso."

I laughed. "What did you do?"

"I almost went and bought me a pack of cigarettes and started smoking again."

I was reminded of being a little girl watching my mother smoke. She quit twenty years ago. She decided to go cold turkey and never smoked another cigarette again. I sometimes wished I had her fortitude.

After more small talk and some gossip about family members, we hung up. I stayed in bed, not wanting to get up yet. Dark gray clouds had collected outside my window and I could tell heavy rain was in the forecast.

I picked up my phone and dialed Margaret's number. I wanted to know how she was feeling. We hadn't talked in four days and I missed her. There was no answer. I hung up and tried again; still no answer or answering machine. Margaret was so old-fashioned. She didn't like answering machines because she thought they disrupted people's lives, so she took back the one I got her and kept the money. I hoped she was doing well. She'd needed me last week and I hadn't been there. That would not happen again.

Margaret

I was still feeling on top of the world when I returned from the hospital. The testing went well and Dr. Kipfer was pleased to hear me sound cheerful. It would be a week before I would know what the results were and I promised myself to live a good, worry-free life during the waiting period.

Lisa came trudging in shortly after I got home. She was dressed in a new outfit, her hair was fresh, and she'd gone out and had her nails done. I wasn't in the mood to deal with her, so I kept my eyes on the television.

"Good afternoon, Margaret," she said.

"Afternoon," I replied.

"Where's Daddy?"

I looked at my watch. "He picked the girls up from Gloria's and took them to have their hair done."

"For what?"

"They needed their hair done and I wasn't in the mood to do it."

"I can't be letting just anybody touch their hair. You know these salons over here don't know how to treat soft, curly hair. They think you fry and gel down everything. Where did he take them?"

"He took them to Tracey's shop."

"That ghetto-fabulous place? Ugh." Lisa trotted to the back. The next thing I heard was her music blasting from the radio she owned. She returned to the den. She grabbed the remote from the couch and started turning the channels. The music still blasted from the back room.

I took my mind to the Lord and asked for patience. I wasn't going to go around and round with her. I refused. This was one devil I was about to rebuke.

"Lisa."

No answer. She looked at the television and laughed.

I rose from the couch and tapped Lisa on the arm on my way toward the hall. "Lisa Jeanette, come here."

She dropped the remote on the floor and followed me. "What?"

"I need to talk to you."

"Well, I was watching television, Margaret, can it wait?"

"No, it cannot wait. I want you out of this house. I want you to turn in the keys and I want you to get your things and move."

Lisa rolled her eyes. "You can't just throw me out on the street. I have two little girls and it wouldn't be fair to them."

"You're right."

"So, can I go and watch television? Once Daddy comes back with Nicole and Shylanda, we'll be out of your hair at least until Monday. Derrick finally invited them over."

"What happened to Carl? That is the name of the young man you were last with, am I right?"

"Carl was just a friend. Derrick is the one who plays football. He wants to marry me and he wants to meet the girls."

I leaned on the wall. Lisa was out of her mind if she even thought that what she was saying made me feel better. At this point, I would testify in a court of law that my daughter didn't have the good sense God gave a grapefruit. I was not going to let my grandbabies be whisked off to live with their mother and a man who they didn't know. "You're not taking the girls from this house. You can get your things now and go."

"What? You must be out of your mind if you think I'm leaving here without my kids."

"Who are you talking to like that? No, *you* must be crazy if you're trying to take Lester and me for fools. Child Protective Services has been by here every day since the police dragged you off from here. I bet that'll stop you in your tracks."

"You called CPS on me?" Lisa walked up to me. "See, I knew you didn't have my back, Margaret!"

I didn't budge. We were in each other's face, woman to woman. Her thin frame was no competition for my thick body. "You best back up off me, girl, before I put a hurting on you." I put my hands on my hips, where they rested comfortably. My breathing remained calm and steady.

Lisa's eyes went from bold to not-so-sure in a second. She slowly moved back, still trying to be pompous about the situation.

"Where were your girls the day you and that woman were outside fighting in my driveway?"

"The police wouldn't have got me if you and Daddy hadn't stabbed me in the back."

I grabbed her arm. My fingers pinched her skin. I wanted to hurt her, but controlled my grip. "Where were my grandbabies? I'm not going to ask you any-more."

Lisa's eyes darted from left to right several times. She was thinking but she was also trying to wiggle herself free. The more she wiggled, the tighter my grip became. She hollered out in pain, but I didn't loosen my hand.

"You better get to talking, Lisa."

"I don't know," she cried out. "They were supposed to come straight home from school, but they weren't in the yard when I told them to be. I'd come home to pick them up."

I let Lisa go, not convinced she was telling the whole truth. "You're not thinking about them," I yelled. "And I want you out of this house before CPS comes back or else I'm turning them over. Lester and I already dis-cussed this."

Lisa's cries became heaving sobs. "I can't leave my girls. They're all I have!"

"Well, you should have thought about that when you didn't come home for four nights in a row."

"I was in jail!"

"You are lying to me!"

Lisa slid down the wall with her head buried in her hands. "This isn't what a saint for Christ is supposed to act like," she spat at me. "You make Christians look bad!"

I grabbed my small Bible from the bookshelf and started hitting Lisa with it. I got her two good times square in the head and shoulder. "Don't you ever bring God into this after I've allowed you to live here and dis-respect me since you moved back. I've lifted you up in prayer more times than the Lord should allow. I want you out!" I walked away, leaving Lisa crouched on the floor, crying.

My pills were waiting for me on the bathroom counter. I took the ones it was time to take then I went to the bed and got down on my knees to pray for Lisa and myself. I asked the Lord to watch over her and to protect her. Then, I asked for forgiveness for lying to her about CPS. They hadn't been by and I would never allow them to take my grandbabies from here. I'd seen Lester use it, and when I realized it was what worked, I just joined in and used it too. After that I just prayed. I prayed till I didn't know where I was anymore. I don't know how long I was down there, but when it was all over and I stepped out of my room, I was alone in the house.

Faulkner

It was the second consecutive weekend that Sunday came before I knew it. I spent Saturday cleaning and getting rest. I thought about Greg and wondered if he was able to get his lawn mowed, but for the most part, I chilled until the next day.

Sunday turned out to be a rainfest. It started out drizzling, and by Sunday night it was raining cats and dogs. I was hanging around the loft, hoping the rain would lighten, but it didn't. I slid on some sweats and drove to the office. I still needed to finalize the editing for the report.

I decorated Brenda's cube first. I'd purchased yellow and gold streamers and miniature baby trinkets. I hung the streamers around her cube and placed trinkets over her desk. It wasn't a lot but it would have to do. After standing back and viewing the decorations, I went to my cube. I turned on my radio and listened to a local jazz station that broadcast out of Denton. The music put me in work mode, even though I felt eerily spooked by being in the office so late on a nonwork night.

Finishing the project was more time-consuming than I'd estimated. My spreadsheet software crashed twice and I had to fix two files by renaming them and deleting the old copies. The time-consuming part was finding them. I used Scan-disk, the built-in fix-it tool. It was after nine when I was finally able to work problem-free. I was pushing to be out by ten-thirty at the latest. I knocked two sections out with no problem. With two more to go and my watch reading a quarter of ten, I knew I'd be able to stick to my schedule. I stood and stretched my legs and rotated my neck to remove the stiffness that had settled in my joints and muscles. I heard the elevator bell and assumed someone else like me was putting in extra work. I didn't try to see who it was and remained relaxed at my desk. A few minutes later I felt a hand on my shoulder. I gasped, startled.

"Ms. Lorraine, I didn't mean to startle you," the voice said.

My breathing was quick as I realized I knew the man who'd touched me. I placed my hand over my chest to calm myself. "It's okay, Mr. Price, I just wasn't expecting anyone to be here."

We smiled at each other.

He rubbed my back and squeezed my shoulder. "I'll bring my bullhorn next time to make my announcement before I enter the floor." He grinned.

"Is there anything I can help you with?" I asked as I sat back down.

"No, no. I was working in my office and decided to take a stroll. I heard the music so I decided that I would come and see who was putting in the extra time. You know, initiative plays a big part in the success of this phone company." He looked over my shoulders. "I see you're working on the project I gave to Joyce?"

"Just editing, mostly," I said, protecting my boss. I could have slapped myself immediately after, but Mr. Price was standing there.

I sat up straight, not really comfortable with him looking over my shoulder. I could feel his warm, liquor-laced breath on my neck. I crossed my legs and scooted closer to the desk to give him the hint that he could leave now, but he didn't. I didn't know if the man was blind or just not paying me any attention.

He grabbed a chair from the cube across from me, pulled it next to where I was sitting, and sat. He had on a shirt that looked like a golf shirt and plaid shorts. His white legs needed some serious sun. They were a different color from his pink face.

"Joyce has been telling me good things about you, Faulkner." He looked at me. "She said you were top choice for manager. I agree with her."

I gave a shocked half-smile. "Is that so? Well, I'm pleased to know that my work doesn't go unnoticed around here." This was proof that Joyce hadn't told anyone about me resigning. Maybe Gail's rumor was right and Teresa's theory about Joyce testing me held some truth. I was now curious, but still uncomfortable with this man sitting so close to me in an empty building.

He nudged me. "Do you mind if I ask you some questions? I don't want to keep you from doing what you're doing, but it's time I think we got to know each other on a professional level."

"Well, I'm a little busy," I said. "This is deadline work that I'm doing. Maybe we can do lunch one day." I didn't like putting an important man like Mr. Price off, but this wasn't the time or place to be developing a professional relationship.

He reached over and planted his hand firmly on my leg. I looked down at his hand and then hit him with a glance that made him know he wasn't doing the right thing.

His hand squeezed and then was gone back into his own lap. "I'll only be a minute."

I tried to relax, but couldn't. I was uneasy all the way to my bones. I kept telling myself to be calm, that this was nothing, but something deeper wouldn't allow me to let my guard down. "Sure, go ahead," I said. I shifted in my seat enough to scoot over and make it look as if I was giving him my full attention at the same time.

"I think you and Joyce have a lot in common and, to be frank with you, I think you'd make a great special services manager, but an even greater manager of customer operations."

"You're talking about giving me *Joyce's* job?" I could not believe what I was hearing.

"Yes. Joyce has been offered a position as executive over regional test and customer procedures and I think you should be next in line for her position."

I was stunned. I could do Joyce's job with my eyes closed, and with her leaving our floor, I wouldn't have to deal with her at all.

"Do you think you're ready for such a jump?"

I didn't have to think about this answer. "I think I'm ready." I smiled. "Thanks, Mr. Price. Your confidence in me is not something I take for granted."

He looked at me as if he were searching for something. His long stare made me uncomfortable. I scratched my neck and fidgeted.

"I'm recommending you make two percent more than what Joyce was making."

I did the math as he spoke. That was putting me at

double what I made now. I thought about finally being able to pay my school loans off, save some money, take a trip, and go on a mini shopping spree.

"Mr. Price, I think that would be fine."

Then came the hand on my leg again, this time up higher and closer to my crotch. He leaned over and spoke in a low voice. "The benefits are outstanding."

I jumped up, knocking some of my papers to the floor. I didn't want to pick them up until Mr. Price was gone. I stood looking at him, hoping that I wasn't reading him wrong, but I didn't want him touching me like that.

He stood and held his hand out. "Ms. Lorraine, are you okay?"

"Yes, sir, I'm okay. I just remembered I left my dog on the patio and I need to let him in. He'll jump if I'm gone too long." I scrambled for my purse. Once it was secure on my shoulder, I kneeled and quickly gathered the papers.

Mr. Price rolled the chair back to the cube across the aisle and tugged on his pants. "Yeah, my wife has a little cocker-poodle that needs lots of attention like that." He extended his hand. "Well, it was nice talking with you and I look forward to having you move up."

I took his hand quickly and let it go. "Thanks. Have a good night."

When he turned the corner and went into Joyce's office, I leaned against the cube wall, still trying to believe what had just happened to me. I gathered the rest of the papers and placed them in the folder. The report would have to wait until morning. I saw light shining from under Joyce's door. I wondered if she was in there or if Mr. Price had a key. My instinct told me to knock and see, but an even stronger urge told me not to knock. I stepped to get on the elevator, when the Gail Perez in me made me inch my head near the door to see what I could hear.

Joyce

When I flipped on the light in my office, it was ten o'clock. I'd put some things off on Friday that I wanted to get done before Monday morning. It was actually Fred's work, but I'd taken the responsibility of doing it. Flashes of lightning lit the Dallas skyline outside my window. I was glad I didn't have any computer work ahead of me. I feared using electronic equipment during storms.

While I sifted through proposals and analysis charts, I heard my doorknob turn and Fred entered. He was smiling that saintless smile of his.

"Joyce, you never cease to amaze me. First I come here and see Faulkner working hard and then she leaves and here you are. Don't you ever do anything but work?"

This time I didn't smile back. I removed my eyeglasses and watched him. Tonight I wasn't drunk and I wasn't in the mood for games.

Fred closed the door behind him and looked around the office. He played with the leaves on the Boston fern hanging near the bookshelf.

"I was actually leaving, Fred," I said, attempting to get him to turn his ass around and walk out the door. I was stalling, but as long as he wasn't in arm's reach of me, I was fine. He didn't leave. I watched him as he took a book from the shelf and leafed through it. He put it back and walked over to the liquor cabinet. He opened it and turned to look at me. "You turn health nut on me, Joyce?" To his surprise, I'd replaced the alcohol with different fruit juices, bottled water, and yogurt cups.

"No, I just needed a change. Leaving work with a hangover is no longer my idea of effective leadership. I'm an executive now."

He laughed. "It works for me." He came over and put his hands on my shoulder and this time my stomach turned all the way. I heaved and coughed a few times. Anxiety rose in me as he slid his hand down my shirt. I pushed him away from me and he almost lost his balance. He struggled to stay on his feet, but not before fumbling into the blinds. "What are you doing?" He spoke loudly.

I stepped away from the desk with my eyes locked on him. "I don't want to do this anymore."

Fred's face was flushed and then the blood receded like a tidal wave. Anger, confusion, and annoyance showed in his face. "Joyce, you've developed a conscience all of a sudden? Is that what this is?"

I remained quiet. I was scared but ready to defend myself. He was between the door and me. All I could do was wait to see if he was going to calm down and leave. Whatever he was going to choose, I meant what I said.

He stepped over to me and grabbed my shoulders, forcing his lips against mine.

I squirmed with the strength I could bring without acting out of character. I wanted him to realize I didn't want this and if he just accepted my new choice, I wouldn't cause any problems, but he didn't seem to get it. He wouldn't let go of my sleeve and ripped it as I tried to get out of his reach. He met my strength with his own, sending us crashing into the bookshelf. Books fell on us and one whacked me near my eye. I could feel the skin lose feeling, then start throbbing as I covered my head too late to avoid any damage. Fred still had my arm in his. He managed to pull me from the floor and palmed the side of my face, which sent my head to the right so fast I thought he'd popped my neck. This man had just slapped me like he was Lennox Lewis. Pain rang in my face as he grabbed my breast. He leaned into me and I tumbled against the desk, with him trying to get on top of me. I raised my knee and caught him in the dick. It wasn't the best knee raise, but it was enough to hurt him. I veered back and pushed him off me. He crumpled against the door, the look of a killer in his eyes. I stood breathing feverishly, then I walked up to him, balled my fist, and swung as hard as I could toward his nose. One blow caught him, but he managed to block the other. My hands burned and I realized some of my nails were gone. Blood dripped to the floor.

"You bitch!" he yelled. "You black bitch!" Blood began oozing from his nose as he turned and opened the door. "You can forget about the job. I want your resignation." With that said, he bolted out of the office.

I stood breathing hard, looking at the door to see if he was coming back. My right hand was on fire now. I needed to get some first aid. I went into the bathroom and ran my hand under cold water. My legs felt like they would buckle at any minute. I wrapped my hand in a paper towel and checked my face. The corner of my eye was closed, with a purple bruise forming. A cut bled on my arm and my fingers burned from the missing nails, but other than that, I was thankful to still be in one piece.

The few books that had fallen to the floor would have to wait until tomorrow to be picked up. I looked around my office to make sure no more damage was done. The awards hanging around my college degree caught my eye. I inhaled and tried to make it all make sense and I couldn't. Without turning out the light or locking the door, I picked up my keys and purse and left.

Faulkner

I hid behind the wall adjoining the water fountain just seconds before Mr. Price came storming out and got on the elevator. My legs shook like I had an uncontrollable condition. My whole body felt heavy and I couldn't remember running to the end of the hall when the tussle had ceased. I had to get out of here, but I couldn't get a grip on myself. I didn't want Mr. Price to see me so I pressed my body to the wall and stood as still as my shaking frame would allow me to.

It took me several minutes to move, even though Mr. Price was long gone. I wondered if Joyce was okay but thought against going to her office. I wasn't in any mood to address what I knew or what had happened to me. I couldn't get to the elevator without passing her office, so I was stuck because her door was open. I decided to wait it out. My knees almost buckled, but I closed my eyes and counted until I felt them lose some of their weakness. I was at eighteen when I heard Joyce's footsteps on the marble floor. I pressed myself against the wall. If she came anywhere near the water fountain, she'd see me, but I was comforted in knowing water was probably the last thing on her mind. Joyce had the same objective as me: she wanted to get out of here and get home. She went into the bathroom, briefly returned to her office, and then walked to the elevator, waiting in her usual

cool-and-collected way. I watched her get on the elevator. After I counted to one hundred, I got on the elevator
and dashed to my car.

Margaret

When the storm came in, my body started aching and
ached ever since. When I got up to get ready for work, my
whole left side felt numb, as if the blood had froze in my
veins. I worked my arm up and down several times before
the feeling came back. Lester massaged me, but I still felt
as if I wasn't a part of myself and I couldn't keep up.

I fixed breakfast and sent everyone off on a good note.
I still had a few minutes before my bus would arrive, so
I sat and made a list of the things that would need to be
done to make the girls' room more suited to their needs.
When Lester had brought them home Saturday, I told
him what happened between Lisa and me. He didn't say
much. At first, he just stared at the television as if he
hadn't heard what I'd said. Then he rubbed his chin and
said he agreed with me and I had his support. Although
he wasn't sure how we were going to raise Nicole and
Shylanda, he was willing to try.

I was no longer concerned about Lisa. I was letting her
and her drama go. It was for my own good. She was
ninety percent of the reason my blood was up. I wouldn't
meddle in her personal affairs anymore, nor would I
keep her father from getting on her once she returned to
this house. She was our problem but his child, and I'd

kept them from each other long enough. All I wanted to do was watch my grandchildren grow up to be responsible women, and I would give that to them until they were able to choose otherwise. Children that age shouldn't grow up referring to every man brought around them as Uncle. They needed good examples of men who would respect them and love them in spite of their flaws, the same way my husband loved me. I wasn't sure how Lester and I would make it raising these girls. I wasn't sure if we had the strength, patience, or will, but we both knew they needed us as much as we struggled with our selfish plans. Before, we'd hoped to be planning a cruise or a country getaway, but now we weren't sure if that would ever happen. Our money was no longer being set aside for home improvements, trips, garden supplies, or additional savings. We would be back to paying for school clothes, field trips, braces, instruments, private lessons, school pictures, and once-a-month hair appointments. And our time would be spent on homework and at the park, PTA meetings, and, soon enough, graduations. I didn't like it any more than I thought my husband did in his own private thoughts, but if we didn't do it the government would, and Lester and I never would let that happen to family.

Joyce

Treating myself to a full-body massage before going to work was the best decision I'd made in a long time. It made it easier for me to walk into my office because I was more relaxed after what had happened last night. The masseuse worked out a lot of the kinks and cramps that I'd acquired from keeping Fred off me. I managed to come to work with no visible signs that I'd been bruised. I put makeup over the welt near my eye, and the cut on my arm was hidden under the sleeve of my blouse, but my mind wasn't at ease. Fred had asked for my resignation and I wasn't ready to accept that. I believed I could get through this and keep my job, but I was in denial about my past and I wasn't ready to open myself to criticism and judgment. The only comfort I could find was revisiting the conversation I'd had with Faulkner, in which she said something about always having a choice. She believed that and I was now realizing how right she was. I did have a choice, and I was no longer choosing to be or live a lie.

I did my walk-through as usual, but with a different attitude and outlook. I was happy to see the team at their desks. Brenda, Margaret, Carmen, Gail, and James were all in place. Faulkner was the only one not in. I wasn't just happy that they were there working, I was sincerely happy to see them. Their faces, hairstyles, clothes, shoes—everything about each of them, I was happy to be around. I attempted to smile at the team, but no one gazed at me as I walked down the aisles. Gail Perez looked at me long enough to report that Faulkner had called in to say that she would be late. I attempted to spend some extra time in the area to see what everyone was busy doing, hoping my newness could be felt. I'd never conversed with any of the team just to shoot the breeze, but today I desired to reach out. I wanted them to know I had made a choice much different from what they were used to.

I walked to Brenda's decorated cubicle. She was typing away on her computer. I congratulated her on the pregnancy. I'd gotten the announcement on the group e-mail last week but never acknowledged it. Brenda seemed perplexed that I was casually talking to her, but she entertained me anyway.

"Brenda, I just wanted to let you know that I think your being pregnant is wonderful. Do you have names yet?"

She looked up at me, her eyebrows furrowed with curiosity. "Thank you, Joyce." She smiled. "I haven't picked out any names yet." Brenda resumed her work. She was too used to me walking through the aisles in silence.

"Do you want a boy or a girl?" As I listened to myself, a smile broke wider across my face. It felt good reaching out.

Brenda returned the smile and looked at me as if she were trying to see into my soul. She couldn't decide if I were up to something or on drugs. "I personally want a girl." Brenda again placed her hands on the keyboard, as if to be busy. I'd thrown her into confusion.

I wanted to talk more, but figured to quit while I was ahead. I couldn't expect the team to immediately warm up to me just because I'd changed overnight. Faulkner's absence made a big difference. Normally, when I did my walk-through, the team would be communicating with her. They went to her for whatever they needed, be it business or personal; now here I was trying to act as if I had the same kind of relationship. I didn't, but I wanted to. To communicate with the team, I needed Faulkner.

As I passed Brenda's cube, I came upon Margaret. She was wearing a gorgeous hazel-and-brown-colored suit. It'd been a long time since I'd seen her dressed to the nines, but she still had it, even with the extra weight she'd picked up. Still, the circles under her eyes gave her a raccoon look, and she was barely smiling, and that was causing the lines around her mouth to sharpen. Margaret used to have so much life in her, but now I couldn't believe that we were once running buddies. Once we were wild women doing whatever, and it had changed in the blink of an eye. As I walked by and looked at her, I found the voice in me that I'd long ago suppressed.

"Nice suit, Margaret."

She looked at me and smiled. Her eyes were somewhat lifeless and tired and I wondered if she'd had enough sleep last night. "Thanks." She smiled. We looked at each other and felt something. I don't know what it was for Margaret, but for me it was forgiving myself for betraying her. I wanted our friendship back. As I headed back to my office, I knew how much had been lost when I'd done what I had. I'd slept with my boss to move up because I was greedy. I was a girl from the country with an illusion of who I was. I didn't want people to know I was from Calvert. I didn't want anyone to know I'd been abused. I didn't want anyone to know that I'd abandoned my brother when my mother died. All my life, I felt like people could sense that in me, so I did what I could to cover it up. When I met Margaret, she let me know it was okay to be who I was. I was comfortable around her until that day Mr. Loomis called her into his office. That event changed everything between us because she came out still Margaret, and I came out of his office a fool, and I spent the rest of my career envying Margaret for being the woman I never could be. She'd walked away from Mr. Loomis and kept her dignity and self-respect. She ended up with a great husband and a loving family. Maybe she had only a modest lifestyle, but all the people at the company loved and respected her. I didn't stay around to talk because I still had work to do. I assumed that Fred had already reported my resignation, so I tried to stay focused on doing as much as I could before word got out.

I walked into my office and sat behind the desk. As I looked at the things around me, instantly I was washed over with a feeling of ultimate thankfulness. Sure, I'd become accustomed to the money, my look, and the ease of my position, but they no longer seemed so important. All of this was nothing because I'd never really earned it, although I could have.

I finalized a few forms to report last week's activity and after that, I pulled up a clean page on my computer and began typing my resignation. I'd printed it out and sat staring at it when my phone rang. It was Fred.

"Joyce, don't worry about making Faulkner the offer. I have it taken care of. Make today your last day and there won't be any problems."

"That's fine, Fred. We're having a going-away party for one of our employees. I plan to be gone before the event is over." I disconnected the call, not caring if he felt that I'd hung up in his face or not. A knock came at my door and when I saw who was standing in the doorway, I felt like the universe was on my side. It was Margaret, and I'd just been thinking of going back to her desk to chat with her.

"Joyce, I thought I'd come by and talk to you."

I smiled. "Margaret, girl, come on in, have a seat. I still think that outfit is slamming."

"Thank you. I was just trying to do something nice for myself, for a change."

I caught myself staring at my old friend. "It's been over twenty-five years since we've sat down and spent any time with each other."

She smirked. "I didn't think you were keeping count."

"You don't have a friendship like we had and just forget about it overnight." I looked at my hands and got right to the point. "I never stopped caring about you, Margaret. Our friendship meant a lot to me. I know you won't believe me, but it still does."

"For a long time I didn't think you knew how to care, Joyce, but I knew you had your reasons, and I never doubted that one day we'd be somewhere having no choice but to deal with our past. I'm just surprised we're at the same starting point. I thought you would have come up with some devious way to get rid of me before now."

"Look, don't rub it in. I would hope that you didn't come in here to belittle me for being a bitch all these years."

"I apologize, because I didn't come in here for that. I just have some other stress on me. I didn't mean to make you feel bad."

"Oh, you meant it, I just didn't want to hear it." I smiled.

"You still crazy." Margaret settled in the chair. "We did have some good times and I still laugh out loud when I think about some of the things we've done together."

"Remember the Barry White concert?"

"Yes, Lord, yes! We talked them two white girls out of their front-row tickets. How could I forget? You talked so fast, I almost went with them."

We laughed.

"It seems like time doesn't stand still until you're

remembering, and at the same time you realize how fast it flies."

"Yeah," Margaret agreed. "Well, a lot has gone on since then."

Now things were going in a direction I wasn't sure I was ready to deal with, but Margaret knew. She had never been a fool, in my opinion. "You don't have to tell me. If anyone knows how much has gone on, it's me. As a matter of fact, I'm turning in my resignation today."

"What? You've worked so hard. Tell me you didn't come this far to just let this job go."

"Letting go isn't a bad thing, Margaret. You know and I know that I've built my career on lies and things too unspeakable to even mention."

Margaret sat quietly. The look on her face showed that she was coming to grips with the fact that I was trying to make things right, not only with her, but with myself as well. "When? What happened?"

I sighed. "Fred offered me the executive position I'd been dreaming about. It was what I'd been working for, but once I accepted, I no longer wanted the other side that came with it. When I demanded that we stop, he asked for my resignation."

"Honey, please. If I were you, I'd file a case against him and go on about business as usual."

I shook my head. "My past is too filled with hurt for me to risk it being brought out just to keep a job. You have to believe that I was really going to make a difference once I became an executive. Things wouldn't be so hard for women who were trying to move up in the ranks at this place."

Margaret looked at me and I immediately felt embarrassed. Aside from Nan Ruth, she was the only other woman who could look at me and cause me to rethink what I had said or done.

"What about Faulkner? You're just going to leave her out there with the wolves?"

I shrugged. "Faulkner has more gumption about her than I could ever hope for. She's got the job. Fred is making her the offer today. If she accepts, the job is hers."

"Joyce, you know what I'm talking about."

"Faulkner has so much of you in her, she'll be fine. If he tries anything with her, he's going down. But I'm not ready to be that woman. Just being me is hard enough." I wasn't in any position to try and go back now and fix everything I helped build for this man. "He'd destroy me."

"That's all in your head."

"Faulkner is your work, Margaret, and Fred couldn't break her if he tried. Like I said, she's got more you in her than me."

"No, she doesn't," Margaret disagreed. "She's a good leader, she's a woman of her word, Faulkner knows and understands business, and she's eager to move up. She's so much like you when it comes to getting the job done that she could be your child."

I smiled. "Thanks, I consider that a compliment in the highest way, but Faulkner will do what Faulkner wants to do. I don't think I have to keep her away from any wolves, because she's like a grizzly bear and wolves don't mess with grizzlies."

"Neither did you. No one could have told me our friendship would be ruined because of something like that. Faulkner needs to know, Joyce, and it's up to you to tell her. We have too much pain between us for things to be like they were, but Faulkner looks up to you and I think it's time you showed her that you are capable of caring." Margaret got up to leave. "Let me get back to my phone. We're busy this morning."

I stood to walk Margaret to the door. "Margaret, do you have any regrets?"

She thought carefully, as I always knew her to do before answering a serious question. "I wish I'd filed a case against Loomis twenty-six years ago. Sometimes my fear gets in the way of what God has in store for me, and I believe if I'd have quit that day and never turned back, my entire life would be different." Margaret smiled and settled her eyes on me. "Unlike both of us, Joyce, Faulkner follows her heart instead of settling or chasing pipe dreams. She's what we've always believed we were but weren't. You still have a chance to go to her and be the Joyce I know you to be and let her know what's in store for her."

"I betrayed you, Margaret, and I apologize for that, but Faulkner is not my child, she's my coworker. It's not my job to tell her about Fred."

"If ever there was a statement I didn't agree with, that's the one." Margaret looked at me and grinned. She opened her arms and I met her embrace. "I'm proud of us, Joyce."

As Margaret stepped into the hall, Faulkner stepped off the elevator. She rushed by, telling us good morning. Margaret and I watched her rush toward her cube. She was a busybody, always making things happen. I smiled and wished for a moment she was my daughter because that would give me something that I'd created and could be proud of.

Faulkner

There was no way I would get to work on time today. I almost called in to say I wasn't coming at all, until I remembered today was Brenda's last day and I couldn't miss her going-away party.

I dragged myself out of bed, trying to get it straight in my mind if I was going to approach Joyce about what had happened. I got dressed and drove to a nearby coffeehouse near Greenville Avenue, wondering what I was going to do. It would be great if Joyce filed charges against Mr. Price because I would have no problem helping her. No, I couldn't prove he'd made an aggressive advance at me, but I'd be willing to get on any courtroom stand and testify that he had. I thought if Joyce knew that I was there, she wouldn't wait another moment. She was a strong woman. Besides, I'd heard everything that happened on the other side of Joyce's door last night. I'd heard the conversation, the tussling, him calling her names, then I'd seen a very scared woman leave her office. The flip side was I also knew that Joyce wanted that executive position and she could be at work right now making Mr. Price an offer he couldn't refuse. Joyce Armstrong wasn't the type to let anyone get the best of her.

I was different and my pride could be withheld for the sake of doing what was right. What that man had tried to pull with me was out of line and I was going to file charges and get me a lawyer. I figured if he'd pulled this with us, then surely there were others, and the rumors I'd heard about him and Joyce now seemed more true than not. But I'd probably lose the case if I didn't have the support I thought was out there. Plus, Mr. Price and I didn't have a relationship. He'd never come to my cube during working hours and no one had ever seen us talking in private. He could deny all the allegations and walk away with his dignity and his job while I'd come out looking like the girl who cried wolf. Whatever the case, I was going to make an issue of this. Mr. Price would know that Faulkner M. Lorraine was the wrong woman to touch.

I looked at my watch and saw that I was now two hours late. I would talk to Joyce after Brenda's party. It was my hope that she would be thankful that she had a witness. Sure, Joyce normally treated me like shit when I tried to be friendly to her, but this was different. This was about an executive abusing his power of authority. I wasn't having it, and the more I thought about the kind of person Joyce Armstrong was, I felt better thinking she wasn't going to have it either.

Margaret

I intended to give Faulkner time to get settled. I was going to apologize to her and let her know that I was wrong the other day when I accused her of being selfish and unconcerned about me. I rose to go to her desk once

I saw her chatting with Gail, but my phone rang. I could see that it was a personal call.

"This is Margaret."

"Hey, Margaret!"

The voice sounded like it was inside a box, but I knew it as soon as I heard it. My eyes lowered as I tried to hear what was going on in the background. I could hear cars passing by. "Lisa. Where are you?"

"Vegas! Carl and I flew up to have a real wedding. He got my dress and had me picked up from the hotel in a limo!"

"Vegas? Married? Lisa, what do you mean, married?"

"We're in love. He wants to be with me. You should see the dress I rented and my ring! Margaret, the ring is off the hook. We're moving to North Carolina."

"So what are you calling me for? Congratulations? I'm not happy about this."

"I want the girls. I can provide for them now and they should be with me. I'm coming home Friday. I need you to have their bags packed and make sure Nicole brings that sorry red Elmo doll you got her. If she leaves that thing I'll never hear the end of it."

I couldn't believe what this heffa was calling me about. "Lisa, I'm not giving those girls to you. If you so much as set foot on my doorstep, I'm calling CPS and I'm turning you in for child abandonment. Try me if you want to, but I won't let you down."

"Aren't you listening to me? I said I can provide for them. Carl wants the girls to come with us. We're even going to have another baby. I'm trying to do right, Margaret."

"Right for who, Lisa? You've done nothing right since you moved back home. You've been arrested for messing around with a married man and his wife nearly killed you in my front yard. You go out and don't come back and to top it off, you fly to Vegas and marry a man that has met your children one time. They think he's their uncle, how in the world does that look? No, you can't take them. You leave them alone, you lie to them, and you expect your new marriage to some football player to impress me? What are you going to do when he leaves you, have you thought about that? You have another think coming if you're assuming my doors are open."

"I'm not coming back. I made sure in the prenuptial that I would be taken care of if that happened."

"Lord Jesus, girl!"

"Margaret, I didn't call you to argue. I have every right to come to your house and take my children with me where I damn well please. I'm trying to be considerate. I didn't call to ask you for my children. I called you to *tell* you that I'm coming to get them and I need them to be ready. It is not my intention to sit on the phone and pay to argue with you."

Lisa's tears were falling by now, but I wasn't in the mood for her drama. I could feel my nerves tightening, but ignored them. Out of all the stunts this child had pulled, this was the one that made me want to disown her. I'd become so mad it hurt. "Lisa Jeanette, you can't have Nicole and Shylanda. This is my warning to you: if you so much as pull up in my driveway even thinking you're going to leave with them, so God help me, you will regret it."

"God will have to help you, Margaret, because I will be in your driveway on Friday and I'm taking my girls with me."

Click!

I was fuming when I ripped my headset from my head. I had a right mind to call CPS for real and report that Lisa had abandoned the girls, but they would only take them from the house, and that wasn't necessary, nor was it what I wanted. I didn't like the government being involved in personal matters even though sometimes it ended up that way. I would just be home, ready for her whenever she came. She wasn't taking those girls anywhere unless it was over my dead body.

I got up and a dizzy feeling washed over me. I waited a few seconds to let it pass. On my desk sat my pills. I picked up the bottle and threw it in the trash, determined to take retirement, move Lisa's things out of my home, and get back to taking care of me.

Faulkner

I saw Joyce and Margaret on my way in. It was awkward for me to walk up and see them standing there. Joyce and Margaret hardly ever talked or acknowledged each other. I didn't have time to try and figure it out, I needed to finish the report. By the time I'd completed the report and printed it out, Brenda's party was starting. I grabbed her gift, asked Gail to go grab the cake, and headed to the conference room.

There were balloons on the table along with the cake and a vegetable platter, and Gail had prepared taco wraps and homemade *queso*. It all smelled great. Everyone was in the room already and Brenda was sitting in the chair at the head of the table. I took the seat between Gail and Margaret. Mr. Price walked in shortly after and the room settled. Joyce walked over and stood nearby. I watched for some sign that she was disgusted with him, but Joyce was the same calm and cool diva that I'd known her to be. She cleared her throat and spoke.

"Most of you know that we're here to bid a warm good-bye to Brenda Jones. Brenda has given three years of service to Southwest Meridian and we're going to miss her."

"Hear, hear," Gail said as gum popped between her teeth.

I nudged her with my elbow, warning her not to be crass. She'd helped me with Brenda's party because I'd asked her to, but she was happy to see her go.

Margaret picked up a napkin to fan herself even though the room was cool enough to have us rubbing our hands together to produce heat. She moved away from Mr. Price and looked at Joyce and it was in that moment I knew that Margaret knew about Mr. Price. I let my eyes drop before either of them could catch me staring in their direction.

Mr. Price held up his hand. "One more thing. Since we're making announcements and the goodies are already in place, I would like to announce that as of next Monday, Faulkner Lorraine will be customer operations manager."

"What?" Gail grabbed me and hugged me tightly. Others clapped and congratulated me. Gail held her hand up for me to high-five her and I did it, but I couldn't believe what I'd just heard come from Mr. Price's mouth. I had a beef with him and he'd still seen fit for me to be promoted. Not only had he promoted me, I'd been given Joyce's title. I should have known she'd still take the executive job. Joyce had officially lost my respect.

"Faulkner, I'm so glad for you," Brenda said as her cheeks turned pink.

"Thank you," I said. I didn't want to make a big deal out of this now, but I needed clarification and I planned on finding out what was going on. "Let Brenda open her gifts and let's eat," I said, trying to get everyone's attention off me and back to Brenda.

James came over and patted me on the back. "Congratulations, boss. Seems like MSCOT just got better." We hugged and he moved on to see Brenda.

I was still allowing the announcement to sink in. I'd worked hard to get to this point and before last night, I would have thought this was the best thing that ever happened to me. I looked at Mr. Price. His nose was puffy but not too noticeably. Just looking at him disgusted me. I felt it necessary to let Joyce know that I knew, hoping that would change all of this. Maybe Margaret would help. I kept motivating myself to do it. I opened my mouth to take the big chance but a hand touched me and then arms took me in.

"Oooh, Faulkner, you did it just like you said you would! You got the job. No, even better, you got the job you earned!" Margaret's smile made her face gleam. She was almost jumping up and down. "That's how faith works." She hugged me again. "I'm going to call Lester right now and tell him. When I come back, I have something to talk to you about."

I watched Mr. Price stand near Brenda as she opened her gifts. He looked up at me and winked. Joyce walked toward the door, but not before patting me on the shoulder. "Congratulations, Faulkner. You'll make a wonderful manager."

I opened my mouth to speak, but Joyce looked somber. I'd never seen such a sad expression on her face before. Her heavy makeup and the hair bordering her face didn't do much in the way of hiding the bruise near her eye. I closed my mouth, not wanting to say anything anymore.

"Before everyone leaves, I just want to give my little thank-you speech," Brenda said. She'd been crying. She'd received a photo album for the baby, several gift certificates, and we'd all pitched in and bought her a foot massager.

"You have to wait until Margaret gets back," I said. "Let me go get her."

"Where'd she go?" Gail followed behind me. I looked around the corner, where I had a clear view of her cube. I didn't see the top of Margaret's head. I thought she'd probably gone to the bathroom, but alarm settled in the back of my thoughts.

"Now, I know Margaret Eddye don't move fast enough for us to have missed her," Gail said. She passed me and headed to Margaret's cube. I followed, still wondering when would be a good time for me to approach Joyce.

In an instant, everything around me seemed to be in fast-forward. Gail let out a scream so loud, I froze as I turned the corner and saw what she'd seen. Gail was on the floor with Margaret's hand in hers. Margaret lay there, unmoving. Her legs were crossed and her head was turned away from me. Gail shook Margaret's shoulder as if she was trying to wake her. "Margaret! Margaret! Help!" She screamed. "Call for help!"

I ran over to Margaret's desk and looked for her medication. "Gail, check to see if she has a pulse."

I heard Carmen's voice speaking to an operator. I grabbed Margaret's purse and found nothing. I opened the desk drawers and checked. The medication was nowhere to be found.

"Gail, is she breathing?" I asked.

Gail shook her head. "I don't know." Her hands were shaking as if they were in ice water. She wouldn't be able to feel Margaret's pulse if she even knew how.

Without warning, Joyce told Gail to move out of the way so she could see what was going on. Joyce lay Margaret flat and uncrossed her legs. She turned Margaret's head upward and placed her ear near Margaret's slightly opened lips.

"Was she like this when you found her?"

Gail nodded. Her eyes were big and her mouth was still mechanically chewing the gum. "I don't know when she fell."

I was still trying to find the medication when my eyes fell upon the trash can underneath Margaret's desk. I pulled it out and there inside lay a medicine container. I grabbed the bottle and looked at it, trying to read its instructions.

"I'm not getting a pulse," Joyce said. I felt my knees go weak. I leaned against the desk, still trying to read the bottle.

Joyce began giving Margaret CPR. My heartbeat felt separate from my body. It was like a drum in the background of a movie. We all watched Joyce place her lips on Margaret's and then place her hands against Margaret's chest. Up and down, up and down, up and down, Joyce counted. I kept my eyes on Margaret's face, looking for some sign that she was breathing.

Margaret

The chest pains hit me as soon as I turned the corner to get to my cube. I stopped and let my body rest against Brenda's cube, which was one over from mine. The worse the pain became the more I realized I'd better get to my medicine. My chest felt like it was being forced into a coin purse. My breathing became staggered and I could feel moisture in the armpits of my dress. Unfortunately, by the time I made it to my cube, I was on the floor, crawling on my hands and knees. The pain tightened in on me so that I couldn't see or take a breath anymore. It hurt to even blink my eyes. I gritted my teeth, thinking only to be seen before the worst happened. I couldn't even cry out. My body was controlling everything and it was making me hurt like I'd never hurt before.

I rolled over and lay still, my eyes trying to focus on the lights above me. I kept trying to tell my body what to do, but I couldn't feel anything other than the blinking of my eyes. One of my hands rested against my chest and it shook like I was having an epileptic fit. I finally closed my eyes and tried to pray, but all I could think of was the pain. My heart was bursting inside me. Then, without warning, I felt it stop. It was as if it had beat itself into not working anymore, and I swear my body died before I did, because I can remember that last beat, that last drain of energy, and a sudden feeling like I was floating in space. I waited for intervention, and hoped someone would find me before it was too late. One thought that gave me hope was being home to confront Lisa. If nothing else, I'd be home to protect my grandbabies, but I'd have to stop floating first.

Faulkner

The paramedics came and picked up where Joyce left off. They performed CPR, stuck Margaret with needles, put electric shocks on her chest, and did other things that made it look like they were hurting her, but nothing seemed to work.

By now, people from other departments were on our floor, some standing with their hands cupped over their mouths in disbelief, while others openly cried. The paramedics lifted Margaret's body onto the stretcher, covered it with a sheet, and secured her. As they rolled her out my legs gave and I fell against the wall. Joyce grabbed me and held on to me. I caved in and every tear in me released. Another hand rubbed my back, while cool flashes of air came and went, came and went. Someone was fanning me.

"It's okay, Faulkner, let it out," Joyce's voice whispered. She squeezed my arms and rocked me. My body trembled, thinking of the loss. Once Margaret's body was gone, I felt the emptiness. I let the tears flow until they couldn't anymore. Joyce sat me at Margaret's desk and handed me a Kleenex.

"Do you need me to stay here with you?"

"No." I sighed. "I'm going to call Margaret's husband and let him know."

"You sure? I can call him if you need me to."

"No, I can do it. I think it should come from me."

Joyce stood over me. Her face was now dark with concern. It had been too much in one day for all of us. Someone had placed a cup of water on the desk for me. I drank it and kept taking deep breaths to calm myself. When I finished the water and stood, my knees no longer felt like they had no bones. Joyce patted my shoulder one last time and headed to her office.

I walked to my desk in grief. People had attempted to go back to work, but we were all still in shock. The green light on my phone was blinking as the phone rung. Out of habit, I answered as if things were normal.

"This is Faulkner."

"Turn my phone on! How many times I have to call this place to have my shit turned on?"

"Mrs. Coleman, pay your bill." I couldn't find it in me to be formal with this woman. "Please, just pay the bill."

"I paid the bill! Y'all lost my receipt and now you tryin' to blame it on me. Folks been callin' me about jobs and I been missing my calls because of you!"

I looked at the ceiling, no longer willing to be entertained. "Mrs. Coleman, you know and I know you haven't paid that bill. Now, I'm telling you today, don't call this goddamned phone company anymore regarding this issue. We've done more than enough for you."

"Bitch, who do you think you're talking to?" Mrs. Coleman asked nervously. I didn't respond. Then without warning, this woman whom I still hadn't pegged asked me a question. "What's the matter with you? Sounds like you ain't having a good day."

"Well, for your information, Mrs. Coleman, Margaret Eddye died today." The tears began to flow again. I must have put her in shock because she changed her tone.

"Look, I'm sorry to hear that. I'm real sorry."

I tried to smile through my shaking lips. "Imagine

how we feel. Mrs. Coleman, I'll delete your account and reactivate your service. You won't have a reason to call here anymore." I pressed the wrap-up button and disconnected Mrs. Coleman before she could get another word in.

Joyce tapped the metal trim to let me know she was there. I looked at her.

I said more than asked, "You heard that, didn't you."

"Yeah," she said. Her face was stern but nonthreatening. "The whole thing."

"Well, will you do me a favor and fire me?"

Joyce folded her hands in front of her. "No, I'm coming to tell you to go home. That's the favor I'm doing for you. Go home and get some rest this week. Come back next Monday and start your new job."

The tears flowed again. I felt fatigue with a mixed sense of displacement. Joyce smiled again and left my cube. I prepared to leave, but first I had a call to make.

Joyce

The day had gone from good to bad in a matter of minutes. I couldn't set foot back into my office because I could still smell Margaret's perfume. I could still hear her voice talking to me. Her presence was still strong. For each year that I'd known Margaret, I could see her in my head, mostly us together when we were friends sharing rides to work, lunch, and plenty of secrets. Margaret and I were once inseparable, and now I would never have the chance to have that again with her, just when we'd come back to our common ground. And even though I'd convinced myself that I didn't want that, I definitely didn't want it like this. Death had ended what we'd tried to make of a bruised friendship. Death had come and set in stone how much I took life for granted. I'd seen people die in my lifetime, but it had been so long since it was someone I cared about. As sick as Margaret was, I still never thought she'd die before I found the courage to say to her how sorry I was for betraying what she and I had. Margaret would never get to know how afraid I was and how much I needed her to remind me how strong I could be. She would never know how I envied her relationship with Faulkner because it was better than what we had. I would spend the rest of my life trying to be at peace with my own shortcomings as a woman in power and as a friend.

I gave the team the rest of the day off, forwarding our calls to another group. Fred said we'd take care of my personal issue later. I kept my composure as long as I could. I kept it for the strength of the team and for Margaret. She'd let me make my peace with her and even though the rest of my life would be filled with what could have been, I'd still have that to remember her by.

I got my things and boarded the elevator. When the doors closed, ironically I found myself going down alone. My chest heaved as the tears began to flow. I wiped my eyes gently to keep my mascara from running, but the more I wiped, the more tears fell.

Faulkner

With the good comes the not so good. It had been a week since we found Margaret dead, and I felt that some great part of me had been stolen. I was full of pain and guilt and more regret than I could handle.

That Monday night, Greg came over and spent the night at my place. He didn't want me to be alone and I welcomed his company. We stayed up and listened to music as I talked about Margaret until I couldn't anymore. I fell asleep on the couch and he slept on the love seat. Teresa was still in New York, but she flew in to be with me the day of the funeral.

Margaret was buried Wednesday morning, and we were all there. Lester had Nicole and Shylanda with him, but I didn't see their mother. I knew Margaret was having a few problems with Lisa, but I found it unusual for her not to be at the funeral. Margaret's two sisters were there and a host of other relatives, friends, and people from her life that knew her.

The funeral home did well with Margaret's body. Her hair was down around her shoulders and she was clothed in a lavender dress suit that had studs on the cuffs of the sleeves. She looked both the same and different. She looked asleep in a way that let me know she was at peace.

Joyce spoke at the funeral. Sitting there, I wondered what had changed her. She didn't appear to be the same.

As she talked about Margaret, I knew her words were sincere. The more she spoke, the shakier her voice became. Before long, the ushers were leading Joyce away from the podium down the aisle. She'd broken down and it was a Joyce that I didn't know. As they walked her by me, I reached out and touched her hand. She gripped me and then let go.

After the burial, I came home and finished typing my story. Teresa had been reading it and asking me to finish it. I hadn't had the desire to until now. It kept me busy and it allowed me to hash out some of my feelings about what I was going through. Sometimes as I typed I would smile or laugh out loud. Writing became therapy for me and I spent my days away from work writing until I was all cried out. I let it all go when I e-mailed the rest of what I'd written to Teresa.

The following Monday I went into the office. To do what? I didn't know. I hadn't turned in my resignation but I hadn't signed a letter of acceptance for the new position either. As I walked the hall and passed Joyce's office, I was surprised to see my name plastered across the door. It was as if all my hard work had been epitomized on a nameplate. I opened the door and the office looked about the same except none of Joyce's things were in there. The desk was empty, the fern was gone, and the blinds were down. I'd dreamed of this moment and now that I was in it, I didn't want to be here. A bouquet of flowers was on the desk with a silver balloon rising from them that read "Congratulations" across the front. I went behind the desk and sat down, resting my body in the tall leather chair. There was a memo on the desk. I read it and was pleased with what I learned: Gail had been moved up to my old position while James and Carmen would take on training new team members. This ultimately meant promotions for everybody.

I leafed through a few folders sitting next to my computer and there was already enough work to get me through the quarter. It would be interesting to know what Joyce did every day besides delegate. I raised the blinds to let some sunlight in but it still didn't make me feel any better. Here I was on the verge of making more money than ever, complete with unimaginable perks, and I felt like a baby bird unable to fly. Three quick raps on the door broke my thoughts.

"Come in."

Gail stepped in the office. I was pleasantly shocked when I saw her.

"Tah-dah," she said as she sashayed around for me to get a better look. Gail was modeling a new hairdo, devoid of any secondary colors. Her nails had been shortened by at least two inches and were a sultry shade of red instead of the usual spray-painted island scene with faux diamond studs on her pinky. She was even wearing a solid navy blue pantsuit with black, closed-toe shoes. "What do you think? Be true with me, girl."

"Breathtaking." I smiled as I got up and walked over to get a closer look. Gail's makeup was subtle. Not too much mascara, and her lips didn't have that dark pencil line around them. She looked five years younger. She looked refreshed.

"I went to the mall and got a makeover. This is the same kind of stuff that stars like Mary J. Blige wear, and her makeup is always right. After that girl was finished with me, I had to buy it. I can barely feel it on my face."

"It almost looks like you don't have on any. You are looking too sharp, girl."

"Yeah, now that I'm Team Lead, I have to be more professional. I told you I would make you proud of me. Everything I know, you taught me."

"Gail, you were fine the way you were, don't forget that."

She held her hand up to stop me. "Nope, you come to work every day dressed to the nines. Now, I can't afford anything from Casual Corner or those fancy stores out at the Galleria, but I learned from looking at you that it takes money to make money. Hey, hey!" Gail danced in place, looking cute.

"It's good to see the clothes haven't changed the woman." I laughed.

"Actually, I used to dress up all the time in high school because I went to Business Magnet and it was a fashion show each day. I don't know what happened. I met my husband, got married, had kids, and if the clothes didn't come from somewhere that had 'Mart' behind the name, I wasn't buying it. You have kids and it's time for wash-and-wear."

I thought to myself as Gail talked. She was a mother and wife working to make a better life for herself and her family. Those two adorable kids would grow up with a mother who would teach them about the value of listening and wanting better.

"Faulkner? Faulkner? Are you listening to me?" Gail waved her hand in front of my face. "Yoo-hoo."

I looked at her. "I was listening to you."

"And I can Riverdance. Your head was somewhere else, ain't heard a word I said."

I motioned for Gail to have a seat. I went back to my desk and sat down. "Now you have my full attention."

Gail seemed pleased. "Good."

"So tell me how being Team Lead is working out."

Gail crossed her thick legs. "It's everything I thought it would be and everything I didn't, you know? For instance, I know it's only been a few days, but I already have two weeks' worth of stuff to do. And since I don't have the same kind of time I used to, Tiffany and Daeshun are already tripping. I don't think we're going to be friends any longer, because I can't hang out with them like I used to. And to top it all off, they're moving my cubicle back to the other end of the floor."

"Get used to it. I've probably been in every cubicle in here. Before you came on board, I was being moved every other month."

"Whatever. I'm ready for what they have to give me. I'm going to keep movin' on up, just like the Jeffersons."

I nodded, feeling good that Gail was taking her job seriously. I'd underestimated her more than I knew. "More power to you."

"And you know what, Faulkner?"

"What is it?"

"I'm not letting Tiffany 'nem ruin my future. For the first time in my life, I finally have a savings account and the kids have accounts that I can put their college money into."

"And your 401K? Are you going to increase what goes there?"

"I already did. I'm still struggling, but it's like a good struggle because it's not for now. This is about ten years from now."

"That's good you're saving your money."

"And when my honey gets his raise, we'll finally be able to get another car and work on getting us a three-bedroom home. The kids can finally have their own rooms and I can get them new bedroom suites."

"Have you looked into getting a HUD home?"

Gail frowned. "HUD? That's for people on welfare. I'm not living in no HUD home," she protested.

I smiled, aware that Gail was serious. She had no clue what HUD housing was. It wasn't for people on welfare. I explained to her that they were government-funded homes that people could bid on for little or nothing in some instances. She said she'd look into it, but that she had to get back to work. We hugged. Gail pulled back. "Margaret would be so proud of us."

I nodded. "She would. She'd be especially proud of you, Gail."

"Faulkner, thank you. Maybe we can do lunch one day. I'll have my people call your people."

"Maybe," I replied.

Gail pulled on her jacket and primped her hair before she left.

"Where's Joyce? Has she moved in upstairs yet?" I asked.

Gail froze with her hands pressed against her hair then she dropped them. "You don't know, do you?"

"Know what?"

"Joyce quit. Yeah, girl, she did it Thursday. Came in here, got her belongings, and left. We can finally get some peace around here."

"Thanks, Gail."

Gail walked back to the main floor. I leaned against the door panel, wondering what in the world was going on. I rushed back to the desk and pulled out the company phone directory. After I made the call, I locked the office up and left.

Joyce

I was now unemployed, somewhat sad, and definitely alone. The night of Margaret's funeral, I called Dennis and broke off our relationship. I was no longer comfortable with his wanting more from me. To me, I was an adult woman who wasn't interested in being locked down with a man young enough to be my son. I wasn't interested in being locked down with anyone, period. Something was wrong with that picture.

Thursday was my first day back at work, and I stayed long enough to turn in my resignation and get my things. It was as succinct and simple as that. That's what I was thinking about when my doorbell rang. My first thought was that it was Fred and I didn't move to answer it. Few people knew where I lived. The doorbell rang again. My car was in the garage so I could easily ignore it until whoever it was went away. Two more rings then two more. I finally got up to see who it was. When I opened the door, Faulkner was standing there.

"Can I come in?" she asked. "I had to pull teeth in HR to get your address, which took half an hour, and it took another forty-five minutes to drive to Plano."

I opened the door. "Come in, since you went through all that trouble," I replied. "What brings you here?"

Faulkner sat in a nearby chair. Sweat beaded her forehead. "You."

I walked to the kitchen to pour her a glass of water. When I returned she seemed more at ease but her face was still flat in appearance. "You don't look so well."

"I'm still working on getting an appetite. Since Margaret's death, I haven't been able to eat much."

"I know the feeling," I said.

Faulkner sipped the water. "I want you to know that I know everything, Joyce. I know about Mr. Price and him being the reason you resigned."

I sat back. "I resigned on my own. Mr. Price had nothing to do with why I left."

"Are you going to talk to me straight up like the Joyce Armstrong I know, or are you going to sit here and lie to me while you protect a man that doesn't respect you? If you're going to bullshit me, I'll leave."

I sat silently.

"Joyce, I know this isn't easy for you. I know you gave a lot of yourself to get that executive position and you deserve to be there. Don't let your resignation be your white flag. You've got to fight this."

"How do you know?"

"I was there the night he attacked you in your office. He had been in my cube just moments before and he thought I was gone."

"Did he attack you? Please tell me he didn't."

"No, but he touched me in a way that I didn't welcome."

I threw my head back. "That bastard. Faulkner, I'm sorry you witnessed that."

"Why? I am *your* missing link. You have proof that lowlife physically harmed you."

"I can't allow you to tell what you saw."

"Why not? Surely you're not going to just sit back and allow this to fall by the wayside. He owes you, and you owe it to yourself and every woman that is coming after you to expose him."

"Faulkner, there are things about me that you don't know, and you don't know what can of worms you're opening when you talk about taking Fred to court."

"*Fred?*"

She sighed. "It's not as easy as you think."

"Then tell me, Joyce, because you're right. I don't understand how anything could keep you from dealing with this."

I got up and poured myself a glass of lemonade with a splash of vodka. I drank half the glass and poured a second before sitting down. "I had sex with Fred several times before that incident. It wasn't a first. We've been involved off and on for years."

Her face remained convinced that nothing I told her would change her mind. "But you wanted the job. Didn't he use his power to force you into having sex with him this last time?"

"No, I did what I felt would solidify the deal."

"But there was still an intimidation factor."

I exhaled because Faulkner was digging and her shovel was about to hit something solid. "Faulkner, I've had sex with every boss I've ever had at Meridian Southwest to get to where I was. Mr. Loomis was where it all started."

She halted. "Mr. Loomis?"

I nodded. "He used to be the Dallas operations manager and I was in account management. He had a thing for black women. I had sex with him and after that became the office manager. The agreement was that if I wore something a little revealing every now and then, let him have his way when he wanted, I would receive a bonus and continue moving up the ladder."

"But I thought—"

"I'd taken Margaret's job? Not really, but we were friends when it happened. She never told me but I think Jack made a pass at her and she refused the job."

"She never told you what happened?"

"Margaret and I were supposed to meet for drinks that night. I think she was going to tell me then, but I stood her up. At work that day, Jack called me into his office after hours and I never met Margaret. She left before me but I was right behind her when Jack stepped out of his office and saw me. He told me about the position and got me all excited about the money. Of course I was thrilled, because I'd come from humble livings. I didn't know any better. Well, after I accepted the job, he started talking about us and taking our relationship in a new direction. We were already involved, but he wanted more, demanded more of my time. In the process, my relationship with Margaret suffered."

"What happened?"

"Well, the first thing that came out of his mouth was that I stop spending time at work with Margaret Eddye. He accused her of being a Black Panther and he said she was going to get fired if I kept hanging around her. I didn't want Margaret fired so I made a deal with him to move Margaret or else all bets were off. So Margaret was moved to a different department instead of fired and I ignored her whenever I saw her."

"And Margaret?"

"She took it personal."

"She had a right. You were her friend."

"I was her friend, but I was also trying to keep my head above water. I'm surprised she never told you all of this."

"I can't believe Margaret stayed at the phone company all this time."

Faulkner was shocked. I'd tried to warn her, and now she'd have to hear everything.

I took a drink. My mind was comforted, which made it easier for me to talk. "That's how she made me suffer. Every day she made it a point that we saw each other and every time I saw her, I wondered if she had told anyone."

"Why didn't you leave?"

"Leave all that money? I came up fast at the company. No other black woman in Dallas was making the kind of money I was making back then. Even now, there are only a few sisters who can brag that they're in my salary range. Being an executive would have sent me over the top. The money was good and as long as I kept my mouth closed, there was more where that came from. Why would I give that up?"

Faulkner shrugged. "I guess friendship would be a lame answer."

"Once Jack left, Fred filled his position and I would soon learn that Fred operated different. After entertaining him one evening I later found out he had it on tape in case I ever tried to hustle him."

"Damn."

"Then there was Dennis."

"Dennis?"

"James. James Dennis Hardy. I called him by his middle name."

Faulkner's confusion became obvious. I could shock her even more if she kept digging. My closet was full of skeletons. She looked at me. "You were having an affair with our intern." This wasn't a question. Faulkner fell silent. "You say that like it was okay to be dating him."

"He's a consenting adult, Faulkner. There was nothing wrong with what Dennis and I had going. Sure, we kept it hidden, but only because I wasn't interested in being his woman. It was physical for me."

Faulkner looked at me then at her empty glass. "Can I have some of that lemonade you're having?"

Her evasiveness disappointed me. I wanted her to have the answer I needed. I wanted her to spring forth with the same fighting spirit she'd had just minutes ago. I wanted to have it in myself. "Do you need any more reasons why I can't help you take Fred to court?"

"No. I understand now."

I poured her a drink and we sat in silence for a good five minutes. I tried to lighten the mood. "So, what's new with you?"

"Nothing. I don't have anything to report."

"Like hell you don't. I just laid out my private life to you and all you have to say is nothing? Come on, tell old Joyce something good."

Her eyes fixed on me. "I'm taking Mr. Price to court. I'm filing charges. I was hoping I could depend on your support."

"I'll support you, but I am not willing to have my life

affect James's. He's still in school and I don't want to destroy that. But I hope you win, Faulkner. I really do."

Faulkner shook her head and downed the drink. She placed the glass on the coffee table and stood. "Thanks for the lemonade," she said.

"Sit down," I said. "I want to share a song with you before you leave." We both could use a little soothing. I went to my Nina Simone CD stash. I wanted to hear something old that Faulkner could probably relate to. I figured she wouldn't know who Nina Simone was, and it was time I introduced her to some good soul music. Faulkner sat as I put the CD on and pressed the play button.

"That's Nina Simone," Faulkner said as soon as she heard the song's intro.

My neck drew back in surprise. "How in the world do you know anything about Nina Simone?"

"I grew up on Nina. As a matter of fact, that song was also recorded live in 1961 at the Village Gate."

I smiled. "I'm impressed."

"I know." Faulkner laughed. She rested her head on the chair and hummed along with the music. "I would have never thought my boss listened to Nina Simone."

"Why?"

Faulkner ran her hand across her hair. "I don't know. I thought you were one of those women who listened to the jazz music you heard on an elevator."

"Don't get me wrong, I have Kenny G's Christmas album." I laughed. "He isn't Sonny Rollins, but he's good for a white boy with midi skills."

Faulkner got the joke and laughed.

"I grew up in Calvert, Texas, where your choices were gospel, country, or the blues. Nina fit all three categories, with a little classical to boot. I couldn't beat it. Before I discovered Nina, I used to write my own songs and my brother would play the drums for me." I laughed. "All we had were words and the beat, no harmony, no notes, because I was as tone deaf as they come, but Jimmy Roy would play those drums like he'd been playing all his life. He was good."

"You have a brother?"

I looked at the floor. "Yes, but I don't know where he is now. The last time I saw him I was eighteen." I took another drink. "You know how it is. Shit happens, the family falls apart, and people don't see each other again."

I didn't know why I was telling this poor child about my sordid history, she really didn't need to be hearing all this, but the vodka had kicked in and I was on a roll.

"I have a brother," she said as she kicked off her shoes. "He lives in Illinois. He's married, with three children, and he just purchased his first house."

"That's funny," I said as I cleared my throat. "I never knew we had that in common."

"Why were you mean to me, Joyce? I never got that."

"Faulkner, who I am is due to years of having to hustle to do simple things like putting food on the table. Money mattered to me. The acquisition of things matters to a lot of people. I was one of them. I spent the most important years of my life selling my soul to the world to obtain the things I wanted. Status, position, vacations. I thought it was worth all the trouble I put people through because I thought I didn't need people if I had the things."

"And I was one of the people."

"I know you may not believe me, Faulkner, but I've told you this before. I pushed you to keep you from turning out like me. I didn't want that to happen. When Fred started showing an interest in you, I hated it. I felt threatened, but I also knew what his motive was. I figured if I treated you bad enough, you'd quit and not have to endure having to make the kind of decisions I've made. I apologize if I came off as harsh, but I thought if

I were more of a bitch and less of a boss, then I'd save you."

"*Bitch* is the operative word." She smiled. "You were a bitch to me but it made me want to work harder at defying you."

I snapped my fingers and saluted Faulkner. "Sounds like somebody I know."

"You gave me so much grief there were days when I knew I wouldn't be returning to the phone company, but once I got in there and spent time with Margaret, she'd always tell me how much the company needed me and that kept me going."

"I thought you were a glutton for punishment, but you hung in there, and sometimes I feared that in you, other times I envied it."

"Why?"

"Because that's what I saw in myself and I didn't want you to make any mistakes once you began to matriculate. It's animalistic the way people act the higher up they move. The politics, the bullshit, no feelings, no emotions, and all the cutthroat dealings—that's what you cope with. I spent a lot of time kissing ass to get a paycheck. I spent time abandoning my friends, faking smiles, eating food I wouldn't give a dog, and remembering names of people who didn't care about me." I shook my head. "But that isn't real. None of it is real."

"What about work? What are you going to do?"

"That's the least of my problems," I slurred. "I haven't paid that any mind. I have enough money to get by, even if I live to be one hundred and fifty." I broke out in laughter then sobered myself. "First, I'm going to try and find my brother. He's all the family I have left and I don't even know if he's alive. That's what is important to me right now."

Faulkner slid her shoes on and rose to leave. She gave me a hug and we exchanged personal information, promising to keep in touch. "If you change your mind about Mr. Price, don't hesitate to call me. What you did in the past is in the past, as far as I'm concerned. Your life is worth fighting for." Faulkner's words touched me. I walked her to the door and watched her walk to her car. As she pulled off, tears rose in my eyes. I was ashamed. Faulkner shouldn't have to face Fred alone, but she was strong. Strong in her will to face him and strong to put it aside long enough to try and fight for me: a woman who'd built the empire that had crumbled beneath her own two feet in a matter of seconds.

The CD changer rotated and Nina began singing. I sat on the couch and listened to her boldly sing, telling me what I needed to hear.

I'm going back home where I born.
First I planned to stay but I can't live this way . . .

I spent the rest of the evening celebrating my grand exodus from corporate America and the life I no longer felt represented who I now was.

Faulkner

I went back to the office for the last time, after visiting Joyce. I went straight to Mr. Price's office. His door was open and he was settled behind his computer staring at the screen, typing. I walked in and dropped the report on his desk. He looked up at me and smiled. "Ms. Lorraine, good to have you back."

"Mr. Price," I said.

He rose from his chair and extended his arm. "Have a seat."

"No, thank you."

His face dropped the smile and he shrugged and sat back down. "What can I do for you?"

"I came to let you know that I will not be returning after today. I'm quitting."

He sat back, rotating the chair from left to right with the heels of his feet. "I'd hate to lose you. Is there anything I can do?"

"No." I stood looking at him. He stopped rocking. "I'm taking you to court for sexual harassment." My voice broke a little, but I stood unmoved. "I know what you did to Joyce and I don't appreciate what you did to me."

"I don't appreciate your coming into my office making false accusations about sexual harassment."

"False?" I looked at Mr. Price like I'd lost my memory of who he was. I held my hand up and turned and walked out of his office.

"You will lose, Ms. Lorraine. You will lose and after that you won't be able to work for another company in this city."

I turned and looked at him one last time. "Fine, if that's the case, then I'll move, but until then, I will see you in court." I swung around with attitude this time. I didn't hear Mr. Price move behind me. I imagined he was sitting there, wondering if he should take me seriously or not. If he had good sense, he *would* take me seriously, because I meant what I said. Now, all I needed to do was find an attorney and get the employment pages from the newspaper. He was probably right when he said I wouldn't be able to find another job. In a matter of a month, I'd gone from up to down. I was back at one. Scared. Unsure and mad at myself for thinking that this would last forever.

It took me no time to get home, drop everything, and pick up the phone. I dialed Joyce's number, anticipating sharing my good news with her, but I got a recording telling me the call could not go through. Joyce didn't want to be reached.

The line clicked as I was about to hang up. I clicked over, wishing it would be Joyce, but it was Teresa, squealing away. We hadn't talked since the day of Margaret's funeral. She had flown back out that same night.

"Hey, girl!"

"Hey. How was your return trip back to New York?"

"Depressing but good. I'm ready to be back in Dallas with you. You need me to be there and I'm slaving away trying to keep the world informed on what's going on." Teresa picked up on my silence. "Girl, what's wrong with you?" she asked. There was more silence before I finally opened up.

"I quit my job today."

"What? No, you didn't!"

"I went to Mr. Price's office and told him that I wouldn't be returning. I'm taking him to court."

"To court? Okay, back up. What did he do?"

"I'm filing sexual harassment charges."

"What? Did he attack you? That rat bastard. I'm on it. Consider this on the news because—"

"No, Teresa, it wasn't anything like that. I don't want to make a big deal out of it."

"What do you mean, you don't want to make a big deal out of it? Whatever he did, he had no right to do it. Faulkner, why didn't you say anything? Do you know how crazy this looks that you've been trying to get a promotion and then when you don't get it you file sexual harassment charges on your boss?"

"I did get the promotion."

"You did? Then why did you quit?" Teresa halted. "Did he give you the promotion in return for sexual favors?"

"Teresa, we'll talk. It's been a lot of drama since you left. There are things I haven't told you because, with Margaret's death, it just slipped my mind."

"You're damned right it slipped your mind." Teresa let out a calculated sigh. "Damn, Mr. Price messed up the good news I was going to leave on your voicemail."

"What good news?"

"I met a guy who wants to buy your manuscript."

"What manuscript?"

"The manuscript you let me read. The one about you working in corporate America."

"Teresa, that wasn't a manuscript. Those were my private thoughts. I can't believe you let someone read it."

"Faulkner, I'm sorry, but it was too good not to share. I was reading it on the plane, and girl, I was laughing out loud and carrying on, you know how I do. Well, the guy sitting across the aisle from me asked me what I was reading. At first I was thinking he was trying to pick me up. You know, some men can be perverts on the side. Anyway, up until he introduced himself I was suspicious. He's an acquisitions editor for a major publisher in Manhattan. I checked his credentials out on my laptop and he's legit. We even knew some of the same people."

"How did he end up with my work?"

"I'm getting to that, just chill for a sec. Anyway, he asked me what I was reading; this was before I knew who he was. I told him about your work. He asked me could he see the pages I'd already read. I didn't see the harm in it, considering he was a total stranger, so I gave him the pages and, Faulkner, when I tell you he read those pages in the blink of an eye, I was like 'Damn!'"

"Teresa, I trusted you with those papers."

"Hold on, home girl, I'm not through. So he reads the pages and a few times he laughed too. I could tell he'd been pulled in. By the time the plane landed he'd read all of it and we were chatting away about the content. That's when he introduced himself and told me what he did. He asked could we meet for drinks and possibly discuss the manuscript more. He thinks it will make a great book, girl!"

"A book?"

"Of course I put my reporter skills on him. I asked all the questions I could think of. He's legit, but I told him I had to call you and see if it was okay to give him a copy of what I had."

I was still in shock. "Lord." I blushed as I realized I sounded like Margaret.

"Faulkner, this could be it! Girl, you'll be like Alice Walker with your books, all over the world. You could tour, and don't get me started on movie deals and hanging out in Hollywood."

I let out an abrasive, cynical laugh. "Teresa, that is hardly Alice Walker material. It's not even Alice in Wonderland material."

"Faulkner, yes, it is. It's a good, well-written work. You have an imagination that jumps off the paper. You just don't see it because you've been too caught up in all this mean-boss, new-boyfriend, no-job business. Girl, I'm telling you, if you don't at least hear what this brother has to say, I'm going to kill you myself."

I didn't know what to say, so I let the first thing that came to mind fly from my lips. "What does he look like?"

"Short, balding, glasses. Great personality but he's got a nice baby on him, about four months due."

When Teresa mentioned *baby*, I knew she was talking about his gut. That was the term we used for men with beer bellies. I didn't know whether to be excited or angry, but I did know that a chance to get a professional response about the things I'd written couldn't kill me. At the very least it would let me know if I should keep it to myself from here on out. "Teresa, this is not an easy position you put me in."

"Faulkner, I can't help it if I was reading your work and got somebody's attention. I didn't put you in nothing. This is all your doing. You created this."

"Whatever."

"Look, you've got talent and I think this writing is good. Granted, I know these people you're talking about and I know you, so it would be easy for me to support your writing as a friend, but this shit is real. Not only do you have a great imagination, but you have the ability to write in a way that grabs people. I should know. I'm a reporter. I never knew you had this kind of gift. Besides, your ass ain't working anyway. Might as well see where this can take you."

"Okay, okay," I said. "You've made your point."

"So what do you want me to do? If you don't want me to give him a copy of your work, then I won't. However, just know that Teresa Mosely, your best friend in the universe, thinks that would be a grave error."

I stalled, letting the events of the day cross my mind, then with a sigh that basically supported the notion that my day couldn't get any worse, I gave my friend the go-ahead. When we hung up, I wanted to call Teresa back and renege on the go, but I didn't have a return phone number. I walked out to the patio and let the evening air brush my face. It was overcast. The sun peeked out where it could, but not enough to bring a sweat to my already heated body. I shook my head while thinking about my confrontation with Mr. Price, hoping I'd done what was right. Hoping that walking away from the job, the money, and friends was a daring move rather than a foolish one. My mother would lose her mind once she found out, and I didn't know what Greg would do, but I wasn't too concerned with him. We'd just met and if he didn't like a woman who left her job because she had morals, then he could fly a kite. I looked up in the sky, watching the clouds drift by. "I miss you, Margaret" came from my lips. I stood outside long enough to formulate a small plan. First I had to find a lawyer, and then my next step would be finding a job. It was time for a new chapter in my life. A new journey. A new way back to me.

Joyce

I t's been two years since I left Dallas.

I visited Margaret's grave the day Faulkner came by. I talked into the air, letting Margaret know how sorry I was for not being able to help Faulkner, but she had to know that I was still scared. I tried to say all the things to her that validated my excuse. Apologizing for the underhanded way I took her job from her. I was the one who should have been in a cubicle dealing with the Jonnie Colemans of the world. And no matter how much I apologized, the emptiness in the wind reminded me that I was still alone. I needed Margaret there with me. I needed to reach my hand out, offer it to her, knowing that she would reach back and touch me, and hug me, and tell me that she forgave me. I cried that day. Cried over her grave, pleading with her for understanding, wanting her to show me in the beauty of the day that everything was all right, but Margaret didn't respond and I never blamed her.

The decision I made that day catapulted me into a whole newness. I came home and within a week closed all my accounts, put my house up for sale, sold my furniture, cashed in some stock, rented a moving van, and relocated back home to Calvert. My hometown. It was where I began and where I would start over.

I purchased twenty acres of land alongside a small stream and had three homes built about ten miles from one another. Hired a few of the local housewives and started a bed-and-breakfast right between Calvert and Bremond. I named it Armstrong's Real Real Bed-and-Breakfast, named after "Real Real," a song Nina Simone wrote that complemented my journey to this point. Business has been satisfactory and I couldn't ask for a better life except I miss my brother. I've mailed letters and even hired a tracking service to see if he can be found, but no word has come back. I'm not giving up hope. Jimmy Roy is out there somewhere. I know he is. If I find him, then my life will be complete.

I'm going to Dallas today for a very special occasion. I was reading the paper this week and saw something that brought a smile to my face and tears to my eyes. There was an event going on today that I wouldn't miss for the world. I was eager to see old faces, and I knew it would do my heart good to make the trip. I haven't missed Dallas, but I can officially say I have missed Faulkner Lorraine.

Faulkner

Life is really good if you stop trying to steer it in the direction you want it to go and just let it happen sometimes. Two years ago, you couldn't tell me that without getting an argument from me. I'd lost a dear friend, I was unemployed, I was suing my boss, and I'd lost contact with a woman I was just getting to know. I thought that the answer to every problem was to have a plan and that if you worked hard enough, you'd have no problems. There was no failure in that as far as I was concerned. At least, I felt that way until the day Margaret died. I thought that a person always had to know his next move, but sometimes life has to happen without a plan. Life can't have the same rules all the time. You couldn't make me understand how easy living could be if you just got in the backseat and let life drive itself where it needed to go. I always had to have the steering wheel and be in control. I can laugh about it now, but then it wasn't funny because I was feeling like I didn't have control, like a baby bird unable to fly. I was worrying myself into a depression trying to answer questions that didn't need answers, but just needed that stillness.

Greg stayed by my side through all of the ups and downs. He turned out to be second best to Teresa. It took me no time to tell him I'd quit my job. I wasn't expecting him to stay around because we'd been dating less than a month and he had no clue what was really going on, but when I told him, his only reply was "As long as you feel okay, then you have nothing to worry about." He ended up being a solid friend, a generous lover, and a wise adviser as I dealt with Mr. Price and the court case.

Speaking of which, I settled out of court with Mr. Price. The cards were stacked against me, without any other witnesses, but my lawyer and I fooled Mr. Price and his attorney into thinking that I had enough evidence to keep him from facing me in court. He thought I had other testimonies from previous employees. His lawyers advised him to settle and he did. I never brought Joyce's name up or told what I saw that night, and that was a big reason why I had to settle. She wanted her life to be hers and I respected that, regardless of how I felt about it. Sure, I wanted Joyce to face her demons and win at the same time, but she wasn't ready. She'll come around when she feels it's time. I know she will.

One afternoon not long after Margaret's death, Lester Eddye visited me. We sat a long time talking about Margaret and what we missed about her. Mr. Eddye had the same look in his eyes that my father had, several years ago, when my mother fell off a ladder and knocked herself unconscious. My father was by her side so fast, I couldn't remember where he was standing before it happened. That's how Mr. Eddye looked.

I still cry sometimes like it was just yesterday that she died, and that was one of those times. Mr. Eddye let me get myself together and we continued talking into the evening. He told me he'd been left with two granddaughters to care for. He said he needed a baby-sitter for the summer and that he'd appreciate it if I could recommend someone trustworthy to him. Since I wasn't working, I volunteered myself at no charge. I felt it was the least I could do to help him with the girls. We both knew how important it was to Margaret that they stay in a good home where they would receive lots of attention and care. I never asked about Lisa, and why she wasn't keeping them, but Mr. Eddye, in so many words, let me know that she'd turned over custody and was starting her own life somewhere in North Carolina.

And here I am today. I'm at Black Images bookstore with a line of people wrapped around the bookshelves wanting my autograph. It's my first book signing. After Pin Oak Publishing secured a small deal with me, they published my book. Three months after it was released it was on the bestseller list and has been optioned for a possible movie on the HBO network. Everything happened so fast that it took me a while to get used to the idea that my story was something people could relate to. I get fan mail, and book clubs from all over call to see if I can come and speak at their club meetings when my book is being discussed. It's a great feeling and a blessing. I'm taking a writer's course to better my technique because I'm hoping to make this a full-time gig. I like writing and I have plenty of books inside of me. I dedicated this book to Margaret and to Joyce because they were my strength and wisdom all rolled up into one. They're the reason I'm here.

After an hour of signing, seeing old friends, and making new ones, I began wondering what Joyce was doing. I hadn't heard from her since that Monday I'd left the company.

People moved along at a good pace. Then, a familiar whiff of perfume caught my attention. When I looked up, Joyce stood, with a book in hand, smiling at me. It was so good to see her that I couldn't wait to get up and hug her. She looked good. Refreshed. Her hair was free of extensions or additions and it was cut close to her head with small curls. No false nails, no three-plus layers of makeup. She was natural and looked seven years younger. She had on a warm-up suit that I could tell she'd paid money for, but it still gave her a casual look that I'd never seen before. I'd never seen Joyce in anything other than an expensive business suit, and as shocked as I was to see her dressed down, she looked comfortable. She looked happy. I rose and embraced her. She returned the hug and it felt like a mother's hug.

"Joyce, I never thought in a million years I'd see you walk through that door. You look wonderful," I said, still looking at her in amazement.

"I wouldn't miss this for anything, Faulkner." Joyce grabbed my hand. "Let me see this ring." She shook her head as she held my hand up. "I see this man doesn't hold back. So you're married."

I blushed. "Yes. We had a small ceremony six months ago. I wish you could have been there."

I signed Joyce's book as she talked to me. "Well, I had some issues of my own to deal with. I'm sorry that I just disappeared the way I did, but I needed to do it for me."

"I understand, but I hope it won't stay that way."

"Faulkner, I'm so proud of you. I read about the book signing in the paper. If they hadn't put your photo on the announcement, I wouldn't have guessed that Faulkner Alston was Faulkner Lorraine. I would not have missed this for the world."

"So much has changed."

"So, have you heard from anyone else?"

"Gail is still Team Lead. We talk about twice a month. Oh, she finally got a house. A four-bedroom with a nice backyard for her kids to play in. She's in hog heaven."

"I'm sure she is. I never gave her the benefit of the doubt. That girl was always so, you know . . ."

"Rough around the edges." I smiled. "She was, but she's doing better. Let's see, Carmen is still there. James finally graduated college and he's in management there, but I'm not sure what department he's in."

Joyce moved to the other side of the table as I continued to update her and sign books. "What about Brenda's baby? Did she have a boy or a girl?"

"Boy. She named him Orion Henry Jones."

"Orion Henry? Lord, today. What kind of name is that?"

"She said that the night he was born, she looked out the window and the sky was full of stars, so it must have been a sign."

"So she chose 'Orion' over 'Big Dipper' Henry Jones, I guess."

We laughed.

"I guess," I added.

Joyce held her book in her hands. "I know Margaret is proud of you."

"I miss her still."

"Me too, and this book will be my reminder of everything that was. I can't wait to read it. Margaret is here in spirit. She's in you, Faulkner, and she's in me. Be strong in knowing that." Joyce reached in her purse and handed me a card. "Here's my information, e-mail address and all. Keep in touch."

"I will."

"And you couldn't have come up with a better title. *Cubicles* is perfect." Joyce leaned over and gave me one final squeeze. "I have to get back to Calvert. I'll be looking for you to come visit me soon. I have a room waiting."

"Count on me, then, I'll be there."

When she pulled away, I knew I didn't want to see her go. I wanted to get to know her all over again. I wanted to sit and listen to Nina Simone with her and talk about what things moved her. I wanted to know why she'd never had any children and why she wasn't married. Joyce was the trunk that I needed to open to refamiliarize myself with that part of me that we shared: the risk taker, willing to change at all costs. The look on her face told me she had it and she would take care of it until we saw each other again. As Joyce walked out into the glimmer of the evening sun, I continued to sign books. One day, I hoped to have a job that allowed me to do what I enjoyed—to work with great people and be fulfilled and never be worried about money, insurance, or pushy bosses—but until then, I'd let my book run its course and continue getting closer to my dream occupation, which didn't involve me sitting in a cubicle eight hours a day watching my life pass me by.